Tales From the

Book One

By Alex Dulson

TALES FROM THE DEAD HEART

First edition. August 20, 2024.

ISBN: 979-8224650798

Written by Alex Dulson.

Table of Contents

For my partner Bella, who always sees the best in me and is my reason to keep writing on those days I feel I can't. I love you.

For my parents, who had the good sense and patience to raise me. I love you too.

For Stevie, my most consistent friend, and without whom this book and every other project of mine would still be drifting around in my head rather than on a page. You're alright.

And lastly for myself, who can't believe he's finished something without being distracted.

All credit to Tabitha Marsh for the wonderful cover art.

Tales

A Tale and an Ale

Year 607

"You never quite feel more conscious of your own mortality than seconds before you die. That realisation, in your gut. It's all at once terrifying and exhilarating, awakening yet deadening. The rush, the thumping of your heart, the prickle through your spine. But Gods, those seconds after you wake up are simply baffling."

The man in the dusty cloak planted himself down and shook himself off. He creaked his hands behind his head with a heavy sigh, kicked his feet up on the table and leaned back against the equally creaky bench, face hidden beneath hood and half-light.

Dex shook his head and brought his bleary eyes to focus. He shifted back in his seat and took a long moment to see if anyone else had noticed. There were only three others in the tavern now - the barkeep, Keln, who sat on a stool 'taste testing' the ale as he always did, and two men he didn't know so well sat mumbling drunken, rambling promises to one another, arm around each other's shoulder, both keeping the other from falling to the floor.

He turned back to the man, who seemed to be looking directly at him, though he couldn't quite tell. Maybe he was looking at something behind him. Was he swaying slightly, too? No, that'd be the drink. He'd been here since late afternoon, after all. The first few hours had been a nice warm glow, ideal for cold ales and good conversations with people he kind of knew. Now, it was getting a little chilly and the coming hangover already niggled at his head. Best to get a drink soon, then. Stave it off for a while.

Dex blinked and stared at the man hard as he could, who still seemed to be looking back, unmoved, the orange glow of the candle between them only reaching a little into his hood.

Dex blinked again, slowly. So slowly he felt his lids clamp and release. He took a sour, malty breath in and became faintly aware of a stench. A vague smell of rotten meat. Which was odd, considering his nose hadn't worked right the last few years.

Then he leant forwards, and careful not to slur his words said, "I'm sorry, do I know you?"

The stranger shrugged. "I doubt it," he said with a grating voice. "I'm not from 'round here. Just came from those woods a few days ago. Finally found somewhere to put my feet up."

Dex thought about that, the stupor of his mind grinding the already slow gears to a crawl. "The woods? They're not exactly..." he searched for the word, "safe."

"You don't need to tell me." The figure shook his head, the shifting light revealing a glimpse of a weary, beaten-edged face. Unshaven and pale. But Dex knew a lot of people like that. In fact, Dex was a person like that, particularly in the mornings. Suddenly the figure raised a hand, and gave a sharp click of his fingers. "Barkeep! A round for my friend and I!" Keln raised his moustached face with a gruff annoyance as he had to set down his fresh ale and grabbed two tankards from the shelf behind him.

"Well, friend," mumbled Dex, "there's no better way to earn my trust than a drink." He raised an eyebrow, before realising he'd lowered it, then raised the other one, before realising he was twice as drunk as he'd thought, so gave up on the whole business and settled for, "my thanks."

"My pleasure. It does, however, come with a price."

"Ah." He wasn't surprised. In Dex's experience, everything did.

"You must listen to my tale," and the man flourished his hand.

"Oh." Dex found himself pleasantly surprised. A tale and a drink. If he played his cards right he could get another few out of this guy. "Go on, then. But I warn you, I'm a thirsty bastard."

"Picture this." The stranger leant forward and spread his hands like framing a painting. "A wanderer in the woods, looking for his calling. A young man, scarcely older than a boy."

Easy enough to follow. Dex nodded along.

"Looking for his call to adventure, perhaps. Looking for reason in this thing we call life. Left his village home, and his family, and his friends for something... more." And he patted the table with a hand. A hand that, now Dex really looked at it, was curiously dark. Not dark-skinned. Dark. Blackened fingers, frail and thin and with receding nails. They looked almost...

"Here y'are." Keln plonked the two frothing drinks in front of them. "One apiece." He stuck out a thick, grasping hand of his own. Always slightly tipsy, always very careful with his money. Never let anything slip. Dex wished he was like that. But instead of wasting time wishing, he looked to the man, who offered the two gold coins to Keln with one of his strange hands. Keln frowned a little and wrinkled his red nose, but took it and shifted off. Never one to interfere in another's business, was Keln. Dex wished he was like that.

The man sipped at his drink and picked up again. "A warm, fresh day in the woods. A young man full of wanderlust." He'd already said it, but Dex didn't interrupt. His attention was on the drink. He took a long swig of the lukewarm ale and let it coat his forever-parched throat. "And what does he find?"

Dex found the man leaning half-over the table, just above the candle, orange light rippling menacingly over his dark face. The rotten smell grew a little stronger. Gods, his nose was shite. Suppose maybe if the man hadn't washed it was doing him a favour, though. And besides, he wasn't one to judge.

Dex shrugged, took another ample swig and said what the man wanted to hear. "I don't know, what?"

"A body." And he sat back, took another sip of his drink and let the word settle in the silence.

"Huh."

"Right." He gestured his hand to the table, as if the body was right there. "So what does he do? He goes over to it, sees what's what. Sees if he can help. It's another young man laid out on his back. About the same age, perhaps. But that's where the similarities stop."

Dex took the final swig of his drink and gestured to the now-useless tankard. "Still thirsty," he said, trying to sound as confident as possible while slurring.

The man clicked his fingers with a sharply raised hand. "Another!" And then downed the rest of his hardly-touched drink in what seemed like one gulp. Maybe there was a barrel under that cloak. Didn't seem much stranger than whatever the truth was.

But a free drink is a free drink. And a man's business is his business, even if Dex involved himself far too often.

"This particular young man is dressed head to toe in blood-red cloth. Silver loops and studs through his nose, through his ears, wrapped around his fingers. Tattoos of black, red, blue, purple, green in shapes like you never saw. Cursed, evil shapes. Harsh, jagged lines and symbols you never thought of. A Druid boy. And not the ones they say have got a little soft as the centuries have rolled on. A true Druid. This was a long while ago, you understand."

The only thing Dex understood was that this whole thing was just a madman's fantasy tale that gave him free drinks. Not that he had any quarrel with that premise. He nodded and looked over at Keln, already pouring two fresh ones. "Mhmm."

"So the first young man checks the corpse, pokes it a little. Can't be long dead, doesn't smell all that bad. Not even all that stiff. No sign of violence, just a little blood coming out the mouth, dribbled over his chin. So he turns him over, notices a blade lodged in his back." And the man pointed a thumb to his own back with a dramatic flare.

"Mhmm." Dex nodded again. He knew what that felt like.

"He checks the wound over, gets his hand a little bloody - careful about it o' course. But he's a curious bastard, this young man."

"Huh." Dex knew that feeling.

"Nothing he can do for him, o' course. Dead is dead, back to the ground as the Druids are apt to say." He scratched at an unseen part of his face. "Or at least the ones I knew did... Anyway, he can't do anything. So he sets about salvaging what he can. He's a good one, this lad, but he's no fool. Not going to let good supplies go to waste. He takes a look on his person, finds nothing much besides the knife in his back and a few scraps of cloth and leather and such, starts digging out the jewelry - 'course if any of it's silver, he can sell it. Then he starts rummaging in his bag-"

"Here y'are," grumbled Keln as he set the tankards down and stuck out a hand. The man offered his coins, Keln took the first two tankards then shuffled off again. Dex took another refreshing, drowning swig as the man continued.

"He looks in his bag. Bits of food, some tools. He's about to get up and move on when... bang!" And he smacked his hand on the table with a hollow thud, making Dex spill the latest sip of his drink down his already-stained shirt as he jumped in his seat. Even Keln looked up from the bar, shrugged and went promptly back to tasting. The other two didn't seem to notice at all, still locked in their stupored embrace. Dex wiped his chin with a dirty sleeve and a grumble.

"Something cracks him on the head, and he's out cold."

"Ah." Dex wished the ale was cold. Warm day, he supposed.

"When he wakes up, he finds he can't move. Something rattles when he moves his hands, when he moves his feet." He paused to lean over. "Chains!" he half-shouted, half-whispered. "Chains, wrapped around his limbs, his body lain on a huge rock, somewhere in the deep dark."

"Mhm," Dex nodded as he finished his drink and gestured for another. The man took his for the first time, and downed in one loud, wet gulp.

"Another!" he said as he clanged it down.

Keln shook his head, and set about his business.

"Then he hears voices. Then into the darkness bursts the light of a torch, lights up this strange place. A cave, full of dirt and vines and moss and damp. Then one of the voices stands above his head, looking upside-downish at him."

Dex just nodded this time.

"It's a woman. Druid, same as the boy. Jewelry, tattoos, red cloth, the lot. She looks down at this young man, chained to this rock, naked, and cold, and confused and she says one," and he raised a decrepit finger, "one thing."

There was a moment's silence as Dex realised the man wanted him to say something. He sighed. "What did she say?"

"You killed my son."

Strangely enough, though it wasn't true, Dex had heard that before too. "Ah."

"Then, she pulls out a bright, shining dagger and... " he smacked his hand on the table again, "right into the young man's chest. That's the last thing he remembers."

"Huh..." well, it was certainly a story, if not exactly a brilliant one. Though he'd hoped it was going to be longer and could at least wring a few more drinks out of the man.

"Until..." and the man spoke softly, like telling a secret. But to Dex, it meant at least one more drink, if only Keln would hurry it up. He'd just finished pouring the second, the prospect of it making Dex's mouth wet and throat dry all at once. "Until he wakes up, in the exact same spot he got conked on the head." He tapped the back of his head with a finger. "He's got his clothes back, got his stuff. All aside from the things he took, 'course-"

Keln put the drinks down a little harder, this time. "Here y'are," he grumbled. He stuck out a hand, got his two coins from the stranger and shuffled off again, muttering something about a smell.

"So he wakes up a bit confused, not sure what to do. He's alive, or at least feels it. Bit sluggish, perhaps. But what'd you expect after that little ordeal?"

"Mhmm." Dex nodded, mouth filled with ale.

"He shakes it off and sets on his way. Only a week later, he starts noticing things. Green patches over his legs. He's a little more damp, a little more foul. A little less tired though. Doesn't make sense, does it?"

"No, I suppose not," Dex muttered, taking his last sip and putting the tankard down.

The man slid over his drink. "Have mine, friend. I'm nearly done."

"Why thank you." The words were barely understandable even to him, but he didn't mind. They both seemed content with the deal. Dex took it with an eager hand and waited a moment for the man to start up again.

"Then more days, and more weeks go by. Skin peels, muscle and bone show, green becomes black, and brown, and filthy dark red. Looks like a long dead, wet corpse at this point. Nowhere's letting him in, people chase out of places

8

before long, has to hide his face. Hopes no one... smells him." The candlelight flickered strangely over his gaunt face, showing a row of browned teeth between thin black lips. But then Dex didn't look much better. And his eyes hadn't been so good recently. He went back to drinking. "He doesn't know what's happening. He's a corpse, but he's fresher than he's ever felt. Figures the Druids did something to him, some sort of blood magic curse, perhaps, but never found 'em again. No one wanted to help him, least not this side of the water, and not like he had much chance at getting passage to the Empire. They say it's been a century and he still doesn't know." He leant back in his seat and gave a gravelly, almost solemn sigh. "He never got the answers he was looking for."

Dex swallowed the last drop of drink and placed the tankard down. "That it?" He had another look under the hood, squinting to see if he could make out anything else. "What about the... uh..." His mind ground to a halt. "The moment before you die thing."

The man shrugged. "Just something I heard, is all. Makes for an interesting conversation starter."

Dex was about to point out that it wasn't really a story if it didn't have a proper end, the words slow to reach the tip of his tongue but there all the same. But then he supposed it wasn't really his business, and the man had bought him enough drinks to earn a little respect. He gave a throaty chuckle, "Bit of an anticlimax."

"Life happens, I suppose."

Dex supposed that was true. He stuck up a hand, shaking and swaying. "Another!" And Keln started grumbling his way through another two tankards.

"My thanks, friend."

Dex shrugged. "In my experience, drink is the best cure for disappointment."

Dead of Knight

Year 383

An icy breeze shivers down my neck as I document the day's activities. The same single, rusty lamp lights my cold office, the candle inside doing its very best not to sputter out. *Never have time to pick up a new one. Well, biting me in the arse now, isn't it? Ah well.* I dip my quill. *One arrest for petty theft.* I write it off. *Two for assault.* I write them off. *Four for brawling in a public place. Drunkards.* I write them off. *And one for... exposing himself in the Church?* I snort. *Good to see someone in this town is having fun. Shame they had to resort to blasphemy.* I write it off and rest my quill. My head slumps into my hand, provoking that elongated creak as it always does. I yawn, my eyes struggling to stay open. *I could just sleep here tonight... no one at home anyway. Guards might wake me up though. Ah, Gods... what time is it?* The blackness outside my window tells me nothing. *Gone midnight, that's for sure. Back in six hours anyway if that's the case. Damn.*

I get up and open the door a crack. Eren and Hal take a break from their dice to acknowledge me with that somewhat concerned look all the guards seem to now. The one that says 'you should sleep'. *What do they know? Crime doesn't rest. Justice can't either.* After a lazy salute I say goodnight and close the door, sliding the bolt shut with a quiet thud. Off comes my chunky pauldron, followed by my gauntlets and greaves. Lastly my chainmail, all dumped in a heap in the corner. I undo the low ponytail in my hair. *Oh, yes.* The dull ache in the front of my head becomes a tad softer. I take the blanket out of my desk, there just for nights like this. Scratchy, old and small. Made by my Ma before I was born. Don't think she meant for me to use it like this. *Can hear her now - 'Mara Oruman come back here!' or 'sit still you!'* I slump back down, blanket just covering my lap. My head falls back, and I allow my eyes to close.

Banging on my door. "Captain! Captain!" I jerk awake. More bashing. "Captain it's urgent!" My eyes flash to the window. It's still dark. *Oh, Gods. Not again.*

It takes a moment for the room to stop spinning but I manage to slur out a response. "Yes, yes." My eyes blink themselves to slumbering consciousness. "I'm coming, Mikael." I know it's him. No other man I know has a voice that cracks so much. Rubbing my aching eyes, I yawn and give myself just a precious few moments more. *Breathe in. And out. Come on Mara.* More bashing. More yelling. I push myself up and start putting on my gear, piece by damned piece. *I just know I'll need it.* The markings where it had dug into my skin are still there from a few hours ago. "Right. Let's have it." I walk over to the still-rattling door and open it. "Yes?" He moves his mouth silently for a second as if he can't speak. *If this is all for nothing...* "Mikael, I am very tired and I'd appreciate it if-"

"Maam!" Hal appears behind him, Mikael resting on his shoulders. "He's wounded. Eren's gone to fetch bandages."

"Oh, Gods... Mikael." His bright blue tunic is stained purple. *Stupid, Mara!* I shake my head. *Wake up!* Hal and I carry him to the chair. Mikael's cheeks are white, eyes wide and breathing quick. "Mikael, what happened?" The wound isn't as bad as it could be. A shallow but bloody gash on his side. But to tear through the chainmail? What beast could do that?

"W-woods." *The Icewood.* "Something attacked us. We were j-just doing a search, one you asked us to do yesterday." His eyes dart to mine. "F-few folk said they'd seen something walking around s-so we went..." His blue hands tremor. I hold them. Cold as the grave. Colder, perhaps.

I keep my voice quiet and calm. *Last thing he needs is more worries.* "Yes, I remember. Go on."

"Well... there is something there. I don't know what. B-but we disturbed it. And it attacked. It got James and Aldwin and Clara. I only just got away." Eren comes back, heaps the bandages on the desk and starts cleaning the wound.

Dammit. Three guards in one night. "Ok, ok. Calm down, soldier. You're safe here. I suspect you rode through the night." He nods. "Eren'll look after you." I pat him on the shoulder with my best reassuring smile. "Hal and I will go check out the woods. See what we can find." *I just wanted some Godsdamned sleep.*

Hal's face falls from concern to fear as he glances at Mikael. "We will, Ma'am?"

"Yes. We will." I snatch my axe from beside the door, sling it through my belt and beckon Hal through the cells and out into the bitter night. "Fetch the horses."

A few long hours later the grass turns to frost and the trees begin to disappear beneath the snow. The chill of the south is famous, and Chilrest is the largest town before the Icewood. *Cold never bothered me but this... this is chilly, I'll admit.* The forest stretches out before us, looming, black as the Void. The crisp night air tingles my lungs.

"Come on. We have something - or someone - to find. And probably kill."

We dismount, tie the horses up and draw our weapons. Hal flicks me a nervous look as he passes me a lantern. *Keep it together.* The snow crunches beneath our boots as we walk cautiously into the trees, lamp held high. *Stupid thing. Not near bright enough to see a damn.* Before long the edge of the forest is already gone.

Minutes later? An hour? Nothing. No signs of a struggle. No blood. No prints. *Could be going in circles for the way the trees share their silhouette.* I trudge through the snow, between the dead, frozen birch trees. I look left and right and back again.

"Captain." Hal comes right up beside me, teeth chattering. "Maybe we should turn back. If there's something out here we're not finding it in this." *A sensible idea, I suppose. But I can't help but feeling-*

A sudden biting wind chaps my lips and I'm grateful for the small amount of warmth the lamp gives my freezing fingers. A crunch from behind us. My head swivels, eyes staring into the dark. I stretch out my lamp, which reaches barely any further. *Useless thing.* Another crunch. A snap. My eyes follow the noise.

"Cap-"

"Quiet." *Something's out there.* I grip my axe tighter. "Whatever you are, come out in the name of the law and the King!" My voice wilts in the breeze. "If you mean me harm I warn there are other guards about and I am quite able to defend myself!" *This is all well and good Mara, but talk doesn't help if a group of ghouls jump at you.* I shake my head. *Focus.* "Come out!" I demand for a final time.

Nothing. Nothing but the whistling wind. Then a rotting stench reaches my nostrils, burning the back of my throat. I stifle a gag. *What on Tarae...*

A raspy voice. "I mean you-"

I spin and my lamp shatters against the figure in a shower of sparks. It doesn't so much as flinch.

"Wait!"

My axe clangs against solid metal and pain ricochets up my wrist. Before I can swing again a steel-firm hand shoves me back through the snow. Hal cleaves for its head only to have his axe batted clean from his grip with one swipe of a huge arm and sent tumbling back with another.

"Wait!" The figure yells and throws up its hands.

Hal stands and gawps at me. *Even in the dark I can see he's shitting himself.*

Even hunched over it stands at least two heads taller than I. The light of Hal's lantern reveals a mismatched jangle of armour. Plate and chain and leather, all worn beyond any recognition. I raise my axe, for all the good it'll do.

It does not move. "You surrender?"

"No." A male voice. Soft and breathy. He keeps his hands raised. "But I mean you no harm, good Lady Knight," his hoarse voice echoes around his great helm. *That helm... I know it. The Ciros on the front. The symbol of the Gods gilded in old silver and wreathed in flames on the forehead. Too dark to tell.*

"I am not a Knight. A Guard Captain."

"Then I mean you no harm, Captain."

"What are you doing here?" *Where do I know that damn helm from? Thinking makes my head ache.*

"That is a question that has a... rather lengthy answer."

"I have time. Did you kill my guards?"

"No. I swear it." He lowers his hands. "But I think I know who did." *Of course.*

"Who?"

"Again," he muses, "a rather long, complicated answer. Is there somewhere safe nearby?"

"I make the decisions here. I'd choose your next words carefully." *An empty threat if there'd ever been one.*

"I swear I mean you no harm." His rasps turn into pleas. *I know that helm!*

"Then why are you wearing a helmet from the Order of the White Flame?"

He still doesn't move. "I am afraid that, once again, the answer-"

"Answer me now Godsdammit!" My throat stings with the cold and the stench and the fear.

He pauses. "Then I can only do one thing." He slowly draws his hands up. My grip on my axe is like a vice. It takes all my effort not to swing for his skull.

"What are you doing?" I ask, voice hard as I can make it. *I can only hope he mistakes the tremble in my voice for cold.*

He places his hands on the side of his helmet. "Showing you." He pulls it upward and tucks it beneath his arm. it looks at me.

"By all that is holy..." My knees wither. His face - where his face should be - is skeletal and gaunt. The little rotted, paper-thin skin it has covers yellowed bones. Its bald, dry head is scarred beyond belief, eyes pale and lifeless as ice. Most features are missing entirely, just a black gap where a nose should be, lips non-existent and teeth like charcoal. There is no breath from his mouth. I want to look away but my eyes forbid it. Hal retches behind me. *I've never been so grateful to have missed a meal.*

"I am... sorry." Its voice makes sickening sense. "I was hoping to avoid this." He steps toward me.

"Stay back, unholy creature!"

"I assure you, I feel the same." His voice is... sombre.

"Meaning what?"

"I abhor the abomination that I am as much as you. As much as anyone. As I said, it is... complicated." His pale eyes pierce my own.

"Am I supposed to trust the word of a... a..."

"Revenant."

"Right." The word feels like slime on my tongue. "Revenant."

"No. I applaud that you don't. Though, I expect you might trust this." His gaze turns to his outstretched palm and mine follows. A bright white flame bursts forth, beautiful and holy. He holds it there, letting it flicker in the breeze a moment. He shakes it away and looks back. *By the White...*

"H-how?"

"I do not fully know. I believe I was a Knight of this so-called Order, a long time ago. May we discuss this elsewhere?"

I pause for a moment. Every fibre of my being screams to end him now, my fingers rippling over the haft of my axe. All undead are evil. *But one with the blessing of the Gods in his hands... I have little choice if I want this matter resolved.*

"Captain?" Hal's voice is filled with disgust. "You're not considering this, are you? We should put a torch to him and be done with it. This isn't our place."

"I can't turn down a lead, Hal." I turn back to the creature. "What do I call you?"

"I do not know my name. Call me what you like, Captain." *Abomination would fit nicely.*

"Fine. But you'll be kept in a cell until I figure out what to do with you. Hal, manacles." *For all the good it'll do.*

I stare at the man - the thing - in the cell. I have been all night. *Still haven't slept. Can't.* Not with that beast in there. He can tell me it's complicated until he's blue in the face. *Not that you could tell, of course.* Doesn't change what he is. *Undead. Unnatural. Wrong.* He, too, hasn't moved a muscle all night. Just sat in the corner of his cell, staring at the opposite wall. I suppose his kind don't need sleep. Hasn't said a word. Didn't even resist when I took his sword and put it in my office. I should have taken his armour too, but I couldn't bring myself to touch it.

"Captain," says a voice from behind me. I shake my head and blink myself back to the moment. I turn to see Nathaniel, arms folded and nose wrinkled. "Captain, would you like to be relieved?"

"No need."

A flicker of concern on his face as he says, "Captain we're all a little worried, you haven't even been home this-"

"You are dismissed."

"Cap-"

"Dismissed, Nathaniel." I grind my teeth. "Do not make me tell you again." He bows his head and takes a long look at the creature before shaking his head in disgust and heading down the stairs to the barracks below.

I'm fine. You're fine, Mara. I turn my gaze back to the thing in the cell. *Right. Time to have this.*

I step toward the cell and rap against the bars. He creaks his head toward me. *Even more revolting in the light.* The lamp reveals every scar, crack and crease of rot.

"Put your helmet back on. If we're doing this, I don't want to have to look at you as well." He says nothing, but slowly does so. *He's used to this then. Good.*

"You are willing to talk beyond the boundaries of this cage?" There's a fleck of hope in his hollow voice.

"Not yet."

"Understandable. I would do the very same if-"

I wave my finger. "When I want your opinion I will ask for it. Got it?"

He bows his head. "Yes." *I wish I could read him.* He stands, heaving himself to his feet. *Ilara's mercy he's a big* bastard. *Abominations are like that, I suppose.* "So, what would you like to know?"

Gods it reeks. A stench of damp mould and many fly-riddled carcasses. "Could you... move backwards a bit? Your odour is..."

"Oh!" It shuffles back to the far wall, raising a hand in apology. "I forget. I haven't smelt anything in years. My deepest apologies."

Sure, whatever. "So what exactly were you doing in that forest?"

"Searching for the man that cursed me this way."

"As in..." I gesture to it. It nods. "And who is that?"

"I believe he was a powerful, powerful blood mage. A Bloodpriest in fact-"

"You believe?" I lean back. "You don't actually know?"

"Well, my memories are... hazy, at best - especially those of my previous life. Being undead and centuries-old... tends to wear on one's mind." *Great help.*

"Apparently so. Go on."

"A Bloodpriest. Ancestors of the Druids of the current Vaskan Empire. From what I've discovered I believe that they invoked some kind of blood magic ritual on me to curse me upon my death. I know not how or even why." *Bloodpriests, rituals... what is he talking about?*

"So did you find this... Bloodpriest?"

"Not quite, but I think I found his dwellings. Whether current or former, there is a cave underneath the Icewood - not far from where you found me." *He sounds sincere, honest. Something about him... but I can't trust him.* "And there is where I think he can be found. I have searched this land for the better part of four centuries and have found no better lead than this."

"Four centuries?" *Gods... he's seen most of history.*

"I spent years, all my existence hunting. I have slain Vampires, Werewolves, Banshees, Liches, even Revenants like myself. I cannot find any more..." his voice turns mournful. "I have hid from the eyes of mortals, and I have helped those I could. But now, I wish only to die. To die and know why I am what I am."

"If you want to die I could have killed you in the forest." I raise an eyebrow. "And I can still kill you now. Save us both the trouble." *I don't think I've bluffed so spectacularly in my life.*

"Death would be a release, yes." *We could both get what we want... he seems sincere.* "Please, Captain." *Why am I feeling sorry for an abomination?*

"Why should I? You have done nothing for me, for my people. You have yet to even prove it wasn't you that killed my guards. The best solution for me is to kill you and be done with it." *I wouldn't stand a chance if he chose to defend himself.*

"But if he is still alive, can you afford not to?" His words turn to pleas, "He may be the one that killed your guards, or at the very least he's a threat."

"He's a potential threat if he's somehow alive after four centuries. You, creature, are a threat right here, right now."

He pauses, and bows his head. "I understand, Captain. I do not wish to fight you." He sits back on the cell floor. "I am sorry we could not help each other."

"And what help could you possibly offer me? More vague answers? Perhaps some other centuries-old criminals?"

"I could... heal you."

"What do you mean heal me? My body is-"

"Not your body." He shakes his head. "Your mind. You are tired. Stressed. Tense. I could ease that."

"How..." My eye twitches. "I sleep fine, thank you."

"I am not deaf, nor am I am blind. I heard your guards' concerns in the night. And even with my old eyes, I can see the tiredness in yours. 'Tis like watching a tree wither."

"Spare me the poetry."

"My apologies. What I mean to say is that I can help you, should you wish it."

"You are not using any blood magic on me, monster."

"It will not be blood magic," he says in quiet affirmation. "The Whitefire can heal as well as destroy. This is a power you know to trust. And I hope, one that leads you to trust me."

Is it true? Is he lying? He gives nothing away. *He has little reason to.* After a quiet few moments of tense silence, I nod. "Fine. Do it. Any slip-ups and you'll be hunted down like the animal you are. Even if I'm not around to see it."

"You have my word as a Knight." He hesitates for a moment. "I think."

I jangle the keys in lock and step into the cell. The smell makes me gag a little but I push the worst of it down. I barely come up to his chest. I swallow. *You're insane, Mara. What are you doing?*

"It may be best if you lay down." He gestures to the rickety cell bed.

I remove the bulkiest parts of my armour and clamber awkwardly onto the bed, laying down on my back, feet dangling off the edge. I brush the hair from my eye and watch as he looms above my head, palms pressed together in prayer.

He unclasps and brilliant white sparks flicker between his hands, followed by a rolling, cylindrical flame. With great care he brings each hand to my temples and gently presses. A heavenly warmth flows through my head as if being bathed with divine light. Calm washes over me. I close my eyes. My heart slows. My breath is released. My muscles loosen. Light cascades through my body, suddenly lighter than air. *Gods...* Blinding light fills my vision. I begin to drift toward it.

I turn over and give muscles a long stretch. *Gods that feels amazing. Where's that draft? No matter.* It's like I'm next to a roasting fire back at Ma's. My eyes open and I squint at the lamp hanging outside the bars. *Huh.* I curl back up, hands grasping at my blanket.

Bars? I leap up and shake myself awake. The cell gate is closed. *He's gone! The bastard's fucking gone!* I scream into my hands. *Idiot!*

"Are you alright, my Lady?" He stands in front of the cell, head tilted in some kind of curiosity.

"You let me out of this cell right now you bastard!"

He gently pushes the cell door open. *Oh.* Then very calmly he says, "My apologies, Captain. I simply thought it would be better for you to wake up without my standing over you. I brought your blanket then made myself at home within your office. I hope you don't mind." *I think... I believe him.*

The words struggle to come forth. "Th-thank you. I just thought..."

He waves it away. "I know. I still don't blame you."

"Sorry." *That feels... strange.*

"No need. Did you... sleep well?"

"Better than I have in a long while." *The first I've had a clear head in years is more accurate.*

He bows a little. "It is a pleasure to serve, Ma'am." *Well, he's more polite than half the guards here. Suppose with a few centuries you pick up things. I think he's earned the benefit of the doubt.*

"Right." I start putting on my gear. "Where's that cave?"

"Really?" His grating voice sounds human for the first time. "I can lead you straight to it. Though I would ask you to be careful and to let me take any risks that befall us. I should, as a Knight and-."

"No chance. I wouldn't be where I am without taking risks." I pull the last strap on my pauldron then sling my axe through my belt. "The horses are outside. Best make our exit quick. I'd really rather not have to explain you to this whole town."

"Understandable. Lead on, Captain."

I clutch the lamp and stay close behind him as he gently brushes aside the frozen branches. He takes great care to not break anything, nor step on anything fragile. *For someone so old you'd think he'd be more jaded. I'm four centuries younger and Gods know I am.* On the way over he talked about nothing but how he once lived in a small hut somewhere in the Pilgrim mountains for a time, with only a dog for company. Raised it, took care of it, watched it grow old. For near twenty years he did nothing else. Barely left the hut from what he said. Said he'd forgotten the dog's name a long time ago, which seemed to pain him. The last stretch was rode in silence. *To say I misjudged him might be an understatement.*

"It's up here," he says, "under an old oak. I discovered records of it in other tomes in similar dwellings."

"Why didn't you go straight in?"

"I..." he pauses for a moment, struggling to articulate himself. "I wanted to but found myself at a loss. I didn't think I was ready, even after all this time." *Ready?*

"Ready for what?" I say, wading through the damp, snowy ground.

"Well," he chuckles and turns to me, "death." *Ah...*

After a few minutes of awkward, silent walking he stops and points to an ancient, frost-bitten oak. "There." He bends down and scrapes away the layers of snow, ice and mud away to eventually reveal a large wooden hatch. Like the top of a barrel.

"Why not simply use the flame?"

"I've found its usage is always a careful balance, but in all truth I simply did not want to harm the tree, nor anything else hidden in the snow. It pays to be kind, even if you don't know if it will bear fruit immediately. Eventually, it will."

"You say a lot of things like that, don't you?"

"Like what?" And as if to demonstrate the duality of his being he rips the hatch clean off its hinges and gently places it up against the tree. *I'm very glad he's on my side.*

"Poetic. Practised."

He shrugs. "I'm not sure. I've been alone with my thoughts for more years than I care to remember. Perhaps some of them would offer some wisdom. And..." he trails and looks off into the forest.

"And...?"

"You're the first person to have held any length of conversation with me in the last... century and a half, at least. I am grateful and perhaps... overeager to have a companion once again. I apologise."

"No, no, please I welcome the wisdom - Gods know I need some. Just curious."

"Oh." Even beneath the helm, I hear his voice falter a little. "Thank you."

"Shall we?" He nods and descends the creaking ladder. I follow close behind.

My feet hit the floor. The smell of damp slaps me round the face, but he's already halfway down a tight corridor, whiteflame aloft. *Well he wasn't lying. This place is certainly old.* Hewn from dirt, stones and roots, covered in spiderwebs both ancient and fresh. Dust loiters in the air like a fog. There's tablets embedded in the walls, scribbled with undecipherable writings. Shapes and symbols I've never seen, scrawled characters and strange drawings. *Scribblings of someone... disturbed. Some kind of Druidic, perhaps?*

"By the Four..." He stops at the end of the corridor.

"What is it?" I stop my looking and rush up behind him into a small, circular room lined and littered with scrolls, books and pages.

"Nothing. Nothing but notes and..." He points to a scarlet-robed skeleton slumped in a chair much like the one in my office. "He's dead. By centuries at least." *Oh.* "It appears you were right, Captain... I am... sorry."

"No matter." I surprise myself. "We had to confirm it. And I'm sure looking through those notes will help." *Look at you go, Mara.*

He is still.

"Are you... ok?"

"Four hundred years," he whispers.

"Take off your helmet, Knight."

"What?

I move my hands to the side of his helm and carefully remove it. *In the low light his scarred skull doesn't look so bad.* I set the helmet down on the floor.

"Come on." I smile at him despite how strange it feels on my face. "Let's look through the notes. There has to be something." He nods very gently, and smiles. An ugly, grim smile filled with blackened or missing teeth but one I find myself happy to see nonetheless.

There's dust-ridden tomes and moth-bitten scrolls. Cracked vials and rusted knives. Half the surfaces are covered in strange stains, and the other half were covered in dark-brown splotches that were all too obvious. *Books on beasts, books on blood magic, books on every vile topic the Church has banned.* All manner of things, but nothing mentioned anything like him.

"Captain," he calls from the other side of the room, "I do believe I've found something." I put down the pages I'm holding and walk over to see his skeletal fingers perusing a crusty, leather-bound diary. "Look here." He points to a faded passage and reads, "I've found the beast that killed my daughter. Caught him and bound him. A member of the White Flame, no less. Abaddon Herasan." He turns to me expectantly. "That's me."

"Abaddon Herasan?" *A Knight's name if I've ever heard one.*

"I remember..." He turns back to the book and begins to read again, "We perform the Revanence ritual tonight. Then my daughter can find peace, and he will walk..." he hesitates for a moment, "forever cursed." He nods. "So... he glances at the skeleton on the chair. "This is the reason for my torment."

"You killed his daughter."

"She must have been an enemy - a blood mage... I would never kill a..."

"It's alright." My hand steadies his shoulder.

And then we don't say a word. I let him take it all in.

"Thank you for your help, Captain. But I have what I came for." He tips his head at me, "It is time."

"Abaddon-"

"I came here with two intentions. I have achieved one - the second falls to you."

"No."

"Captain, I ask you as a friend."

"No, Abaddon. I will not kill you."

"Then you leave me no choice." My heart skips.

"You want me to defend myself then I have no choice either." My axe creeps to my hand. *Don't fight me. Please.*

"No." He picks up his helm and places it in my hands. "Thank you, Mara," he says, extending his arms to his side, "I have enjoyed this last day more than the past few hundred years combined." Holy fire bursts from his palms, bright and furious. "Except perhaps the dog. Felix, I think his name was." He smiles at me in jest with those dark teeth.

The flames crawl up his arms. The paper around him catches alight, and the ground beneath him begins to smoke. I step back and through the crackling flames I swear I hear him chuckle. *This whole place is just a set pyre.*

"Go, Captain!" His hoarse voice roars louder as the flames crackle and start to tear through the tree. "The fire will die not long after I but you must go!"

A roar of flame sends me sprinting down the hallway and springing up the ladder. Out the hatch and bounding across the snow, not stopping until I reach the forest's edge.

I catch my breath and watch the thick white smoke rise high above the Icewood and drift into the black sky. *Good luck, Abaddon. May you find peace.* I tuck the helm in my satchel, tie the horses together then hoist myself up to the saddle. We start the long journey home.

The Executioner's Dread

Year 338

Today's the day. The one I hoped would never come. The one I pushed far from my mind, thinking, hoping, praying that if I never thought about it, it wouldn't. But I've known it for months. So has my wife. So have my daughters. So have the people of Edefall, those bloodthirsty nameless who just need some excitement.

Blood's as exciting as it gets to most. The endless struggle of life and death, a small reminder that all we are is flesh and bone and blood. Whether a gaping wound, a nick in the back of a hand or a scraped knee, that shot of excitement as you feel your heart beat loud in your chest for just a sliver of time, all at once fascinated and afraid. All the better if the blood isn't yours. I was like that, once. When my Father made me pick up the axe for the first time, and told me what an honour it was to kill in the name of the King, the thrill of judgement done and blood spilt. Now I daresay I've seen as much blood as I've seen water, and it makes me feel very little. It gives me no more pleasure, no more thrill, no more feeling of a job well done. It gives me no feeling at all.

But today, it gives me fear.

I kiss my wife goodbye, and she looks at me with those big, ever-loving green eyes like there's something I can do to prevent the inevitable. I kiss both my daughters on the forehead, each twice, and squeeze all three of them in my arms, resting my head there for a moment, taking all the time I can. All so alike, my family. My wife breaks her head from my chest for a moment to look at me, but I know she knows there's nothing I can do.

"It'll be alright, my darlings," I say, knowing that it is a lie, and yet unable to say anything else. "I love you." Nothing could be so true. Strange, how a person is able to switch from one to the other, all in the name of love. Love is the downfall of many great people. Love of their family, of their city, of their nation, of an ideal. Makes people do the strangest things and the darkest deeds.

And with that I'm out the door, out onto the narrow, cobbled street filled with houses that look like mine, all filled with those that perform duties like mine. The maids, the servants, the House Guards, their barracks right at the end. Two outside the door turn their helmeted heads as I step out into the morning and nod at me. Do they know, or are they just being polite? It makes little difference. No one's sympathy can stop the inevitable.

I turn left, past the short row of huddled houses then stop just short of the end, in front of the door. The dark, wooden door with the big, heavy ring handle. To the cells of the damned, and my little armoury, full of my many implements of death. I fumble the heavy key in the screeching lock, feel the weighted thud as it opens and then take the cold iron ring in my hands. Then I open the door.

Dark, and cold. No matter what time of day, or the weather outside. It's always dark and cold here, the light barely filtering in from the heavily-dusted windows. No one ever wants to look in, and it helps me to never look out. Coils of rope loom in the grubby corner, a rack of assorted blades hanging over them - rusted and old, shiny and sharpened to lethal points, needles and cleavers attached to worn-down wood, tired from years of hands, many here before even I was. Before even my Father was, no doubt. There's one around here somewhere, I forget where, from before even his Father. I always wondered if one of my children might take up the blade after me. Seems unlikely, now. I never wanted this for them. And after this I doubt I'll be able to wash the taste of guilt and steel from my mouth for the rest of my days.

I shift over to my leathers left on the bench. The thick, black vest that stinks of sweat and salt and still feels damp. The equally thick, black gloves that make sure when I grip the blade I swing strong and aim true. The black mask, my other face, those eyeholes staring at me accusingly as I run my fingers over it. Looking into my heart, as if it knows what it is I'm about to do. I stuff it in my trouser pocket. No need for that just yet. Not until I leave.

I slip the vest over my undershirt and button the sticky, heavy thing tight. By Duw, it weighs heavy today. I pull on my leather gloves, flexing my hands in them, just like I do every time, pretending that anything about today could ever be normal. Just another execution. It'll all be over soon.

I move to the shelf, and run my finger before the selection of blades, stopping at the largest. The Headsman's axe. A large, curved blade bolted tight to a thick wooden pole. Thick and daunting as ever. It seems heavier today. I run my finger softly over the blade, just enough to feel the kiss of the metal. It barely breaks my skin, nought but a drop of blood. Good enough for some, good enough for some common criminal, perhaps. Too good for a murderer. Not sharp enough for today.

Back to the workbench, then. I pull a whetstone out from one of the gnarled, dusty drawers, and put it to the blade. Scrape, hiss, scrape. The stone moving up and down each side of the blade, the thin edge getting thinner with each stroke of my hand, all the more ready to do its dark work. Hiss, scrape, hiss. The blade gradually picking up an evil shine, my face reflected clearer all the time. Scrape, hiss, scrape. Shining now like a freshly-forged blade in the dim morning light, my face clear as in a mirror. My eyes. Tired, dark, and hollow.

Life loves to test a man.

I used to love the way the whetstone made the steel ring, tuneful and bright as it prepared for its use, excitement flushing through me as the blade grew sharper, more deadly with each stroke of a hand. My father used to say it sang to him. But with the last, solemn scrape of the stone against steel all I hear is a mournful sigh. It too seems to know what it is about to become party to.

I set the blade down for a moment and take the hood from my pocket, looking once again into empty eyes. Maybe wearing it might hide some of my shame, but only from those who don't know who I am. Only from the gathered crowd, who care not for the beheaded nor who does the beheading. I pull it on slowly, letting the still sweat-damp leather cover my face bit by bit. As irritating as always, and yet a sore relief today. I pick up the blade and head out through the back door.

Into the yard, into the pale light of morning again. More guards. Servants and stable-boys rustling around, tending to the horses. I move across the yard, then soon enough through another door to the jail cells, back into the darkness. More specifically, the cells of those condemned to die. Only one today. My heart beats dully in my chest, the breaths I take sharper than they should be. I look to the two guards posted outside his cell, leaning and muttering between themselves.

"Ready?" I say, more to myself than either of them but they both bolt up and nod, one of them fumbling for a set of jangling keys. He creaks open the cell gate, they both step in and after a short, muffled exchange they drag out a man by his armpits, shins dragging across the floor, face thankfully covered in a hood much like my own, only without eyes. Comforting, in a dark way I know shouldn't be comforting. "Come on." I nod to the far door. "Let's not keep them waiting."

I swing the heavy wooden door and step out into a waiting, bristling crowd in the city square, a path only created down the middle by a few dozen guards desperately trying to keep the bloodthirsty masses at bay.

I don't think I've ever really looked at a crowd quite so much. The twisted faces of impersonal hatred, the married eyes of pent-up anger, just waiting to be directed somewhere other than the true cause, the stinking fruit and vegetables ready to be thrown, squeezed soft in their waiting hands, the stench of sweat and anger radiating from all around. All of them here, just for something to do.

Then the man's dragged out, and all at once I hear the deafening roar of the crowds as their rage is finally able to be directed, the whizz of projectiles past my ear just moments before they thud into the prisoner, or splat into the ground at his feet. The guards push back against the waving, rippling, hollering crowd. I take no notice. I have a job to do.

The slow, aching creak of my heavy feet on the wooden steps up to the gallows. No ropes today. His crime was deemed worthy of the blade. Over to the executioner's block. That gnarled, bloodstained, sweat-dripped, ugly lump of wood. A crescent cut out just big enough for a human neck. I'd never thought of it until now, but did the carpenter who made it even think about how many lives it would help take? I gaze over my axe. Did the blacksmith know this was its fate? Did the farmer know their crops would be used as rotten projectiles? How many people are party to my profession?

Just one, I suppose. It's the man that swings the axe. I'll have to live with that.

Then the man comes dragged up the steps, shins smacking against each one before being manhandled to the block and forced to his wilting knees as if he might have the strength to resist.

I look out to the crowd, the nameless waiting faces, suddenly quiet with reflection. With awed, bated breath, Or perhaps just bored, waiting for me to swing the blade and have it done so they can get back to their guiltless, bloodless lives. They'll forget about the man at the block just as soon as they turn their backs. It's up to me to remember the faces, each one of them. Young and rebellious, old and haggard, men and women, screaming and silent, tearful and stoic. Every single one passes through my thoughts at least once or twice. This one, I fear, will never leave for a moment.

I remove his hood and throw it down onto the platform.

The boy stares up at me, his sunken green eyes and squinting in the morning light. Then he nods, and settles his neck in the crescent. He knows his crime, and he knows there's nothing to be done.

I grip my axe with two hands just like always. Strong and secure. The swing must be perfect, after all. I raise it high above my head, the glint of the light glimmering on the freshly-sharpened edge.

It seems like an age I leave it there. A single breath, mine and the boy's and the crowd's all at once. I could keep it there for an eternity. I could stop it all, throw down my axe and declare that I will not do it. But I can't, not really.

So down, a swift strike, a deep thud into flesh and wood. A splatter of blood on the platform, a bright red coat on the blade. The crowd cheers. The head rolls, the body slumps. The breath is released.

My duty is done and my son is dead.

Dream Thief

Year 564

Dreams are unique things. They show us our fears and our hopes, our hates and our loves. All in such fantastic detail yet so often masqueraded by self-delusion. We feel the need to protect ourselves from our own thoughts. And that is why our subconscious captivates me so. What we are when the active mind fades away and leaves behind a tangle of suppressed thoughts. The things we refuse to know about ourselves. Things we refuse to believe. The lies we tell ourselves and the beliefs we hold despite the unforgiving nature of reality. We know who we are in the light. We fear what we are in the dark.

When I was a younger man I had yet to fully realise my potential. I was talented, of course. But I inexperienced. And as you'll well know Cheans look upon the use of any blood magic with scorn. They detest and vilify the Empire, the druids, the Elders themselves. Had I been born across the water like my parents perhaps it would have been different. I wouldn't have had to teach myself, for one. But then, it led me to where I stand now.

It was a dark night about fifteen or so years ago when my journey truly began. I had just slipped past the guards outside the front gates of Grahel. Oafs couldn't guard a single coin without a drunken beggar claiming it. I was on my way to a house of a young girl I'd met just a few days before in the town market selling flowers. The same age as myself, dark red hair and, I must say, a true beauty. I remember the scent of her perfume mingling with the floral notes of the basket tucked under her arm. She told me her name was Heather - I recall making a vapid remark about her being akin to a flower and she blushed. We made conversation and I purchased a bunch, claiming they were for my Mother. I remember the split second our hands touched as I passed her the coin. Her skin was gentle, soft and smooth. The shimmering silver sliver in her bright blue eyes told me she concealed something. A small vision of her wild mind just through the way she looked at me. She was a perfect fit. Eventually I inquired about her residence and after some playful back-and-forth she gave it to me, inviting me to come around when it suited me best. She warned me she lived with a protective father, but I didn't much of it. The best time for what I was interested in was in the dead of night anyhow. And protective or not, we all sleep.

I crept low to the old town walls, careful not to step into the torchlight lest the guards see me. For years being of a small frame had been a curse. Now it was a blessing, allowing me to stalk the night with ease. I came to her small abode, a little cottage near the edge of the town not fifteen strides from the wall, and the same from the nearest neighbour. I studied the quaint building and the windows suggested two separate bedrooms with an open ground floor. No smoke came from the chimney, which meant they were asleep. That would be my way in. I took a look around and noted the sewer grate just a few strides away. That would be my escape. I proceeded to climb up the stonework of the house, fingers digging into the crumbling mortar and onto lichen-covered ledges, only stopping to peek through the window. It was her. Red hair and porcelain skin. It seemed almost a shame, at the time. I recall thinking I could have pursued her traditionally had I so wished. But she was, frankly, a bore and my desires lay not with the flesh. I continued past the window, up onto the roof. I took a quick look around, careful not to be seen. There was no one in sight, and so I took a breath of the cold night air and stepped into the chimney, bracing myself against the walls on the way down. Thick with soot but otherwise easy enough.

Just before I hit the bottom I peered out, careful and quiet. The room had not a single candle, black as the night I had just left. I dropped down and stepped out, ever careful of making a sound. Feet light on the floorboards, crouched down low as I could. I saw the stairs and slipped toward them. As I went up each one I pressed it with my fingers, being sure it didn't creak before I moved. Once at the top I headed to the room on the left - the one I had seen Heather in. I pushed the door open, little by little. She was still sound asleep. There was a candle on a nightstand next to her, giving me just enough light to see what I was doing. The evening was going wonderfully. I made my way in, latched the door behind me and slunk to her bed. I could still smell the flowers lingering over her. Examining her body, I noticed a few bruises on her arms I hadn't seen before, as well as a fresh black eye, which hadn't been there earlier that day. No matter, I thought. She must have taken a fall. She had some other job, perhaps. A thousand reasons. She was still perfect for my wants.

I took a rag from the inside of my shirt, which had been soaked in a mixture of herbs I'd perfected. It could knock someone out cold in a matter of seconds. I held it to her mouth gently, so as not to shock her. She had to still be comfortable or it would not work. Deep sleep works best, you understand. Once I saw her hand go a little more limp I knew it had started to take effect. I set about what I had to do.

I took the knife and vial from my satchel then made a small incision on the girl's wrist and pressed the vial to it. Drop by drop, blood filled the vial. Once full, I capped it and wrapped a small bandage around the wound. I didn't intend to cause more harm than was necessary. I had what I needed. I often wonder that, if I'd left as I should have, things would have been different. But we cannot change the past.

As it was, in my eagerness I went to the other end of the room and sat down cross-legged on the floor. In one hand I held her vial and next to it, one of my own. I took out a small bowl from my satchel and placed it in front of me. I poured the two vials in, watched as two dark shades mixed and became one. Like a river meeting the ocean, the two blending seamlessly as nature always intended. I gazed into the pool before me, hands on my knees and breathing slowed. Concentration is the key to all blood magic, but particularly of the mind. Breathing in, breathing out. Then I began to feel that pull. The calling of my blood outside my body, a connection that cannot be broken, mixing with a foreign entity. Her blood pooling with my own, beautiful and mesmerising. Before I knew it my mind was falling, spinning, back and back again. A swelling pressure, a cool breeze in my mind.

I opened my eyes, and I'd arrived.

Her mind was even more beautiful than her. I saw her imagination in perfect detail.

Everything was etched in silver. A dark forest with impossibly tall trees. A child with burning red hair on a winding path. Perhaps thirteen or so. Birds twittered magical songs in the starlit treetops whilst critters scuttled quick and unseen through the undergrowth. Everything felt so real and though I knew better it was hard not to believe it. It was absolutely glorious. I followed her as she strolled the woodland path, but I was careful not to disturb her. Behind trees, in shadows. I came to observe, not participate. She came to a small river. A hop, a skip and a jump over it as a child might and she was over the other side, water splashing and glittering dark around her.

But as I approached, as I crossed the river itself I caught my breath at its darkness. A deep, ugly, thick maroon. Almost bloodlike. An odd thing for such a bright-eyed dream. I shook it off and kept up with her. Back into the bright forest.

And then as abruptly as I had found myself here, the forest ended. A black void beyond. No light, no silvery trees, no sound. She was still for a moment; a girl against the blackness, facing away from the beauty she had left, teetering on a precipice.

A great, scarred claw broke the void from below and gargantuan roar shook the trees. It tore through the blackness and rose - a beast of pure, fiery evil. Flaming hair and two great horns atop its head, a thick, fire-red beard upon its gnarled face. Another great roar, the trees shuddering as it brought its hand crashing down. It froze mid-air, barely a palm from Heather's face.

A woman, nearly tall as the monster itself held its hand, pulling it back. A woman of pure white and silver, shining like The White itself. The two giants fought, a battle of raging red fire and heavenly white as Heather stood in place, helpless and frozen. I could scarcely describe the colours, the feeling of foreign emotions whirling through. But as soon as it started it was over. The beast proved stronger, clawed hand choking the life from her and tossing her aside, flung into the void. It turned its eyes to Heather.

Once again it raised a hand. And once again it was stopped.

A man appeared underneath it. A real knight in shining armour, radiating just like the woman that had come before him. Blade brandished, shield raised in virtuous defence. He let out a fearsome yell as he drove a sword deep into the beast's hand. The monster roared again, a shriek, almost - loud and hollow and full of rage.

A black hand broke from the void and shackled around the knight's ankle. Then another. And another, another and then hundreds of hands, clawing, grasping, pulling until he was swallowed. Soldiers of darkness, come to take away the hero. She was alone again. And she began to cry, hands clasped to her face, knees sunken into the dirt. The beast raised its evil hand once again. I could sit idle no longer.

I rushed out from behind my tree. Stupidly. Foolishly. "No!" I screamed, "NO!" The beast and the girl turned to me. Their eyes went wide, and then the blackness swallowed us whole.

I was ripped from the dream as I fell into it. I snapped back into this world, eyes wide and heart pounding.

There was banging on the bedroom door, the wood creaking and shaking beneath the weight of the furious knocks. My eyes darted to the bed. She was stirring. It was time to leave. I leapt up and sent the bowl spattering crimson over the floorboards. No time to do anything about it. I rushed for the window. Locked. No. *Sealed* shut, two iron padlocks either side. Breaking it would draw the guards. My eyes flashed around the room, desperate for a way out.

"Heather!" A brutish voice called out from behind the door, "Is someone in there with you?" The bashing on the door and the snarling behind it only got louder. "I'm coming in!" I had no choice. I grabbed the candlestick off the nightstand and smashed it through the window. Heather bolted up, eyes staring at me, face frozen for a split second. She opened her mouth to scream. *She'd seen my face.* I took the dagger from my belt and leapt on her. It went right through her throat, blooded point sticking out the other side. No sound. Only a trickle of blood.

I brought my lips to her ear. "I'm sorry." I pulled the knife out with a wet scrape sound as the blood bubbled gently from the wound and down my gloves. I backed off the bed and smashed the rest of the broken window with the pommel of my dagger then leapt down, knees nearly buckling under the fall. I heard the bedroom door crash in, wood splintering. Then a deep, wailing scream. The guards would be there in moments. The night had turned from perfect into the only time I was nearly caught. I rushed down to the sewer grate and tore it off, slipped down and pulled it back on just as I heard more voices coming my way. I ran through the dank, stinking underground and out through the sewer's slime-caked exit. Through the ditch the sewer emptied into, through the grasping, sticky mud and through the whipping trees.

It was raining something evil by the time I finally reached home - a cave, then - cloak sodden with rain, boots sludged with mud, gloves sticky with blood. I banged the makeshift door hurriedly shut behind me, threw my satchel to the ground and grabbed a bottle of foul-tasting spirits I had opened a few nights previous. I had never killed before. And at the time I had only been practising that little routine for a few years, moving from town to town every few months to ensure I was never caught.

But in that time I'd never once sought to affect a dream. I'd observed, listened, watched with intent. I lay on my bedroll next to an unlit fire and took large swigs of burning drink in hopes to ease myself. I had never killed before. A shame it was her. I recognised the unique mixture of thrill and regret that it brought me even as it happened. But it wasn't really that I'd killed that bothered me so. It wasn't planned but I knew it would likely happen eventually. No, it wasn't that. It wasn't simply the barbaric rush of taking a life. I could see people's dreams, their true selves and I would be the only one to ever know their deepest, darkest secrets once they were gone. The thrill of untapped knowledge. Knowledge belonging solely to me.

But along with that was something else, nagging at me. What were the bruises on the girl's arm? Why was her window sealed? So many questions rattling around in my drunken, adrenaline-pumped head. About the girl, about the world and about myself. My conscience and my curiosity were at war.

I drank enough that night to drown them both.

A month later I had still not left my forest cave. Initially, it had been to avoid arousing suspicions from any curious locals. But now it was a habit; days spent not seeing the daylight except through the slits of my door. Days spent pacing, mind mulling over nought but that night. Days spent sitting in one spot, watching at the dusty shafts of light move across the damp floor, disappear into night and reappear the following morning. My spirit was restless. And so I finally decided the time had come to leave this place behind. Thinking, hoping, praying it would help me forget. That a new home might help me begin to make things normal again; allow me to ruminate properly.

That evening I was arranging the vials in my pack; each one placed carefully in folded cotton to keep them from breaking. I heard a slow knock on my door and a low, careless groan. I reached for the knife behind my belt - I'd never been much of a fighter but precautions are always wise - and approached the door.

Another low groan, followed by a series of scratching knocks and a feeble cry for help. I removed the makeshift rope latch and pulled it open, just a crack. A pale man with a mess of matted red hair stood in front of me, two arrows sticking out his shoulder, one out his leg, blood down his leathers and two blue-black bruises marring one half of his face. A familiar, helpless look in his big blue eyes as they widened at me. I hurriedly put his arm on my back and helped him in, closing the door behind us.

Upon inquiry he told me his name was James, and that he was a soldier returning home. On his way back he'd been set upon by a small group of bandits. He'd not been able to reach Grahel in time and they shot down his horse. After losing them in the trees, he'd come upon my cave only out of sheer luck. He told me all this as I removed the arrows from his back, careful so as not to make the wounds worse. I patched him up reasonably well. Always had a way with bodies. I set him on the ground, cleaned and gave him a simple mix of healing herbs on his wounds, wrapped a thick bandage around his thigh then the same around his shoulder. Not much I could do for the bruises, but nothing was broken.

He thanked me and told me how lucky he was, and that he was faring much better. As typical a soldier as any he asked for a way to repay me for my services - with feigned surprise I asked politely if I might try a herbal remedy I'd been practicing but had yet to try. I don't blame him for believing me - a friendly, stranger out in the woods with all sorts of tools and herbs and vials? How could I not be a healer? I of course told him it would put him to sleep, but he was stupid and eager to repay me so agreed without hesitation. He joked that he'd be thankful for the rest, and I laughed along with him.

I washed and rinsed the cloth in my mixture of herbs, handed it over and explained to cover his mouth and nose. He was out in seconds. I set to work.

As with the girl I took my knife, made a cut just under one of the arrow wounds in his thigh, careful not to rip my own fine bandaging and took some of his blood into a vial. I took a vial of my own, took them to a corner, mixed them in the bowl and started to meditate. Breathing slow, mind slow. Mine and the foreign, mixed yet pure. The draw of it, the gentle, washing pull. My mind fell backwards.

I found myself on a dark hill overlooking a raging battle. Nameless, silver soldiers fought terrible creatures in utter silence. Figures moved as if in the ultimate, ridiculous fairytale battle of good and evil. I saw James on a brilliant white steed charging through the mad fray, his shimmering blade a beacon through the dark, cleaving down his enemies left and right. An almighty roar shook the earth, a rumble reached the soles of my feet. Thunder crackled in the sky, almost as if in reply. A gigantic hand came up from the ground. A great, bestial hand that caved the ground in as its owner drew itself up onto the field, soldiers and monsters alike falling into the abyss left in its wake. Another hand, this time clenched shut and punching up through the earth as it reared its horrific head.

I knew that beast. Right down to the burning red beard and ugly yellow eyes. James saw it the same time I did, rushing towards it sword raised and bellowing. He struck the beast's legs, leaving a great yellow gouge. The beast was lumbering and slow, fist always just where James had been, the hero landing blow after blow. Then, in one mighty leap from his steed he cleaved the beast's head off and landed just as the two parts of him thudded into the dirt. The clenched hand smashed against the ground and unfurled. Inside was a young girl with wild, shimmering red hair. No older than fourteen. She took James' hand. They embraced and exchanged hushed words.

The pieces clicked into place.

"Oh no." In an instant the whole field turned its gaze to me. Creatures. Soldiers. James. And the girl.

My eyes shot open, lungs heaving for air. James thrashed and scrambled backwards, kicking me in the teeth and sending me reeling. He looked at me, then at the bowl, then the knife by my side. He staggered backwards, gripping his thigh and panting.

Blood mage. That's what he screamed at me. Called me filthy. Unholy. Vile.

He stumbled his way to the door and gripped the handle. I had no choice. I took the knife and charged him. A stab in the shoulder, a howl of pain from him and we bundled into the wall. I dragged the blade down his back, hot blood spattering into my face as I tore through my own stitches. An arm around his neck as he flailed, pulling, pulling, twisting the knife in his back until he fell limp.

I'd done it again.

I let go and he slumped to the ground. My hand was drenched with blood. Warm spots dripped down my face and the taste lingered on my tongue. Crimson pooled around his leaking body. I felt the urge to collapse to my knees. To tug at my hair. What had I done? Such waste that could have been avoided if they hadn't been so stupid...

His dream. So familiar. The beast, that girl... I squatted down beside his still-leaking body and patted him down, rifling through the pockets of his leathers. I turned him over and something poked out from inside his shirt. I reached in - a small letter written in a shaky hand, spotted with fresh red as my fingers opened it.

James,

I hope this finds you well.

Father's only gotten worse. Nine years since Mother died. Seven since you had to leave. It's becoming harder and harder to hide. Just the other day I met a young man, invited him to visit. It was stupid of me but he seemed nice enough, and I thought Father might approve of me looking to find someone, to marry. But when I told him he flew into another rage, said he was going to kill him if he ever came around. He's put locks on all the windows, put an extra bolt on the front door. The flower stall makes me some money, but I'm sure he knows about the stash under the boards.

Please return. I have no one else. Do anything you can.
With all my love and hope,
Heather

The note fell from my hand. The familiar face, the dream, the beast, the bruises.

I tore at my hair until nightfall, pacing around my cave, trying to stitch it all together, my conscience and my passion at odds again. I could leave, never return and no one would be any the wiser. I could go on, pursue my passion and leave the whole sordid mess behind. The safest option, that my morals would not allow. Or I could risk it by going back, and taking it just one step further. After all, it was the Father's fault they were dead. If he'd been a real Father, if he'd looked after his children, loved them instead of treating them like dirt they'd never have been around for me to hurt, never have found themselves there. If he hadn't locked the windows, if he hadn't barged into the bedroom, if he hadn't sent his son away.

I knew what I had to do.

Under cover of nightfall I slipped into Grahel for one last time. Past the guards, close to the wall. The rain was torrential, my footsteps splashing against the puddled cobbles. When I reached the house, the window was still broken. No smoke came from the chimney, and no light from any windows. Asleep, then. I crept up the side of the house as I had before, peeked in through the smashed window to check it was empty then slunk through. The room was bare aside from the basic furnishings. An entire month, and he'd done nothing but clear her memories away. It made me sick.

I checked the floorboards first - I knew there was gold somewhere and I wasn't about to let that brute have it. After a small while tapping, one sounded hollow. I dug my fingers underneath it and flipped it up. It was empty. Had he already found it? No matter, I thought. That wasn't my main goal. I slid my hand to the door and opened it a crack. The Father's room was opposite. I crept across the landing and took the doorknob in my hand. I hadn't even thought about what to say when I had my knife to his throat, if anything at all. He needed to know why. Why it had to happen. Not for me. For his children. For their mother too, no doubt. I gripped the knife hard in my hand and eased the door open.

The room was empty. Bare. Not so much as a sheet on the bed.

I reeled back, fury creeping up my throat. I shook myself off and marched down the stairs, eyes sharp for anything.

Empty. Dark, cold, and empty.

He was gone. I wanted to scream but found my throat thick with disbelief. My revenge was ruined. Heather's revenge. James' revenge. Their Mother's. I ran out into the pouring rain, the door left open behind me. Drops pounded down heavier than I'd ever felt, slamming onto my head, the great weight of my failure heavier with each one.

I fled through the sewer, back to my cave. Once there I gathered everything I had and left. There was nothing for me there now. But in the months following it never left my thoughts. It stewed like a vile illness, sickened me to my core. It preyed on my mind like a leech growing fat with blood off my torment until one day I cracked. On that day, I vowed to find the man that was the cause of all of this misery.

"And now... we come to you." I turn to the old man kneeling before me in chains of his own design. His sunken blue eyes look up at me, skin around them a mottled grey-white. He's been here a month now. I keep him fed and watered - but only just. Only enough to keep him alive. "I found you. It took me fifteen years. Fifteen long, failure-ridded years I hunted you down. I lost you in Grahel, but I tracked you from town to town, never stopping, never giving in. I didn't know your face, but I knew your soul. I know why you ran, too." I slowly move my hand through his withering red hair to the back of his scalp then grip it, the man's face scrunching up in pain, tears lining the heavy creases in his face. "You ran because you knew the guards would blame you for Heather's death. One look at the bruises, a read of any letters she sent to James and you'd be in for life. But you've outrun justice long enough." I take the knife, cloth and vial from my satchel.

"Yo... You killed my children, r-ruined my life..." I pay no mind but he continues mumbling, "You're a-a m-monster..."

"You would know, wouldn't you?" I drag the tip of my knife down his arm and he squirms, blood trickling onto the stone floor. I put the vial to it to the wound and once there's enough I prepare the bowl, pouring the vials in as I have done hundreds of times before and set it to one side. "These events have shaped my life in many... undesirable ways. But my Father always taught me there was a silver lining. And it's true. Without your children and their dreams, I never would have known that I could be heard in someone else's mind. I never would have known that not only could I see dreams, but I could make them." I don't bother to hide the grin on my face. His pain is my pleasure, my knowledge, my reward.

"What are you... talking about?"

"Let me show you." I shove the rag into his mouth. His head falls limp. I stay standing, no longer needing the meditation of my weak youth. The blood calls me, my veins flowing with pure power. I no longer fall. I walk in, free.

I walk over a smoking, barren field, laden with corpses of nameless fallen. In the centre, a lone creature sits hunched and naked in a cage. Not a man. Wizened and decrepit, a far call from the beast I'd seen before. He shrinks back, eyes wide and weak.

"You-"

With a snap of my fingers, his cage disappears. With another his arms and legs are wrapped in white-hot chains. A long-awaited shriek erupts from his mouth as his skin bubbles and sears. Another snap and four dark horses appear, each with chains wrapped around their bridle, each linked with one of the man's limbs. "Pull." His body contorts, arms and legs moving outwards, skin writhing, bones squirming free of their sockets. He thrashes, his ugly face a picture of perfect agony as his skin tears. His eyes stream, his bones pop from their joints and with another great pull the horses wrench him in two, hot guts and flesh painting the dirt.

I snap my fingers. The man is back in his cage. He whips his head around, eyes wide with fear. I smile at the blood-drenched ground.

"Let's have some fun."

As the Gardens Fade

Year 250

The Elysha wanes, sinking behind the edges of the rift and giving way to the darkness of the Void. Light echoes through the leaves, sprinkles down the canopy and brushes the floor. Birds trill in the trees and creatures scuttle through the undergrowth. A breeze touches my skin; a warm whisper of the forest. Four others lay in the glade, bodies growing cold, ground beneath them blackened. Not Elves, however. Strangers with pale and earthen skin, with dark hair and rounded ears. Strange, small eyes glassed over.

"Sorry, my friends." I whisper not to the bodies, but to the scorched clearing. I tried to avoid this. To every leaf, every blade of grass, every blooming flower. *We breathe as one. We feel as one. We are one, after all.*

My own waning body rests against a Bardyr tree, blood seeping into the bark behind me and dirt beneath. I move my hand from my aching stomach to check, my glove stained a sticky dark red. The laceration is deep, a slither of bone visible through the torn flesh and crushed armour. *Not even Bardyr bark could stop that axe. Say what you will about Humans, they are a tenacious bunch. And stronger than many of my kin give them credit for.* My vision blurs in and out, the many greens of the clearing melding into one. My hearing whistles, and dulls. *I will be departing soon, then.*

I cough, an evil hack at the back of my throat, blood gurgling down my chin. *One hundred and thirty-seven years and it all ends here. Though I could not wish for a better death than in service to the Elwydd.* I'd say it were too early, but in many ways I am glad. I would not wish to grow old and have to leave the Elwyddan. To leave my clan. *I wish I were not alone, however. Death is lonely enough without being alone.* My lungs strain, heaving for air as I notice another puncture, lower down near my thigh. *I wonder which one got me there.* My breaths become more laboured. I grunt, gritting my teeth, straining with all my withering strength to push myself upright against the tree.

Few come to this part of my homeland. Even Elves. The Elwyddan is only visited on pilgrimages. I know not why the humans came. I cannot guess at the mind of something I do not know. They live far from us, beyond the western gate. They are welcome in our lands, but not without an escort. And certainly not here. We will protect this land with our lives. *I already have.* I give a breathless chuckle, which soon turns into another harsh, bloody cough. *I should know better. I never learn, do I?*

What little remains of the Elysha's light still trickles betwixt the trees, glinting off the human's ugly metal blades and armour. Through the highest leaves I just make out the white sliver that still shows. *It won't be long until I'm there, I suppose.* The Gardens of Elysha are supposedly beautiful. More wondrous and heavenly than even our lands, than even the Elwydd itself. Long have I marvelled at its splendor from afar. I have held a portion of its power and grace in my own hands, as all the Elwyddan do. *I shall see it for myself soon.* A pained smile comes to my face.

A single, shining leaf breaks from a high branch. The breeze cradles it downwards, floating softly. Down, down until it lands on my thigh. A Bardyr leaf, dark green swirls and bright white veins recognisable in an instant. I reach for it, sides splitting as I'm barely able to. I snatch it up and wheeze in relief. *At least I'm going out the way a true Elf should. Nothing is more fitting.* I roll it between my fingers. Tight, into a thin green cone. And for one last time, a small white flame bursts from the tips of my fingers. I light it, flick away the flame and take the thin end to my lips.

Inhale, deep and slow.

And exhale, a little smoke wafting from my mouth as it fills my body with calm. I slowly puff at it, the leaf burning bright white each time. The ash is scattered to the winds and the smoke dissipates in, leavin behind only its earthen scent. The forest begins to glow. My pain begins to ease, the harsh throbbing of my chest and lungs become a dull ache, far away now as the place of my birth.

After a short few minutes the leaf is nearly done, and so am I. Euphoria seeps into my being, serenity flows through my veins. The leaves become glittering emerald, the vines and branches become gentle, cradling arms. I can hear all the sounds of the forest as well as my own heart. The wind, the scurrying of feet, the sighing of branches. My breathing eases, the adrenaline from the fight fading as the Bardyr works its magic. *I feel more alive on the brink of my death than I've felt in a century.* The forest breathes with me for the last time. The Elysha vanishes. *I will see you soon.* The forest falls dark. *Spirits, let me finally rest.*

Corruption's Light

Year 107

"Knight Onan Edas, recite the Order's oath," said the Knight Commander.

Onan bowed his head and took a breath. This was it. A tingle flooded his skin as he readied himself for a moment that was years in the making. He spoke the order's words, resonant and true as he could.

"We are the light in the dark, the flame that guides,
May we never falter,
We are the light in the dark, the flame that persists,
May we never yield,
We are the light in the dark, the flame that protects,
May we never neglect,
We are the light in the dark, servants of the four,
May we use our flame wisely."

"Good." Knight Commander Jadon unsheathed the gleaming ceremonial blade from his belt and planted it in the flagstones. The daylight poured in, coloured all the vivid hues of the stained glass windows and sheening off the bright stonework. "Now present your flame. Light the pyre." He stretched out his hand to marble column behind him. About as tall as Onan was, with carved gilded ribbons wreathing to an unlit leaf-shaped sconce at the top. Onan had seen it many times before. When he was younger, he'd spent nights musing on when it might be his turn to stand before it. Spent days dreaming of the moment, going over every detail. But not for a long time had he wondered about this overblown ceremony - only what it meant for him afterwards.

The Church of the Four was still. He made his way to the pyre and raised his hand, coming just before the kindling. He took a breath, and felt that familiar, warming tingle in the tips of his fingers, in his chest. Gods, it felt good. A burst of white fire from his palm sparked the kindling alight.

That Holy glow. The familiar crackle, lower-pitched than normal fire, to the trained ear. Calmer, if fire could be such a thing. The only thing about the ceremony he found himself enjoying. Onan stared. Even after all this time, the flame was still one of the few things that he thought was truly beautiful in this world. And the rush of using it was just the same as ever.

Knight Commander Jadon spoke again. "Then from this moment, in the name of The Four, you are now a Paladin of the White Flame." He gave that dry, thin-lipped smile he reserved only for very special occasions. "Congratulations."

Onan turned to face him, his own relieved smile barely concealed beneath a veneer of stoicism he'd cultivated over many years that everyone in this order seemed to naturally possess. His heart swelled. Sixteen years. More than half his life. But it had paid off.

The old man approached and extended his hand. Onan gripped it tight. "Wear your title with pride, Edas," he said, voice lowered.

"Yes, Knight Commander." Onan turned to look at the many faces sitting on the pews, some familiar and some unknown. Paladins. Knights. Scribes. Squires. All giving their applause, each offering their well-wishes as he started to walk down the aisle. Assuredly insincere, but he kept that thought to himself and kept smiling. Their congratulations didn't matter. There was only one who's opinion counted, and she couldn't attend. They didn't even know she existed. She wasn't allowed to. He waved a hand in a vain attempt to ease the uncomfortable clapping. He wished once again the ceremony had been quicker. Less faff. Eyes needled him all the way down the aisle. All assuming they knew him. All assuming they knew where he was going next. Training, perhaps some celebratory drinks with his comrades or simply some well-earned rest. Wrong on all counts. Sweat clung to his brow as the Whitelight seared at him like through an eyeglass, made his undershirt all sticky, the back of his neck squirm. Gods, he wanted to be out of here. The doors were only a few strides away now but still people tried to usher him, tried a word or two, clapped him on the back and he had to fend the urge to clap them back harder so they might rethink their choices.

"Thank you," he said, unconvincingly, "thank you." He nodded as he did, hoping they might believe him.

Then he was out.

A warm breeze washed over his face and the afternoon light bore down as he stepped out into the streets of Godrall.

He began his journey to the barracks, brisk as he could. Children ran on the cobbles, the odd one stopping to gawp and awe at the new Paladin, with his bright sword and glittering silver-white armour. What a lie it all was. Nevertheless Onan smiled, slowed down a little and let them marvel at the radiant champion they believed him to be - though not for long. He had somewhere to be.

Through the streets, around the buildings and around the edge of the market to avoid onlookers. From the light into the shadows of the back streets, taking longer but less populated routes. In no time the barracks were in sight. The open courtyard full of Knights and Squires drilling, swords scraping against each other, clanging against dummies, laughter and shouting all around. The barracks itself was a small fortress with four floors - that towered over the courtyard, over the burgeoning city, enveloping it in its shade. The resplendent standard of the Knights of the White Flame flapped lazily in the light breeze, the Ciros stitched across it in silver and wrapped with white flames rather than the simple gold of the church. Over the grand iron-studded doors stood open. He swept through the doors, nodded to the guardsmen on either side all whilst managing to not look them in the eye.

He told himself he was just trying to look busy but was keenly aware what a rush he seemed to be in. Then again, he was a Paladin now. Amongst the heights of the order. Above reproach from most. That would help with what was to come. Through the entrance hall, past a trio of young squires struggling to carry a variety of armour, into the second corridor on the right, past a pair of bickering priests, past the familiar collection of weapons, shields and banners along the walls. Under an arch and up a flight of stairs, around a corner and at the end of a hallway. Past a Knight just coming out of his quarters and around one more corner, then he was outside his door. Finally.

He took a breath, wiped the collected sweat off his brow with a bit of his tabard, then turned his key in the lock.

There she was, sat on the bed. Head of dark brown hair deep inside that poetry book she was reading, '*Words from the Water*'. The one he'd bought for her, hoping it'd help her to read a few years ago and she'd not put down since. He closed the door with a soft clunk. She looked up, little eyes wide and smile even wider.

"Papa!" Abigail leapt at him and sped across the room, her small arms wrapping around Onan's waist like a vice.

He embraced her with a gentle hug of her head as she squeezed up against his breastplate. "Hello, Petal," he beamed. Onan thanked the Four for his armour or she'd crush him. He wriggled her off and hoisted her up onto his arm. She pressed her forehead against his, and he caught a sparkle of those honey-brown eyes. So much like her mother. Honest. Precious. And more than a little troublesome.

"Oh, I missed you," he whispered.

"I missed you too Papa." And they hugged a little tighter.

"You sit here," he said, gently putting her back on the bed. "Let me take my armour off and we can do whatever you like, alright?"

"A story!" She squealed.

"Shh, shh." He brought a finger to his lips. She nodded. It wasn't any life for a child to live in secret. But she knew he loved her. And he did all he could. Was going to do all he could. "You've heard all the ones I know three times over by now, Petal."

"I want to hear them again!"

Onan chuckled. "Ok, ok. Story it is. Give me a moment."
He bent down a little. "Can you undo the strap just under
my pauldron?" She nodded, quickly slipped her hand
underneath and pulled it loose. Onan set it aside. "And the
breastplate?" She did the same, small hands wriggling for the
straps. He gave a heavy sigh as the weight started to come off.
"Which one would you like to hear?"

Her face scrunched in thought for a moment, the lit up
again. "Ooo! The one with you and the doggies!"

"Ha! You mean the Barghests?" He began to take off his
greaves and felt the cold sweat clinging to his underclothes
as each part came loose. Gods this felt more a prison than
even the rest of the order, at times. To think it once brought
him such pride. "Of course, sweetheart." He removed his
sabatons last and set them down. He rolled his shoulders,
stretched his arms and legs then gave a heavy, aching sigh,
feeling her eyes on him all the while.

He sagged to the bed and tapped his leg; to which she
responded by leaping on him. Onan gave a sharp grunt as she
landed. "Oooh, be careful Petal. You're not as little as you
used to be, you know." She giggled as he wrapped an arm
around her. "So, you remember how this one starts?"

"Uh-huh."

"Go on."

"Y-you're near a little village, with some friends. And
the-" she stopped and he saw her eyes roll for a moment, face
clenched with thought, "-*barghests* had been attacking farms
nearby."

"Well done," he said softly, "we were in Dawrest, east of here. The Knights and I had been told to go and protect these farms from the nasty beasties." He wiggled his free hand's fingers in front of her and produced another bout of giddy laughter. "We'd had letter after letter from the village, each one mentioning these animals. So, we set out to try and track them first. But what happened?"

"Uhh... Barghests don't leave prints!"

"Yes!" She really was his. No other ten year old knew as much of the arcane or beasts as she did. Perhaps It wasn't a normal childhood, but it was hers all the same. "Barghests don't leave prints, which meant we had to wait until nightfall for them to show. And so when it came-".

A sharp rap on the door. Onan flicked his head up. Abigail looked at him. "Wait here Petal, Papa has to check the door." She slid off his knee. He approached and slid the shutter back. In the hallway, a familiar armoured figure leant against the wall, arms crossed and scratching at a dark beard, managing to smile and frown at the same time. "It's your uncle, I'll be one moment." Not her blood uncle, of course. But the only true friend Onan had. He opened the door.

"Hirah! Good to see you."

Hirah held up a hand. "You too. My apologies for missing the ceremony earlier." He shut the door behind him then leant up against it. He dropped his frown for a moment and flashed Abi a grin. "Hello trouble."

"You didn't miss much. Far too long."

"You'd have killed for it once upon a time."

Onan grimaced. "Mhm, never thought I'd see the day." He glanced at Abigail, already lost again in her book. "But things change."

Hirah ran a hand through his cropped hair. "It hasn't changed for ten years Onan." He shot a glance at Abigail himself then spoke a little softer. "You know what you've got to do, don't you? Now more than ever."

Onan shook his head, even if he knew Hirah was right. Even though he'd already been planning it. "I stay for her. The order provides for us, and so I can provide for her."

"I know, Onan. But if they find her - especially if they find her now-"

"I know," Onan hissed, and from his peripheral he saw Abigail glance up from her book. This wasn't a life he wanted for her. She was far brighter than he ever was. The sly looks, the small smiles, the nods of her head. Just like her Mother. She hid her knowledge of it all well, though. "I know," he whispered, so quiet it was barely more than breath, "I know what I'm risking. What they might do. I knew the risk when I married her Mother and I knew the risk when she was born. I know where we're going, but I need to clean up before I leave. I can't leave a trail."

"Good," Hirah sighed, "glad to hear you speak some sense." Their eyes met. "But let me worry about the trail. I can cover your back once you're gone. You need to focus on getting out."

Onan grimaced again. Hirah was right. He always had been, when it came to Abigail. Otherwise Onan would have done something stupid a long time ago.

"You're a Paladin now. More responsibility, more eyes on you." He became agitated, eyebrows twitching as if in fear. "It's only a matter of time Onan. If they find her, it's not just about what they'll do to her-"

"Not here." He turned to Abigail. "You stay here sweetheart, Papa just needs to talk to Uncle Hirah outside alright?" She knew a lot, and she was clever. But she was still a child, and not nearly ready for anything like this.

She nodded slowly. "Ok Papa. I love you."

He walked over quickly and kissed her softly on the forehead. "I love you too." Hirah opened the door and sidled out into the dimly-lit stone hallway. Onan followed and clunked it quietly shut behind them. "Go on." He crossed his arms.

Hirah sighed and started again. "Look, I'm only trying to look out for you. You know why we're not supposed to have children."

"Yes." Onan had spent the last decade trying not to think about it.

"Then why do you insist on staying? To them, she's a walking bonfire just waiting to be lit."

"I need-"

Hirah cut in again, "I know you think you can always do more. I've spent a lot of time these past years talking sense into that thick skull of yours, but this time I'm telling you." He put a firm hand on Onan's shoulder and lowered his voice once more, "It's time to go. It's what Lea would have wanted. What she always wanted for you three." His stomach churned and heart fluttered at the mention of her. As usual, Hirah was right.

A moment of silence as the thoughts passed through his head, slow. This was it, then. The last few days. From a recruit from a small village, an idealistic servant of the Gods making his vows, to rising through the ranks like he was their only champion, to finding love with a girl he met by pure chance, to the birth of the child and the loss of a wife, to a jaded man living two half-lives, and someone who now only wanted the best for his daughter. This was his real chance to end it all. The happiest ending they would get. He had to take it while he could.

"Yes, yes. I know." He took a sharp breath in, then out. "What do you propose then? That I just up and leave? They'll track me down and find us the second we leave the city."

"I've thought about that." Hirah dug into his satchel, took out a rolled-up notice and handed it over. Onan studied it - a notice for a Revenant seen around the north coast, a day or two's ride. Undead warriors three times stronger than any living man. You may as well stab boulder with a paring knife. The only tactic was to wear it down, dismember it and keep burning it until it stopped twitching. Raised from death by ritual blood magic. Deadly, rare, but he'd fought them twice before. Hirah continued, "We fake your death. Me and you go tomorrow, slay the beast. I come back, telling them you died ever so valiantly and tragically whilst you sneak back into the city, collect Abigail and be on your way."

"I'll be dead?"

Hirah held up a finger and spoke fast, like it all had to come out at once. "Well, it's near the Amberfalls. I can tell them you were pushed, and I can take some of your armour, knock it around a bit. Even dig a makeshift grave somewhere near the falls. To really sell it."

"You really have thought about this, haven't you?" He handed the notice back. "But won't they come for my body?"

"Well, I can tell them I buried what I could but that most of it was..." and he gave a slightly uncomfortable smile, "unrecoverable."

Onan nodded. "Oh, right. I see." He couldn't help but share the same smile.

"So what do you think? I know it's grisly, but-"

"If it works, it works. You know I trust you." And Onan felt a wave of relief as the plan was formed. Without much forming by him it had to be said, and he was grateful. He hoped Hirah knew just how much. "But let me spend tonight with Abigail."

"I can't guarantee no one else will go after it before we do, so we set off at dawn, alright? I'll let the Quartermaster know."

"Alright." Onan offered his hand. Hirah took it, and yanked him in for a hug, clapping him on the back. Onan gasped, then chuckled and returned the embrace in kind. "Thank you, Hirah." They let go. "I couldn't have done any of this without you."

"I know." He gave that smug, half-smile half-frown again. "I'll see you tomorrow." And with that he was off down the hallway, footsteps fading into the quiet distance.

Onan stood there a moment, then went back into the room.

"Papa!" Abigail beamed.

Onan's smile grew wider, and he returned to the bed. "Where were we, sweetheart?" For now, this was all that mattered.

A jet of white fire burst from Onan's left hand, lighting up the cave and sending the Revenant reeling backwards, ancient mail clattering. Its ruined skin crackled with flames and the air stunk of burnt, rotted offal. Sparks flew as it shrieked and swung its heavy blade, clanging dully against Hirah's sword. Always there. Always in the right place at the right time. Both of them in sync, moving with each other. Onan kept his blade waiting in his other hand, ready until the moment came. Years of hunts together, of unholy creatures slain, as in tandem as blade and shield. He gave a yell of his own and kicked out at the creature, staggered it backwards then felt the fire, true as he ever had.

Adrenaline burst through him, collected and unleashed all at once. The righteous white-hot fire in his veins, in his chest, in his very soul. He'd scarcely felt closer to the Gods. Moments like this were why he'd joined the order those years ago. Another growl, another torrent of roaring flame burst from his fingertips, forcing the creature back further. Hirah battered the beast's sword down, blades screeching before he bit into its side then swiftly again through its arm, black blood gushing from the withered stump.

It screamed, grating and piercing, thrashing its black blade through the air, over itself and into the cave wall. Hirah cut clean into its shoulder. It screamed again, writhing and twitching as it hit the cave wall. Its death throes.

Another burst of flame, catching the monster's ragged cloth under its mail. Hirah nailed it into the wall with a wet crunch. Onan finally brought his blade up, caught it across the jaw and felt a waft of wet, foul breath hit the back of his throat. He stifled a retch and drove his sword into its shoulder, pinning it as he sent yet another jet into its eyes. It had to die, it had to burn, and he had to be the one to do it. His last victory for the order. Every moment the fire felt like it was filling him up, making him fit to burst at the seams yet never quite enough to sate his hunger. Hirah followed up, sword cleaving into its flame-wreathed skull. Bone cracked. It shrieked, twisted face spasming as it gurgled some unholy noise, their strength keeping it fast against the wall.

Then it slumped, suddenly much heavier and held up only by their blades. Onan yanked his out, followed by a slick of black gunge. Hirah did the same and it sagged to the floor a broken, bloody, burned heap.

Onan took a breath. A wheeze, more than anything. He m a fist with his hand, eyes lingering on the flames, suddenly gentle and inviting again. Water steadily dripped from somewhere around, and he could hear the rivers of the Amberfalls running somewhere overhead, above all the rock. It was a comfort to the slight ringing in his ears. He glanced at Hirah, already wiping his blade with a rag.

"Shit." Onan broke the silence first. "I'll be glad not to have to fight one of those again."

"Lucky bastard."

"Not a nice job." Heavy breaths between words. "But someone's got to do it, and you can't say it's not at least a little fun."

"I don't know, you seem to enjoy it more than most," Hirah jibed, eyes on his blade.

"Well, it's the last time. Had to go all out." He shook his hand again, still flickering with flame. The passion was gone from his chest for the time being. The need of the moment. The desire. But it was still beautiful. And the only light in this damn cave.

"Suppose so." Hirah passed him the rag. Onan took it and started on his own blade, using the already-filthy rag to wipe the worst of the blood off. "Anyone sees you doing that the Order'll hunt you down in no time. Not exactly used by the common folk."

"Still, got to expel it." Which Onan was admittedly glad about. "Just got to be careful. And like always - never too much."

Hirah suddenly deepened his voice and made a comically serious face, drawing in his brow and cheeks to imitate Jadon. "It's all about balance." Then he gave a chuckle and went back to normal. "Wise words."

"All about balance..." Onan echoed, glancing at his hand. It couldn't be that hard, could it? He'd gone days without it before, but a lifetime? A lifetime of just dealing with it as if it was some kind of annoyance? Never having the relief, that righteous, euphoric feeling again? He felt a pang of loss as he stared into the ethereal white around his hand, and then of guilt for even doing so. He wasn't doing it for him. He wasn't blind to how much he needed it. Perhaps he had been overusing it lately. A break would do him some good. A couple of weeks in their stead. Just him and Abigail. A normal life. He'd use it very rarely, just expulsion. Couldn't go too long of course, but long enough. All about balance.

"Onan?" Hirah's voice snapped him back to reality.

"Uh huh. You know me. I'm always careful," he said, unsure of the words as they came out. He nodded to the body. "You get the arms, I'll get the legs. We need to chuck it off the highest cliff we can find."

"Yeah yeah," Hirah said as he hoisted up the monster's stumped armpits. Onan put his hands under its decayed, stinking calves.

"Gods, this thing reeks."

The night was quiet, nothing but wind whispering through the streets of Godrall. Onan's cloak billowed as he kept a quick pace in the dark, narrow backstreets. He clutched the brooch around his front, holding the hood down. No one would recognise him, especially not in his armour. But every precaution had to be taken. He'd spent a good two weeks away from the city camping in the woodlands to the east before he risked coming back. He'd arranged transport. He came through the smallest city gates, on the southwest side where traffic was light even at its busiest. The guards on the way in had taken the bribe he'd had prepared as persuasion. The only thing left was to collect Abigail. And he was close. He turned a corner, his head flicking left and right. The guardsmen of Godrall were notorious for stopping people at night. He turned another corner, down a narrow alley. The orphanage was in sight. He quickened his feet yet again until he arrived at the low wooden door. He rapped once, coughed, waited few moments, then rapped once more. He heard shuffling. An elderly lady opened the door, squinting up at him, holding a candle in one hand. Martha.

"Yes?" she croaked.

Onan kept his voice low. "Abigail, please." Martha gave an understanding look and simply nodded before retreating back into the building. Onan looked behind him, taking in the dirty back alleys. Nothing he would be sad to see the back of. The city was founded mere years after the Dawn but already had a clear divide. Onan sometimes wondered whether the Order was one of the few things they had in common, now. Protectors of the people. Hunters of evil and purgers of blood magic. They'd split from the Heralds before he was born, stuck true to their purpose whilst the Heralds kept to running the nation. But politics was beyond him. That's why he was a soldier.

Shuffling from behind the door, a few mutters. Martha appeared again, Abigail in front of her. Onan knelt down.

"P-Papa? What's going on?" Abigail's voice was weary, her eyes blinking.

"Shh Petal." He took her in his arms. "It's alright. But we have to leave now, ok?" He looked up at Martha and patted the small sack on Abigail's back. "Does she have everything?" She nodded. "Good. Thank you. Come, Abigail." She shut the door, leaving them alone in the alleyway. Onan glanced around before turning to look her in the eyes. "We must be quick and we must be quiet, do you understand?"

Her big honey eyes gazed back. "Y-yes Papa."

"There's a good girl. Stay close, hold my hand." And she took it, gripping it tightly. He led her back the way he'd come. Through the alley, through the streets, checking each corner for guards before they stepped out. He heard his breath in his hood, felt his heart like he'd scarcely felt it before. He had no fear for himself. But for his daughter it came in spades. As they neared the gates he stopped at a corner. He peeked around it and saw the two guards stood either side of the heavy wooden gate, torchlight flooding the space around the city wall. He took a breath.

"Keep close to me." He kissed her forehead. "Do not let go." She nodded.

He stepped out, clutched her hand tighter than he probably should have but couldn't bring himself to let go. Approaching the gates he was cautious but not slow, trying to strike a balance between being quick and not being overly suspicious. He'd paid them already, but there was always a chance.

"Halt!" Onan's heart skipped but he didn't flinch. "Who goes there?" A different voice. It was a different man to the one he'd paid. Two different men. One thick-set and grumpy-looking, gripped his spear like it might try to run away. The other was wiry and was leant back up against the wall, arms folded. The big one did the talking.

Onan wracked his brain for an answer. "Uh-I am a simple farmer sir. This is my daughter. Just making my way back to our stead." He swallowed. Hot fear flooded him for a moment, but he couldn't surrender to it.

"At this hour?" The guard looked across at his partner, who shrugged.

"Sorry, Sirs. I had to leave my daughter at my brother's house." His voice was shaky. He'd never been quick enough

74

to lie convincingly. "My wife is taken quite ill and I needed my daughter to be safe. I now fear she may not last the next day." He glanced at Abigail. "I would like her to see her mother once more."

The guardsman stepped forward and studied the two. "What illness has your wife been taken with?" Onan's hand twitched and he was struck by a sudden urge, a hot tingle in his hand but pushed it deep down. Now was not the time. hese were innocent men.

"I know not, Sir. A magical one, I am afraid." The two guards shared another uncertain look. The tingle came back. Abigail squeezed his fingers as she pressed up against his side. The urge faded completely. He breathed a silent sigh of relief.

After a moment of studying them, he grunted. "Be on your way." And the wiry one unlatched the heavy gate and started to usher them through.

"Thank you Sirs." Onan took a small bow to each, gripping Abigail's hand. "Come, Petal."

"Be quick, wolves outside the city this time of year."

"Thank you again."

They made their way to the waiting horse and cart. Onan lifted Abigail up and sat her in the back before climbing up himself. One last look at the city and he placed an arm around his daughter, enveloping her in his cloak for the warmth. The carriage started moving, clattering off over the cobbles. She drifted off in his arms as the dark countryside moved around them and before long, his own eyes grew weary. He allowed himself some rest. After all this time, he was free.

Onan brought his axe down again and split the log down the middle. The daylight was waning, the last remnants trickling through the sparse forest treetop and shimmering over the grass ground in thin slices. The White was falling past the breach and would soon gone for another day to reveal the blackness beyond. Seventy-seven days they'd been here. It was almost normal to him now. But he still couldn't stop counting his days, couldn't stop the worries of the mind, founded in reality or no. He picked up one of the split halves and set it up on the makeshift stand. A good clean swing and he hefted it in two with a nice thud. This had been much of his life for the last few months - uneventful, anxious at times, but mostly peaceful. The cabin they'd settled in was only a few short miles from the nearest town, isolated between a small forest and a few fields. The farmers and the folk of Earch largely left them alone. They were pleasant folk for the most part too. The lifestyle had taken some getting used to and he still wasn't quite there yet. It held little excitement, and no use for the gift he'd earned nor the skills he had honed - except perhaps being able to split logs with unnecessary precision. But every day was better than the last, and every time he worried or had a yearning for the life he'd left, he thought of the reason he'd done all this. Put things in perspective. He set the half-log up and swung his axe down. He stuck the wood axe in his belt loop, took the logs under his arms and started the stroll back home.

He thought about his previous life, all he had left behind. Hirah was surely fine - he was a few years younger than Onan and would surely make Paladin himself one day soon. He attempted to recall other friends but his memory failed him - or perhaps he never really had many. There never was much point. Half the friends he could have made would have sold him out to the order the moment they'd found out about Abigail.

Months without the pleasure of the flame had been difficult, but necessary. All about balance, of course, and every night once she was tucked into bed he felt the pull on his mind, the tug on his soul. But he couldn't ever bring himself to. What if someone saw? He still felt that tingle in his hand. An occasional heat in his chest, somewhere deep. Headaches of a morning, lately. Many nights he had been close - the temptation of just a spark, to light a candle, to let himself hold it in his hands. But he had stopped himself. Sleepless nights and cold sweats be damned. He would prevail.

The trees started to thin and the cabin came into view. One floor, all logs and timber and in dire need of repairs when they'd come here. A small well outside he'd dug himself, with the help of some friendly folk from town. An old but solid stone wall grasped with weeds and lichen. Patches of upturned earth - root vegetables mainly, with a few choice herbs that couldn't be found in the forest. He was never much of a cook, but he was determined to try. The odd natural flower. Chickens were out the front in a small pen. Some steps up to a porch and slightly rickety back door.

He nudged open the back gate. "Abi? You there sweetheart?" Fast footsteps from inside. Her dark hair flew past the window, then the door opened.

"You're back!" Excitable as ever. Onan had no clue where she got the energy. Well, maybe a small clue.

"Uh-huh, Papa's back." He walked over to the hearth at the far end of the room, dumped the logs by the side and placed the axe down with them. Abigail's arms wrapped around him from the back, squeezing him tight. "Slow down there Petal," he said, trying to prise her off, "Papa's covered in dirt. I've been out all afternoon." She let go and he turned around. Specks of mud over her shirt, dark brown flecks over her face but she didn't seem to care. A big, toothy grin that never seemed to fade these days. He raised an eyebrow, to which she responded by sticking her tongue out. "Go on trouble, get cleaned up before dinner."

"Do I have to?" She faked a pout.

"Well, at least get that dirt from your hands and face, alright?"

"Mhmm!" She beamed and sprinted off down through the back door and down the garden to the well. Onan watched her a moment as she wound up the bucket, water sparkling in the dimming light. A shadow of a smile reached his lips. She did love it here, and though he had his struggles he did too. Everything really was worth it, in the end.

"I wish your mother were here." His eyes wandered the room - small, but safe and quaint. Homely. "She would have loved this."

A while later and the two sat outside on the back steps, crackling fire in front of them. The White had set but the night was still young as Onan laid the finishing touches. A pot sat over the makeshift campfire, filled the air with the smell of meat and herbs as the steam wafted over them. Stews were really the only thing he could make. Many nights on the road cooking for many very tired, very hungry men. But she didn't seem to mind. He gave the pot a stir and she peer over his shoulder, eyes wide like she'd seen something amazing. She'd wanted to sit outside tonight, for some reason. Not that he complained. The fire was warm, if a little smoky, the breeze of the night air was lovely in his hair, and Abi was wrapped up warm in her blanket. Just like he imagined she'd always wanted.

"Is it ready?"

"Give it a little longer," he said gently, as he watched the meat start to fall off the bone, prodded the potatoes and noticed they were just turning soft enough. "Just a little longer."

She gave a small sigh, then sat back and leant against him as he did the same. They watched the night sky in quiet for a moment. The glittering stars, so far up above them. That yawning black gap in the sky where there wasn't a single one. '*The window to the Void*', as it said in The Chronicle. By day, the way light came into their world from the heavens. By night, utterly devoid of it. A stark contrast. Abi leaned into him a little more and he put his arm around her.

"Papa?" She looked up at him.

"Yes Petal?" He looked back.

"Why did we have to leave?"

The question struck him like an arrow to the chest. He felt his breath stop a moment, the calm of his heart suddenly disappear. All this time she hadn't asked. He'd assumed she

79

was simply all too happy to let it be in the past. Perhaps just that she knew already.

"Well..." he started, tongue stuck in his mouth, face scrunched. He wasn't sure where he was going. How to explain it to a child? That the order didn't allow children. That the only reason her mother wasn't here was because of them. Because of him and worse yet, because of her. That he had a rare magical power that singled him out among many, gifted by the Gods themselves. That because she was his daughter, his blood, she had an uncontrollable, unstable connection to this power? The moment drew out and he felt her eyes on him, expecting something. Anything.

"Well sweetheart... do you remember the friends of Papa's?" She nodded. "They're Knights, very special Knights."

"Special?"

"Yes, we can do special things and... we go and fight things that other people can't."

"Like the barghests?"

"Yes, like the barghests." He chuckled nervously. This was going well. "We would make the world a safer place. A better place." And he felt a little tingle in his hand. "But I had to leave those people because we didn't agree on a few things. And if they find us, Papa will be in trouble. And we might not be able to see each other again." He squeezed her gently against him.

A silence hung between the two, until she spoke up again. "What didn't you agree on?"

Another startling question, but this time with a semi-prepared answer. "Well, remember how I told you you were born?"

"Uh-huh." She nodded eagerly. "In a forest."

"That's right, a forest. Well, those people are why that had to happen. The order doesn't really like children, sweetheart"

"Why not?" She screwed up her face. "I like children."

Onan chuckled softly again and continued, "So do I. But not everyone does, sadly. Your mother and I had to keep our marriage hidden and when you were born, that meant hiding you too." He swallowed. His mouth continued for him. "There were difficulties with your birth." White sparks, red blood. Scorching and screaming. "And we couldn't find a healer for your mother." A tear rolled down his cheek and he wiped it away before Abigail could see. "But I got you didn't I?" They looked each other in the eyes a moment, then he gently kissed her forehead. "And I wouldn't trade you for the world."

"Oh..." her little face fell, and even the one word sounded strangled. "Why do they not like children Papa?"

"I'll tell you when you're a little older, ok?"

"Why?"

"When you are older, Abigail." His voice was harder than he intended. "I promise." She shuffled a little in her seat and sniffed. He moved the blanket over her a little more and drew her as close as he could. "But it's alright. We're safe here. And it's all in the past."

"Papa?"

"Mhmm?"

"Am I special like you?" Her voice cracked a little.

Another question, another half-truth. "Fortunately not quite like me, Petal." No, she had potential for far worse. He sighed. "But you are more special to me than you'll ever know." He squeezed again and she giggled as she tried to wriggle free.

A thought crossed his mind. He looked up. The woods were empty and quiet, save the wind. All around were the silhouettes of other steads, spotting the farmland. No one was around but them.

"Abi? Let me show you something. Make it up to you." He brought up his left hand in front of them both. He felt that tingle. The gentle heat in his palm, soft burn in the tips of his fingers. "Watch my hand." At last, he opened himself to it. A slow, torching white flame in his palm, the campfire dull in comparison. It made such a soft sound for such a violent thing. He flashed a look at Abigail - her mouth open in awe as the flames reflected in her eyes, dancing. Divine bliss rushed through him, hot and righteous as the flame grew by its own accord, as it took him over. As if his very soul burned with light. As if he were pure fire.

"Papa?" It was far away. A voice. "Papa?" High and sweet. A gentle tug on his arm. "Are you ok?" The flame broke and his eyes flashed open. It was dark.

Onan shook his head. "Uh, yeah. Sorry Abi, just got carried away." He smiled despite the sudden burning in his chest. "What did you think of that?"

"That was amazing!"

"I thought you might think so." He kissed her on the head again and then leant forward to the pot. He took the ladle with his left hand and caught a breath in his throat. His fingers still burned, still lingered with white flames. He shook his hand off and then they were gone. A caw came from the garden and Onan saw a single crow perched on the stone wall, staring at them both. It cawed again. He shook his head and checked on the stew.

"It's ready, Petal."

"Papa! Papa!" Small hands on his arms, tugging. Daylight stinging through his eyelids. Papa wake up!" Her voice was shrill, made his head ache more than normal. He grunted. "Wake up!" Her voice was piercing. He blinked, just once. Abigail was a blurry silhouette against the window. He blinked a few more times and strained himself to consciousness. Gods, his chest felt heavy. He tried to push himself up, wiped the cold sweat from his brow.

"W-what is it sweetheart?" He managed to groan.

"There are people coming to the house."

Onan's eyes flashed open. "Shit." No need to guess who. Stupid- what was he fucking thinking? He heaved his legs out of bed, shook himself awake. Pain could wait. "How far?"

"I... uh... I don't-"

His hands gripped her shoulders. "Where from? And how far?"

"From the town. They're coming down the road."

"*Shit.*" Onan looked frantically around the room. They had to leave. Now. "Abigail, go to the kitchen and pack any food we have. If you need anything from your room you need to get it *right now.*"

"Papa?"

"No questions. *Now!*" Her face flickered in fear then she ran back out of the room. "Shit." He pressed his temples, shook his head again. He couldn't be the one to panic. He knelt and scrabbled under his bed. Felt the familiar grip of his sword, felt a spark of that righteousness as it fit perfectly in his hand, and put it on his belt. Back for the cheap leather vest next to it and as he slid it over his shirt he wished sorely Hirah hadn't taken nearly all of his armour. Boots on, then he was out into the front room where Abi was waiting with her bag.

"Ready?"

She nodded, lips tight, eyes red. That burning pang of guilt struck his chest even harder.

The curtains were closed, but vague silhouettes moved behind the windows. Likely at the end of the garden.

He grabbed Abi by the hand and snatched the axe from the fireside. "You ready, Petal?" He tried a smile but knew it came off as pained. She nodded again and he took her to the back door. "Stay behind me, no matter what?" Already he felt that surge, that tingle deep inside. Focus, he needed focus. He shouldered the door down and sped out into the early morning light, axe readied and Abi safely behind him.

"Stop in the name of the White Flame, traitor." Three young Squires, in their white mail at the end of the garden, just inside the gently-swinging gate. One barely more than a child himself, likely not even worthy of his flame yet. Surely this couldn't be the strongest they'd send. Three lives to be wasted. They drew their swords, and the girl in the middle spoke.

"Do not make us draw blood."

"Step aside," said Onan. But there wasn't much want behind it. His hand grew hot and twitchy. A need for release in his veins and with just the opportunity he needed. No one would touch her. "Step aside, and you can all go free."

The three readied themselves, feet grinding into the ground, muttering, sparks flickering in the girl's hands. Onan couldn't stop himself from smiling. In righteous defence of the innocent once again.

"Brothers, attack!" The moment they moved Onan flashed his hand up and out came a cascade of fire. He roared as the flames roared and grinned as bright as they. There were screams, somewhere over all the glorious noise. Then it was over. He shook his hand free of fire, swung the axe and chopped deep into a flame-wreathed head. He kicked the body to the ground, shoved another over the wall and dashed through the gate.

"Abi, follow me!" She was running after him, hand outstretched. He went for it and saw his own, still enflamed. A ghost of the fire, lingering.

"Shit." He stopped a moment and closed his eyes. Felt the hot pleasure of it, tried to ignore it, tried to be rid of it, to purge it. "*Shit.*" His eyes snapped open and it was still there.

A crash from the house. Wood splintering, glass smashing. Shouts and cries and the faint screaming of those poor Squires. He looked at Abi again her eyes starting to stream, lips trembling.

"It's alright, Petal." He stuck his other hand out, realised it was still holding the axe white-knuckle tight and spotted with bright red. He retracted it. More shouts. "Come on, we need to move. Run."

They were off through the woods. Between the grasping branches and over logs and through shadowed trees. He in front, feet slamming against the ground, fast as he could without leaving her behind.

Voices echoing. Hooves pounding at the ground somewhere in the distance. His heart pounded, lungs strained, head thumped. They couldn't be far behind. He shot a look to Abigail, face red and sweat pouring down her face, hair flying in the wind. A shadow beyond her. Hooves pounding rapidly on the ground. A shout.

"Here they are!" A horse and rider burst into the open as the woods began to thin, flickering through the trees. His bow drawn, aiming. For her.

"Abi," Onan shouted back, "don't stop!" He heard her quick breaths behind him, saw the glint of the steel-tipped arrow as it was loosed. He ignited his hand in rageful bliss. The arrow flew by and thudded into a tree. He hurled the flaming axe at the horse and watched in grim pleasure as it bit deep into its flank, brought it crashing down with its rider in a shower of sparks and dirt.

Abi was further behind now, starting to slow. Onan bit his lip and kept running, eyes forward. Where were they even running to? Open fields? More trees? It was useless but he couldn't stop. His lungs heaved, chest burned, left arm still wreathed with fire. Hooves got closer. Shouts got louder. A squeal and thud from behind him.

"Abigail!" She was rolling in the dirt. Onan swerved on his heel, sped back and picked her up with his free, trembling arm. "Are you hurt?" He looked her up and down. Just a few scratches. Tears sheened her face, honey eyes stained with red. Something bright flickered in them. A look over her shoulder and more shapes became clear.

"Come on Petal." He tried to tug her along but she refused to move, straining against him.

"Papa-"

"Abi, we need to *go.*" His voice grated in his throat. Anger like it wasn't even his. The fire inside.

She stumbled back, eyes wide and sparkling with white. "I'm sca-"

"*Now.*" He caught her and yanked her along. He'd save her. All he'd done for her, and it was going to end like this because of her. His eyes darted to the rapidly approaching figures - the daylight glinting off white and silver armour, off sheening blades. "Shit." He pulled her arm with him, dragging her through the forest if she would not come on her own. She thrashed but he could not let go, even as her feed dragged on the ground, slowing them down.

Then two horses sped past them, wind and leaves whipped up as they fled into the forest, turned and came back, arrows levelled directly at him, stopping twelve strides or so distant. More trotted up behind, the sound of defeat heralded with soft hooves. They were circled. Near a dozen Knights, a number of them already holding aloft flames in their hands, no doubt smiles hidden beneath their helmets. No doubt some he knew, no doubt at his ceremony all that time ago. Cowards. He locked eyes with Abi. Swore he saw that a white flicker in her eye. He sighed, pulled her close behind him with his right hand and drew his blade with the other. She did not resist this time. He tried to breathe. Found he couldn't without rasping. Every breath was hot.

A Paladin in full, gleaming white armour drew his black steed closer. A flash of what Onan could have been. Was, nearly. It made him sick and envious all at once. His hand tingled again. They would burn.

The Paladin spoke first, voice echoing from his great helm. "Former Paladin Onan Edas, you are hereby placed under arrest by the Order of the White Flame on the charges of treason, cowardice and heresy." Spoken as if he was reading out something incredibly tedious and not the death sentence of young girl and her Father. "Come peacefully, and we will allow you to live out your days in a cell, in relative peace."

Onan gripped his blade tighter. He tried to not let the anger twist his voice but couldn't seem to stop himself. "What about my Daughter?"

"She will be cared for." A lie if he'd ever heard one. He tried to place the Paladin's voice but couldn't. No one he knew. "You have my word as a man of faith, and as a member of the Order."

"I lied for ten years to the order. A Knight's word is worth dirt," Onan spat. He felt the heat rise in his veins. Perfect and just. This is what the flame needed. What he needed.

"You have nothing *but* my word." A flame burst from his hand and he held it there. "If you think you are in a position to bargain, you are gravely mistaken. I have orders to kill you if you resist," he scoffed. "And I would very much like you to resist. There's nothing I hate more than traitors."

"Papa-" came a nervous, raspy whisper from behind him.

"Let me speak with my Daughter."

"You are in no posi-"

"I am *not* asking." The Paladin remained silent as Onan turned to Abigail.

Her eyes were full of tears, sparks at their edges. Her irises danced with flaring white and Onan flinched at the sight of it again.

"What is he talking about Papa?" He put a hand on her shoulder but she pushed it off and backed away.

"Nothing, shh..." And he reached out to grab her shirt, pull her in but she recoiled. She took quick breaths. Sweat on her forehead as her eyes darted around. "It's ok," he said, "we'll be ok. Come back here." He tried to be gentle but his entire soul felt hot, angry, hungry and he found his voice was the same.

"Bu- but he said-"

"I know what he said-"

"I don't feel right..."

"Back here*, now*," he felt himself growl. Fire in his mouth. Scorching. Evil. Unholy.

"Papa-" she started, then her eyes went wide as a hand clamped around her mouth. "I-"

The Paladin spoke again, voice unwavering as stone. "Your time is up, Edas." Abigail's eyes streamed as she was hauled up by one of the Knights.

"Let go of her!" Onan lurched forward but something crunched into his temple and toppled him sideways. A knee in his back pressed against his lungs. Hot breath. Fiery breath. A mouthful of dirt.

Abi kicked and screamed.

"Stay calm, Papa's here-" A boot sank into his face. His vision turned blotchy.

"Papa? I don't feel right." Her voice was hollow. He stared up from the dirt and spat out a mouthful of muddy leaves.

He could only watch in horror.

"No!" she shrieked, eyes bursting with white flames. The Knight dropped her, armour smoking, gauntlets glowing red-hot. "They're here to hurt us Papa!" The leaves smouldered beneath her feet, smoke curling up into the breeze.

"Finish this!" The Paladin roared. A chorus of drawn blades.

"Shh, Petal," he tried to shout but it came out as a whimper. Tears stung on his burning face. Useless. All this infernal rage, useless. He could see nothing now but a sliver of the ground.

"Papa!"

A scream. A brilliant flash of white. A rageful boom. A burning wave over his skin as if it were water.

Where was he? It was dark. There was flickering light. Near him. No. Coming from him.

"No, no, no..." His lungs ached, mouth dry. Onan crawled across the scorched earth, hands grasping for anything and finding nothing but dirt. The fire encasing him was agony. Numbing, scorching, dull, endless agony.

The stench of charred corpses and wood was overwhelming. His hand touched something soft. Charred. Sticky. He looked up. A dark honey eye looked back, still perfect as ever. He pulled her in tight. She was still warm.

Onan wailed as tears turned into steam on his skin.

Onan shovelled the last of the dirt into the hole. A makeshift headstone stood atop it, the evening White making it cast a long shadow across the blackened ground. Surrounded by the charred remains of the stead. The stench of burnt timber and guilt. Dirt and blood clung to his face, knotted his hair together. The salt of his own tears mixed with the taste of iron in his mouth. He dropped the shovel to the ground and took a long, slow look at the white flames staining his arms, covering his shoulders. Felt them gnaw at his back and creep up his neck. Burning hot ache everywhere. He'd been stupid to think it could be avoided.

He wished he could cry again but nothing came. No tears. No sound. Nothing.

Rain began to fall, drops clinking on the shovel as others thudded softly against the dirt. A single crow flew down, perched atop the ruins and watched him in silence. Godrall was miles away. Another crow landed next to the first, cawing bitterly. He wasn't even sure he would make it all the way before the fire took him for its own. A third crow came down, this time perching on the headstone and squawking.

It looked into his soul, beady black eyes daring him. He had to try.

He took a last, sombre look at the pile of the rubble that had been his home, then at the pile of dirt that covered his little girl. No doubt some of his last lucid thoughts, and they were all he'd ever feared they could be.

He turned and started on his long journey to Godrall.

Hirah grumbled as he trudged into another spot of soggy cave. "Stupid muck." Nonetheless, he kept going as the cave went ever deeper, followed by the gently splashing footsteps of the two Knights behind him.

After the detachment that had been sent to apprehend Onan didn't report back they'd assumed the worst. It had been a week since. But the Onan he knew wouldn't have killed them. At the very least not without good reason. Men of honour, and of the Order. Maybe they'd threatened Abigail. Maybe they'd struck first. Maybe they were just taking their time coming back, or couldn't find him. But whatever had happened there would be a rational explanation. But Hirah had always been a worrier.

He had mixed feelings about finding his friend and he could only think the Knight Commander had chosen him to lead the second hunting party for that reason. Maybe Jadon thought that Hirah could convince him to come peacefully, he didn't know. It didn't matter. Hirah loved the order. It was his home, had been since near his birth. But if you can't see the problems within your own family, where can you? It was flawed, but also the best defence the people had against the darkness.

He didn't have a plan but as long as Onan and Abigail were safe he'd find a way. He had reasonable pull in the order now. Hopefully, they'd surrender and Hirah could at worst get some kind of reduced sentence for Onan. At best perhaps he would run into them alone and get them to safety. The men following him were trustworthy in a fight, but not so much in nuanced matter. Both young Knights, both too idealistic - you've got to bend the rules a little or you'll break under the pressure. Gods, if even he thought they were too idealistic what would Onan think? He smiled softly at the thought.

As they'd conducted their investigation, they'd heard few leads. Their latest was mixed reports of a bright figure moving northbound, along the river Uras. It had spooked him when he'd first heard of it. Made him think the worst. But he knew he was just overthinking again. Common folk always embellished the truth. Maybe Onan had been careless and lit his blade or a torch. Camped along the riverside. They'd found remnants of char marks along the river bank. Wasn't outside the realms of possibility. Onan was a phenomenal warrior but by the Gods he could be an idiot sometimes.

That must be it.

Hirah and his men wandered ever further into the blackness, each of their hands lighting the way with their flames, the walls of the cave thick with black lichen and stinking undergrowth. Roots and rocks grasped at their feet as they waded through the sludgy dirt.

"What exactly are we looking for in here, Sir?" One of the three spoke up.

"A man and girl. The man has the fire just like us, so be careful - but I doubt he'll-."

Faint splashing from up ahead. Followed by a faint... sizzling?

"You hear that, sir?"

"Yes..." he tuned his ear to it. "This way, come on." They picked up the pace down a narrow path and came out into a crosspaths. A steady drip-drip and their breathing were the only sounds around.

A deep, echoing, rasping growl.

"Draw your swor-"

A blinding flash. A scream as one of his men crunched into the wall. The light fled and disappeared down one of the tunnels. The Knight's throat smoked and the smell of burnt meat sickened Hirah's stomach.

"Gods..." murmured the second Knight. Their swords rung out simultaneously, whitefire making them gleam.

Drip-drip. Shallow breaths now. A new tightness in his chest, too. It couldn't be. Not Onan, surely?

"Sir, I-" the blinding light sped past. Hirah swung his sword far too slow and the Knight crashed against the wall, slumped in a smoking heap. A glowing, fist-sized hole ran through his armour, cave wall visible the other side. Hirah raised his blade again, tried to breathe slow. He saw his own face reflected in his sword, his own terror looking back at him. He looked into the dark instead, shot a jet of flame into one tunnel. Nothing. Then the other. Nothing. It seemed like eternity, deep within the blackness.

"Come out, whatever you are. Beast or man I mean you no harm unless-" A growl. Deep, and unforgiving. A blinding, pale white light from behind him. From the way he'd come. A bead of sweat rolled down his face and dripped to the sodden floor. He turned.

A being of pure divine fire, flooding the entire cave with holy light. An Infernal. Everything was suddenly quiet. The drip-drip. His own terrified breathing and the fast thumping of his heart. The Creature's rasping, breath-like growl.

"Onan?" He took a small step forward. The being remained silent. "It... it is you... isn't it?" His eyes went wet, his voice gave a pathetic crack. "What happened to you?" Nothing. "Onan it's me. Hirah." Another step. "I'm your friend."

The thing took a step towards him and Hirah's flame went out.

"Onan..." He flinched, started to backpedal, and desperately tried to produce another but nothing came. His veins and soul ran cold. His back touched the wall. "Gods..."

The inferno spoke. "There are no Gods here."

The Rogue Drone

Year 207

We are one. We are the hive. For the hive to thrive, we must expand. This land is ours and ours alone. Vkathi are all. We are one.

This one digs and digs and digs. *The hive must grow to sustain us.* Drones build, as Warriors protect, as Servants keep our Nestminds. *To sustain we must grow.* We Drones work, we ferry materials, we bring food and water, we nurture young. *This one has worked for years.* Near since he was a nymph as all do. This Drone peels away the rocks and dirt with each of his hands, digging for the nest. The others around this one do the same, working for the good of the hive, scurrying this way and that. *Click. Click. The beautiful chorus of our voices. Parts of a greater whole.*

'Brothers, sisters. Come skywards, to the lake. The time nears.' The Nestmind calls. The Night of Summoning is upon us. As one, we cease. The scurrying stops, and the work halts. Then as one we climb. We climb the tunnels, the halls, the sheer, sandy walls of the nest and ascend to the opening. This one helps his brethren, his siblings, giving hands as they need, if they need. *But we all know our home well.* As this one gets closer to the top, the stars are more vivid than he had seen in a long time. Not since this time last year, when the summoning was last performed. As he brings himself over the cusp of the nest and onto the desert sands, he stares out at the many Vkathi making their way to the glittering lake in the distance. *Thousands upon thousands, all committed to a singular goal. For the hive.* The trek through the dunes begins. We are swift.

The Founder's lake glints in the starlight, a heavenly memory of our ancestors' beginnings. *Of where the Vkathi began. Where we clambered from the deep.* This one stands at the very edge, lucky to be among the first. He has never been this close, and he has been many times. The numbers of Vkathi are now tens of thousands, standing around the softly rippling mass of water, encircling it in murmuring quiet.

Nine Servants in thin, web-like robes befitting of that honoured status - each on a raised platform at the edge of the water. A Warrior kneels before each of them. Silence befalls the lake, the only sound lapping of water and the whispering of the desert night winds. The central Servant clasps two hands at the abdomen and raises her other pair above her head. She unsheaths her stone blade. The other Servants do the same, all in perfect unison. A chant begins in our head, one we have heard many times before. There are no words spoken. There is no need. We hear it in our souls.

Tonight we give praise to the Founders, to our great Guardian. May he protect the gate between this world and below.

Give praise to the Founders, who gift us this water,
This water that nourishes us,
Give praise to the Founders, who gift us this blood,
This blood that feeds our souls,
Give praise to the Founders, who gift us this Guardian,
The one that watches the lake

Give praise to the Guardian, who with his watchful sight
Looks upon us this night.

The Servant raises her dagger high and slams it into the chest of her Warrior, cracking it under the heavy blade. The sound of crunching exoskeletons ricochets around the lake as the other eight do the same, all the Warriors giving their life for the glory of the Guardian. They make no sound nor protests, for they are glad to die. Their blood pools beneath them.

The lake is once again silent. Then it trembles. *He is risen.* It trembles again, water rippling slow at first. Those around this one raise their arms, as does he. The ripples turn into waves, and waves wash over the Vkathi at the lake's edge. We bask in its lukewarm embrace. *We give praise to this gift.* From the centre of the lake he emerges with a writhing leap, black-scaled and roaring like thunder. The giant serpent, dwarfing any other creature this one could imagine. *Our protector is risen!* He falls and slinks through waves of his own creation. He brings himself to the Servant's plinth, all of whom bow before his majesty

For a moment, nothing. Then he rears his great head, nostrils flaring out with a deep breath. He looks upon them, upon our sacrifice, his enormous yellow eyes betraying nothing. Then he nods, once. *The great Basilisk accepts our sacrifice! May he bathe in the life-blood of this world!* His eyes turn to the servants. *And may we bathe in its blood ourselves.* They each look up to the eyes of the guardian as one. It is their time to sacrifice.

The blood around their feet swirls, climbing up their legs and crawling around their bodies, becoming dark and grey and hard. It creeps along their limbs, encasing them frozen stone. As they transform they are as silent as the warriors, glad to accept their fate. *Yet more gifts to the great one. The Guardian blesses us!* This one watches as the petrified Servants and sacrificed Warriors are taken to the bottom of the lake one by one, held delicately between his mighty fangs.

Once the last is taken he rises for a final time, gazing at his subjects. This one stares at his majesty, his power, his awe. He sees each of us and we are grateful. With a great leap he slithers back beneath the lake, ripples leaving a trace of what was just there.

'Come, children. Back home. The desert nights are not kind.' The Nestmind calls us home.

The Nestmind was correct, the night sands blistering even the most hardened Warriors, whipping furiously around this one's feet and eyes. Never has he seen a sandstorm so violent. We huddle together, shoulder touching shoulder, sheltering together as we move towards home. The darkness makes it hard to see, the storm makes it worse yet. *Stay close siblings, we all must return safely.*

Eventually we near the safety of the nest. Yet the storm still rages around us, bitter rain turning the ground slick, angry lightning striking sand to glass. Thunder shudders the sky. *Beware.* This one looks around but is unable to see anything less than a short distance from his face. His antennae twitch. *Something is coming.* He stops moving and others around him do the same. Then we see. A vicious whirl of dark wind, surging at us, hurtling through the dunes. *Quick, to shelter!* A cry rings out in this one's mind, echoed by the many voices around. This one looks around, panic in his throat, panic for himself, panic for his brothers and sisters running for their lives. He runs too. *Hurry, hurry.* The sand trips our feet, the wind batters us back and yet still we charge for the nest. *To safety.* The tornado chases us like a hungry dunespider, quick and lethal. We can see the shadow of the nest now over the horizon, a beacon in the sand. *Hurry, hurry.* He feels the terror of his siblings. The rolling stampede of their many feet. The pain as some are snatched by the vicious, roaring wind. *We must not fail the nest.*

A cry. A sibling stuck in the sand. The decision is made. This one rushes and gives him his hand. *Help is here, brother.* He drags him to his feet and pushes him onwards, then looks behind.

It is upon him. He turns on his heel, legs moving as fast as they can scurry, looking left and right as his siblings beside him are caught in its wrath. He is too close. The vortex catches his feet and sweeps him under. It envelopes him, batters him with sand and smashes him with rocks, twisting him this way and that before slinging him out far, far into the wastes. The vicious sands bury him and he is too weak to fight it. This one's vision turns black.

My eyes snap open. I splutter out a mouthful of sand. The grains shift over my body as I wriggle free of its warm clutches, dragging my weary body up. The desert's heat is warm on my exoskeleton, I must have been here for some time.

I... I...? *I? What is I? Who am I? What am I doing here?* The desert, my home. Not this place, though. *Home is the nest. But where is the nest?* I try to listen to the song but there is only the shifting sands around my feet. I try to hear the nest and there is nothing. *Nothing? The nest does not call me. Where is the Nestmind? Where are my siblings? What is this strange voice?*

The silence is deafening, the emptiness terrifying. I am alone, and yet my mind deigns to speak in tongues with a voice I feel I should know.

I collapse into the sand. The Nestmind is gone. *Gone, and I am alone. How can this happen?* I shriek upwards to the sky, to the blinding light, cry hoarse until my throat burns. *Curse you, vile sky spirits. Have the Founders forsaken me?* My mind is loud within myself. It is not right. I yearn to hear my siblings again. *I must find a nest.* They will welcome me. I am Vkathi. No matter my single mind I am Vkathi. I stand again. I will find my home. I look around to see nothing but drifting dunes. I know not where to start, but I cannot stay here.

I begin the journey back to safety.

My mind ponders. It likes to ponder, seemingly without my input. I try to keep it quiet, to deafen my ears to the strange sound that sounds like me. Thoughts like none I've never had run wild and loose and enthralling. *How is this possible? The Nestmind will know. The Nestmind always knows. It will heal.* The light from the break in the sky is hot this day, though it does not yet bother me. The desert shimmers with its heat, the horizon hazy. But Vkathi are made for the desert's harshness. *We are harsh in kind. We are survivors.* I keep moving, slogging through the drifts, searching for a haven. But the wastes never end.

It is nearly nightfall. I still find no sign of life for miles. *No nest opening, no tracks, nor even another creature.* I must dig a place to rest, lest the night's predators find me - I am no Warrior. I kneel, and with my hands scrape away the sand. *If nothing else I still dig well.* I keep digging down. Down and down I go until I am hidden below the surface. I rest, and will resume my search in the morning. I want nothing but to hear the voices of my siblings. *I so wish the Nestmind would say my name.*

Morning. I dig myself from my hole, pull myself from the sand and look around at the endless, vacant dunes once more. But the work begins again. The work never ends. I set off, ever wary of the dangers the desert poses to single Vkathi. My eyes are wide and my steps fast. As I trek once again, my unfettered mind seems to talk, and talk, and talk without purpose. *Am I to be stuck like this? Will the nest welcome me? I do not know. Oh to be sure again. To know safety once more would be sweet.*

Many dunes, many steps later and the heat starts to take its toll. It is a heavy burden. My feet drag on the ground, my breaths grow shorter and a hunger begins to gnaw. I must find shelter soon, lest I perish. I tire of this journey, But I know I must press on. *Am I to die alone? Is this the fate the Founders have assigned to me?* My head hangs, and I stare at the many grains beneath my feet. Vkathi are like sand, I think. Apart, we are weak. Small. But together? Together we are strong. Together, we are like the tornado that led me to this fate. Together we are a force of nature. I push myself once more off the sand. *I must be together again.*

Shapes move in the distance. Dark blurry. A small group of Vkathi. *Founders, you are generous.* They have not seen me yet. I gather my strength and run.

"Brothers! Sisters!" I shout, to no response. "Brothers! Sisters!" This time louder, screaming for them, voice loud as my dry lungs will carry. I wave my arms and leap, I can see them clearly now. Three Warriors no more than a few hundred strides away. *They must have heard me now.* I keep shouting, pleading. One of them turns. *They see! They see!* I pick up my pace, weary legs carrying me as fast as they can. I trip over myself and flail headfirst into the sand but I scrabble up, racing towards my brethren. *They do not move, but they see.*

Twenty strides away now. I slow, and look up at them. All Warriors, larger than I by at least a head and stronger, too, each with heavy raktooth spears. Unfamiliar faces, unfamiliar scents, but at last my own kind. Their big, friendly, black eyes stare at me inquisitively. I stare back. *I... I cannot feel them. It is as if they are not there.* Their presence is simply void. They tilt their heads, antennae flicking back between each other and myself. *They cannot feel me either.* Their antennae curl and they flicker the tips toward one another. They raise their spears. *Oh no.* I bow my head so as to not provoke them. My mind screams, tries to scream, tries to tell them '*I am a friend*' but they do not hear it. Their hands grip their spears tighter, all three of them hulking down and snarling. I take a tentative step forward and reach my arm towards them. *Please, understand me.* The closest hisses, mandibles chittering. Then he lunges, spear aimed for my face. I jerk back and stumble to the ground. He tilts his head to his nestmates. After a moment he points back to where I came from.

"Leave now," he growls, "and do not return, stranger." *Stranger? I?* My pained mind races but I know when to give up. I squirm, averting my shamed face and shrink back from my former brethren. My chest heaves. My gut aches as I go back the way I came. Another long walk to nowhere. After a small while I look over my shoulder. They are gone, disappeared into the sands. *They are right. No nest would have me now. I am an outcast. An abomination of my kind.*

Thirty-eight days. I claw my way up the next great bank, pushing myself onward. I take a look back. The dunes behind me are the same as those in front, bleeding into an endless sea of hazy, hot beige. My feet ache. My legs ache. I haven't eaten since I was last in the nest, nor have I tasted the purity of water. *This cannot go on much longer. I cannot go on much longer.* I keep slogging, my knees just one more step from caving each time.

I will perish soon. Yet I do not feel sad. *I do not wish to be a part of a world without the hive.* I have not enjoyed my final days here, wandering aimlessly. I wish to be part of a collective again, part of a whole. *Myself again.* My single mind is all too loud and all too quiet, the duality of my being eating away at me as savagely as the desert has eaten away at my body. I near the top of the drift, my footing loose against the sand. I use my forearms to steady myself, turning my walk into a steep crawl. I pull myself up, up and over the dune and roll onto my side. I stare up into the sky, into the great blue emptiness. A deep breath, readying myself for the last push. *I do not wish to push anymore. I wish to let go.* Maybe it is better I lie here. Maybe it is better if I accept my fate rather than make it worse. *I do not wish to be alone any longer.*

I turn my head, expecting to see more sand, perhaps the gratifying shade of rocks where I can spend my final moments. But no.

The sand melts away into earthy brown, into vivid green. Tall, strange plants with great green leaves and impossibly bright flowers like I've never seen, the colours refreshing upon my eyes. Short, beautifully emerald shrubs, like a purified reflection of the dead weeds that grow through the nest. Life of all kinds, an oasis at the very edge of the barren desert sea stretching the length of my vision.

I push myself over the cusp and tumble down the sand. Towards the trees, towards my oasis saviour, my legs as strong as they have ever been. I see animals too, now. Strange animals, foreign and wonderful to my eyes. Small hairless ones, scurrying between the undergrowth and swiftly followed by a ravenous red lizard. Larger grazers, thinly-furred and with odd, round noses sniffing at the trees and munching on their leaves. Birds of bright blue and fiery yellow trilling in the branches, bright and content.

Water. Water! Nothing more than a large pond, but clear and bright as the sky. I race over and dive to my knees, hands eagerly cupping it into my grateful mouth. *Oh, sweet founder's blood. Water.* My hands flash in and out of the pool, water dripping down my face and thorax. *You have never tasted so sweet.*

After a few moments I have had my fill and pause to look around me with clearer eyes. This land is so far from my home. Vkathi never normally venture this far. *But I am no normal Vkathi.* It is glorious here. Only moments ago I was accepting of my death. *Maybe this is my true fate.* Not to die forgotten in the desert, but to bring this haven to my people. I must. *Maybe that is why the Nestmind let me go. The Nestmind always knows...* This oasis is surely the land that we were made to live in. The stolen land that the Nestmind sometimes talks of. How far does this wonder reach? I must know.

Wonders I hadn't ever even dreamt of pass me by, the trees greener and more lush with each step. Soon even the thin sands turn to damp dirt. The leaves glint in the light and raindrops trickle gently between them. There is vivacity like nothing the wasteland I call my home.

A small bird perches on a branch above my head, eyes locked on me. A bird with green and gold feathers and a bright red beak. It sidles along the branch, making its way toward me one tiny, careful step at a time. It chirps and cocks its head toward me. *Curious.* I click back. It does it again, a little louder. It looks deeper into the forest for a moment before it turns back to me. Then it chirps again. I point at myself, and then into the forest. Another chirp. Then off it goes, flying away and into the trees.

I rush after it, after the glimpses of gold and bright little chirps. Deeper into the forest. Twigs snap under my feet as I dart through the undergrowth. The bird is swift but I keep it in my sights, running through this strange land as if I'd known it my whole life. *Where does it lead me?* Farther yet. I keep pace, feet darting over every obstacle and before long I am deeper than I ever thought possible, in a sea of brown and green. Even the sky is hidden now.

The bird comes to an abrupt stop and perches atop a large pile of rocks. It chirps again.

"You want me to move them?"

It chirps, seemingly in confirmation. I start clearing the many stones away and before long I can make out some sort of tunnel, stretching far and dark. The bird takes off, soaring high into the trees before swooping back down and disappearing through the hole. *I've come this far.* My antennae twitch. *Forward.*

The tunnel is narrow and steep. It hasn't been used in a long, long time. Faded markings score the walls. Claw marks? Footprints? *Other Vkathi?* I move carefully onwards and eventually the last of the light from the entrance fades. I am left only to trust my other senses. *The closest to the hive I've been in ages, the dark underground. Calming.* I am sure I can hear water lapping against rocks but I can't sense any around me. *Strange again.* A chink of light twinkles up ahead, through leaves and vines.

I reach it, brush them aside and step cautiously out into the light once again. My feet touch warm sands. I look around. A gigantic ring of stone, as if a mountain were hollowed. Trees cling to the edges, the wall wrapped in thick vines all reaching for the light. *Founder's blood!*

A great beast to rival the Basilisk itself lies in its centre, sleeping. Scales just as the great serpent has, only brilliant green instead of deathly black. Bladelike teeth, four colossal legs all ending with razored talons. Two vast, furled wings lie over it. *A Dragon. Stories of such things exist, yet I never thought...* Its scales shimmer like the leaves of the forest, emerald flecked with gold.

I stare at the magnificent slumbering beast before me. The Basilisk is friendly to us because we appease it - will the Dragon be the same? *Do I leave? Do I dare stay?* I look around as if for a sign. Nothing. I could turn back now, try to find a hive that will listen to me, tell them of the beauty I have found here. *But I cannot let my decisions be dictated by a hive that no longer wants me. I've come this far and I cannot go back to any nest now.* I take a breath. *If I am to be doomed, then let me meet my doom by a Dragon.*

How to wake a sleeping beast? A fist-sized rock on the ground catches my eye. I pick it up, feeling the weight of it in my hand. I hurl it at the creature and it bounces off its head, echoing through the chamber. Nothing. Another rock, this time thrown a little harder bounces harmlessly off its wing. Still nothing. I shout and the birds on the closest tree take off, obviously upset. But still the Dragon is silent. I approach the great beast. *Maybe it will sense me.* I creep up to its head and stay away from the teeth, the smallest of which still dwarfs me. Placing two of my hands on its eyelid, I peel it upwards with great effort. Its brilliant golden eye shines with all the hues of majesty and power but... not so much as a flinch. I look into its huge, slitted pupil. *Maybe it cannot be woken.*

The pupil flicks to me and the Dragon blinks. *It's awake.* I stagger backwards and land on my back, hands scrabbling on the sand to get myself as far from its gigantic talons as possible. Its cavernous jaw opens, yellowed teeth sheening with wet. *Founders...* A great shadow looms over my face. Before I even have time to think about the possibilities a great foot thunders down next to me, blasting me sideways and battering me with sand. I scramble along the ground as it trembles. My heartbeat is deafening. It rears its head and stretches its legs, wings not quite spreading the width of the chamber as it shudders them out and back in. It is a wondrous sight to behold. *Wondrous and terrifying.*

The Dragon brings its head down, great golden eyes upon me, snout about ten strides from my face and breath like steam. It observes me silently for a few moments, then seems to furrow its brow. My breathing stops. I am still. With a whoosh of wind it whips its head up and from the bottom of its throat comes a deep roar of flame, just scraping the edges of the crater, hot on my body even from this far below. It lowers its head once again.

"I have waited long for you, little one." *It speaks! Its voice in my head as if the hive were with me once again.* "You are later than expected." I do not know what to say.

"I am sorry, great one." I sink to my knees and bow my head.

Its voice is soft and deliberate, that of a queen speaking to larvae. "Do not be sorry. I never said you were late, only that I expected you earlier. Your time is whenever you decide it is."

"Yes, great one." I keep my head down.

"We are equals, you and I. Rise."

"Yes." I stand up and look into its eyes. They pierce me right to my core. Like it knows me without even knowing me at all.

"You are lost, are you not?" The Dragon takes a great breath in. "Unwhole."

"That is true. My connection to the hive is lost."

"I can feel it." It closes its eyes and muses. "Your new state of mind has been a source of much turmoil for you." It pauses and smiles for a moment, great lips curling. "And yet such an adventure it has brought to you as well." *I have nearly died, been threatened by my own kind and by the desert itself. But also I had found this Oasis, and its life and was the first I had ever heard of to see a Dragon.*

"Is this the experience of a single mind? Only extremes?"

"Oh, nothing is ever that simple, dear mortal. But for you, it has provided a lease on life very few of your kind will ever experience. But I sense you are conflicted."

"I feel the call of the Nest... it is home to me. But I cannot return."

"Indeed you can, if that is what you desire. I can reconnect your mind, but I..."

"You can?" My heart flips. *I can go home.*

"Yes, little one. But..." and it pauses, thinking a moment, "allow me to make another offer before you decide. Step closer." It moves backwards, quaking the ground with its massive steps. It nods to where it had been laying. A large, sandstone circle, with a rough ring of steps all around. I walk beside the Dragon's lowered head and it gestures forwards. I take the steps slowly, then look down.

A swirling abyss of ethereal crimson, a deep red glow cast over its surroundings. Hypnotic and beautiful. I feel... pulled in only one direction, now. I shake my head free.

My head swims with questions but I ask only one. "What is it?"

"This is one of the many portals that connect Tarae... this world." A great claw gestures around. "They are the very veins of this world, all guarded by the Leviathans." Its head turns to me. "You are the first Vkathi I have seen in centuries. You are not like the others... And you are ready." I cannot believe it. *New lands, new life. A new beginning.*

"Where does this one lead?"

"To the lands of Humans. Far removed from what you know. A diverse people with many... nuances." Silence befalls the two of us for a moment. "But they are often as warm as any you will find. I know not exactly what you will find beyond, but I believe you may enjoy it." It smiles once again. *I must. The chance will never come again.*

"I am ready."

"Are you certain? You are welcome back, of course - but this is not something to be undertaken lightly."

"Yes." Though my nerves say anything but. "I must do this."

"The guardian on the other side of this gate, unfortunately... " the great being holds a note of sorrow in its booming voice, "is long since dead. But I wish you luck little one, I hope I may see you again one day. Mortals, for the most part, truly are a delight."

I stare into the abyss below me. It stares back. I let myself go. It catches me in its lukewarm clutches and I spin, faster and faster as red rages into blistering white then flung out the other side, plummeting face-first into the mud.

I'm in a cave, the portal behind me shaped like some kind of strange, circular door in the wall, not a pool like the other. It is cold here. Rain lashes and wind howls outside.

The exit is wide open and the land is full of green. *Oh, it's so wonderfully green.* I run to it, through the muddy darkness to a new world. Trees thick and damp with rain. Squawking birds and skittering insects and the twitching of the undergrowth. *So much noise, so much life!* Moss and vines cover everything I can see, wrapping themselves around even each other.

I think I will like this place.

Gravedigger

Year 653

The evening was bitter and the service was almost over. Kildreth watched from his porch, just good and out of earshot, though he knew well enough what they were saying. His waterskin wobbled dangerously in his trembling right hand as he brought it to his lips. He'd thought that, maybe, he should start trying to use his left. It'd stop him from missing his mouth and dribbling it down his wrinkled chin quite so much, but he wasn't one for letting anyone tell him what to do, especially if that bastard was him. As it was this time he caught the bottle opening well and sipped on it about the same, steady pace the coffin was lowered into the ground.

"A fine waste," he muttered, to no one.

Seventeen, he'd been. Just two days ago the fever took a grip of the boy, and now Kildreth watched him return to the ground. Kildreth remembered when was born. He'd been a nice lad. Helpful, hard-working. Had a good clear head on his shoulders. Would have been just like his Father. Every village needs some foundations. Leaders, organisers, farmers, woodworkers, smiths, Druids. Priests, if you were one of those godly people across the water, Kildreth supposed.

And gravediggers. Which made Kildreth one of those foundations. For the last sixty-odd years, in fact. Maybe if he'd had children he wouldn't be the grimmest bastard in the village. But he'd never been bothered by that sort of thing, and as it was here he stood on his battered, damp old porch he'd built all those decades ago, and watched as yet another corpse was hefted into a hole he'd dug. A life far shorter than it should have been, and one Kildreth had seen near every moment of. Just as he'd watched the lifetime of most the dead in Alkvyn.

"Damn shame." He took another shaky swig of his water, carefully pressed the stopper in with his aching fingers, and tucked it in his breast pocket.

He could see the final words were being said. Vren finishing his piece. Old Druid bastard wasn't so spry himself no more, but he was still a good decade shy of Kildreth. Wasn't many else there. Just the father, his daughter, and a few close to the family. Kildreth remembered burying the mother a few years back, whatever her name was. Just another bit of bad luck, really. Got bit by something nasty, and not even Vren could figure out what. Two days later and she was cold as the grave Kildreth had already dug for her. You spend long enough around death, you can tell it's coming. A sense for bad luck, more than anything. Kildreth knew the only thing you can change less than luck is death. Though recently, he wasn't so certain.

The people started drifting away, going back to their homes or to their work. But the father and the daughter came this way, she holding his hand. Only a few years younger than her brother, and already gone through so much. Her face buried in his side, his sullen and drawn, pain visible even in the way he walked, a far cry from the lad Kildreth knew those decades ago. He stopped just short of the porch steps, arm pulling his girl close.

"Kildreth."

"Davin," Kildreth replied. "Sorry about yer boy. The whole bastard thing." And he tried his best to look and sound like he wasn't numb to it, even it was an awful shame.

"Thank you." Davin's hand squeezed on his girl's shoulder. "Me and Reya just wanted to say thank you. Know it's a bastard of a job, and you were good to us when-" And he swallowed, taking a moment to steady his voice. "When their Mother-

"Aye, I know," Kildreth stopped him in his pitiful tracks. "I take no pleasure in my job, but someone's got to do it. Glad I could be of service." He nodded his head. "His soul's back to where it came from, now."

"Aye." He leant his head down to Reya and said, "What do we say, eh?"

She let out a large sniff and took a long moment to take her head away from her father. "Th-thank you," she whispered.

He gave her the smallest of smiles. Just a sharp curl of his lip. "You're welcome, my dear. I wish you both well, and my shack's always open, Davin."

"Thanks, Kil," Davin said. He gave her another squeeze, held a solemn, lingering look at Kildreth, and then another at the fresh hole over the edge of the graveyard. Then they left without another word.

Kildreth took a moment to breathe, then grabbed the shovel leant up against the porch and began his walk through the many stones.

The shovel hit the coffin with a hollow clunk.

"There ye are," Kildreth muttered, half-smiling, half-grimacing. He'd only covered it this afternoon. Was a bastard to be digging it out again, especially this late in the night, but if this was what it took this is what he'd do. Wasn't exactly like he could do it in the daylight. The dirt still hadn't settled yet. An easier job. He shovelled away the last few clumps before setting it on the earth just above his head.

"Hmpf." He rubbed at his face, soil-caked hands catching his nose with that damp stench they always carried. Folks here often joked that he stank of death. But Kildreth had long since lost his sense of smell. "Time to get you out, lad."

He set to work on working off the lid.

Set the hammer at the nail, and yank just right to be quiet as he could. Once, twice, thrice normally did it. Clink. Rinse and repeat, the coffin creaking under his feet. Never snapping though, not once. He had Kark to thank for that. Youngish lad, his father buried only in the last year. Mother not far off. Though she wouldn't be much use. But Kark had picked up the craft like anything, and these coffins never once broke, never once splintered. Every nail out clean as you like. Kildreth often supposed he should enlist him to help him improve the shack, but it'd mean time away from his work. And he couldn't afford that, not now.

Once, twice, thrice. A soft clink and the last nail came out. Kark was good, but no one knew coffins like Kildreth. He scurried the tools away in his pocket and stepped back onto the earthen ditch he'd shovelled out for himself. Then, with a grunt and a great pang in his decrepit bastard of a back, he knelt and slid the lid up to the side.

There he was. Whats-his-name. Davin's boy. Pale as anything. Didn't help he was red-haired, Kildreth supposed. Didn't help he was dead neither. Without ceremony he grabbed him by his waif-thin ankles and hauled him up onto the dirt steps, head and limbs flopping in that strange, stiff-limp manner they do. He set him down, dug out his hammer and nails again and set to work. Made sure they were in the right place. One, two, in. And soon enough it was done.

He hauled the body up to the bank, not even bothering to check if there was anybody about. There never was. Strangely, no one visited the graveyard at night. And Kildreth had long since been used to the noises of the wind, the hooting owls in the trees at the far end near his shack, and the cats mewing at the other. Sometimes the crafty buggers made their way to his shack, hoping for some food. But never such luck for 'em.

He once again set about shovelling the dirt over the coffin for the second time that day and before long, that was done too. He picked the boy up with a grit of his teeth and sharp niggle in his back, hauled him over his shoulder. Good thing he'd lost some weight before he passed. Age might have finally caught up with him, but Kildreth had always had a little good luck.

"In we go lad," he muttered, and strode over to the shack.

Kildreth leant back in his chair and caught his breath, trying to stretch his aching legs. He'd have to find someone of a like mind to give him a hand with his work, soon. If he could find anyone. Bastard age. He worked his right palm around that knot in his right thigh that never quite seemed to leave, gave his creaking shoulders a little flex, a little rise-and-fall, and of course, eventually tried with his left hand - the one that wasn't quite so shaky - to prod at that niggle in his back. Leant forward now, tried to stretch his right arm all the way - no. He shook his head out and fell back into the chair Kark's father had made all those years ago. Didn't creak, even now. And the cushions his wife had made for it still had feather in, after all this time. Soft against his rickety spine. A crackling fire over the other side of the shack spread a little warmth through the room, surrounded by the stone hearth he and Davin's Father had made.

"Hmpf." Kildreth closed his eyes and let out a happy grunt. Like a pig in shit. There were some perks to being in his profession, he supposed. Everyone wishes you well when they know its you sending them off. A lot of the things in his shack had been gifts.

What to do about the boy? At the moment, he lay over on the floor by the door, wrapped up loose in a load of old burlap. Kildreth had found it soaked up any overnight leaks. He'd take it downstairs come the morning, lay it on the table, set to work. He'd probably be able to get a good day's work on it tomorrow. Not many came to see him the day after funerals, for some reason. There'd only been twice anyone had knocked for him while he'd been downstairs. One time they'd left before he had the chance to get up, the bastard, and the other had only come to offer condolences a few flowers when Pick died. Couldn't remember who it was, though.

Poor Pick. That dog had been with him for over twenty years. Poor old girl. Kildreth felt his lip go a little wobbly even thinking about the silly mutt. Stupid, she was. Stupid, but honest. Everything he wasn't, he supposed. That had been a hard hole to dig.

He opened his eyes to wipe a little wet from them, and glanced at his bed in the corner. Lovely piece of woodwork that was and all, but it seemed awful far away at the moment. Busy day today. Besides, he had a blanket right over the armrest for this very reason. Through a big, weary yawn he shook the soft, hand-woven blanket out and drew it over himself. Another busy day tomorrow.

Kildreth took the razor to his left forefinger and in one quick motion, smooth as he could, sliced it open. He gave it a squeeze at the base, getting as much blood as he could. Drip, drip, into the bowl, nice and steady. He'd become good at this now. He didn't need a lot, just a good enough measure to afford some spillage. Nearly always some spillage. He put the blade back on the shelf beside him and picked up a slightly larger, far sharper one beside it.

As soon as the small bowl was filled about a third of the way up, he wiped his finger clean and wrapped a little rag of cloth around it to stop the bleeding. Then, steady as possible he picked it up and shuffled over to the table in the centre of the cellar where the boy lay and left it beside his head.

"Where to start..."

This was always the question. It was a bastard getting them down the ladder, and even skinny as this one was it was no easier. Then Kildreth had to undress them, of course, which was a venture in and of itself. Luckily his years in his particular profession had rendered him quite immune to any retching. Still, it wasn't pleasant. He never wanted to waste a single precious resource.

"Perhaps a wrist... a hand..." Yes, it'd been a little while since he'd done anything quite so simple. But it was often simple pleasures that brought the most glee.

And so, with his tongue sticking out his mouth for concentration he strained his right hand to get a good angle, determined to not let it get the better of him. He gently pressed down so that it just punctured the skin, slit it parallel with the smallest bones.

Off to a good start. He put the knife down beside the bowl and dug out the small spoon from his pocket. An odd tool for this, he'd often thought, but it served its purpose with little mess. Especially after that time he'd dropped the bowl over himself. That had been a bastard to get out. So he dipped the spoon in the bowl, got just enough, and with his right hand peeling open the incision, dribbled the blood into it and set the spoon aside.

He rolled up his sleeves despite the chill of the earthen cellar and closed his eyes. A breath, in through the nostrils and out through the mouth. A clear mind was best for this.

He felt a tug, in his mind. In his veins. That familiar, brilliant tug of the blood. He had to stop a smile, had to stop himself from getting carried away. With his mind, he reached out for it. Reached out for his own blood within another's veins, warm amongst the cold, living amongst the dead. He'd often thought about what it would feel like inside the living. Not just to control the dead, but command the living. But now was not the time for speculation.

There it was. His blood inside the boy's wrist, a warm pulse in his right hand. As real and as true as if it were his own years younger, more supple, more pliable. Oh, that glorious, simple pleasure. He opened his eyes, aching joy spread across his face.

The boy's arm from the elbow down stood straight up, fingers moving as Kildreth's moved, only more carefully, more considerate. Turn by wonderful turn he extended each jittering finger of his own with great effort, yet felt the boy's hand flex each digit like a newborn child. The duality could be maddening, the echo of his true body forever there, every niggle, every pang, every twitch just out his mind's eye. But for some truly beautiful moments, it was like he was young again. Like he was himself. To see a hand move as he desired, to see the tendons move as he intended, to have the shakes gone from his being, even falsely, even temporarily, was bliss.

He wiped a tear from his eye and let out a childish burst of laughter as he saw the corpse poke its face, arm flopping as he momentarily lost control.

"No, no." He forced himself to stop, to retain that hold over his blood, lest it be lost. "Don't get carried away." You had to take your time. He steeled his face and let the blood flow freely, twisting and turning his wrist in ways his real couldn't quite anymore.

Both he and the corpse scratched at their chins. "Now, what next?"

Thunder cackled in the distance. Rain battered the roof and howling wind pummeled the shack, wood groaning a sombre groan. Kildreth sat on his chair, and grumbled.

"Bastard storm."

That drip of water in the far corner of the roof was more bothersome than ever. He was grateful he'd chosen to have no windows when he built the place. No doubt the lightning would be right in front of them, trying to distract him from his rest. Yet none of that was what worked his mind tonight.

He couldn't draw his eyes from his hand. Couldn't draw his eyes from the ugly, parchment skin. From the age spots. From the dirt-encrusted nails. From the popping veins.

And try as he might to ignore it, when he closed his eyes he felt his body failing. The pain of stretching his fingers a little further than they'd like, the ache in his bones from trying a little too hard.

Elders, he wished he had more time.

The boy's legs, with them he was free from that eternal knot in his thigh. The freedom, the litheness of his spine, being able to stand as he liked even just for a little, even if it wasn't quite him. The quickness of his mind translated to a body that still agreed. It was beautiful.

He might get another small go at it tomorrow if he was lucky. After then the body would be too far gone. He'd cleaned it before the funeral, of course. That was another one of his jobs. That's how he knew it'd be a good one. The best he'd had yet, perhaps, but they never lasted long. He always had to return here. To this barely-functional husk.

He'd cleaned it again after the day's work, tried to preserve it as best he could, of course. Crawsalt over it the flesh and in the wound. A little trick he'd picked up years ago. Salt and powdered crawberry, which grew in abundance in the woods behind his shack. An ugly little black fruit the size of a fingernail, smelt like lavender. Made your throat choke something awful if you swallowed it, but clogged up wounds a treat and kept bodies fresh. Strange, the way people fussed over keeping their bodies living was the same way he fussed over keeping them freshly dead. No matter what he did, though, they'd all start to smell, and he'd have to get rid of them. And simply putting them back in the coffin wouldn't do neither - better to risk an exhumation of nothing than a body chopped up and sewn back together. So tomorrow evening, before it started to stink, he'd have out to get the cleaver and sack to haul the bits down to the river, or dig a hole somewhere in the woods. An ungraceful end for the boy, but the dead don't tend to care what happens to them.

Kildreth didn't fear death. In fact, he often wished it would hurry up. But he could at least try to make himself more comfortable before it happened. He only wished that comfort would stick. He shrugged. Or at least, he attempted a shrug, felt that pang in his left shoulder and decided against it. The chair again, tonight. He pulled his blanket over him and turned his head, eyes clamped tight as they could be, trying to find most comfortable discomfort he could manage.

Thump, thump, thump. Kildreth's weary eyes snapped open. Three knocks at the door, loud even over the wind howling outside, even over the battering rain.

"Is anyone in there?" A man's voice. One he did not recognise. He scowled at the door a moment, watched it wobble again as he knocked again. Thump, thump, thump. He was, once again, grateful he opted to not have windows in here. "We need shelter, me and my girl!"

He had no obligation. He did not know them. The boy was downstairs and it seemed like an awful risk. But then Kildreth could always force them out come the morning. And he wasn't inhuman. To leave anybody out in this unsettled him a little. Maybe his skin really was that thin. Or maybe the note of terror in the man's voice had just got under it.

"Please!"

Curse his damn good heart.

"Bastard," he grumbled as he rose from his chair, hands steadily making him rise fast as they could.

"In anyone in there?" The voice climbed higher in pitch as the wind picked up outside.

"I'm coming, I'm coming!" He shouted as loud as he could, which wasn't very.

He shuffled over the floor, it creaking near as much as his bones, reached the door, unhooked the heavy latch and turned the handle. All at once rushed a hoarse roar of wind that half-staggered him, a thick spate of rain, a man, sodden and filthy and wearing nothing but rags and a big, shaggy dog in much the same state, aside from the rags. Kildreth banged the door shut and fumbled the latch over.

"Oh..." Kildreth mumbled, "your girl is a dog." Though he knew he sounded disappointed, he actually much preferred that it that way. He looked over them both for a second.

The man was doubled up, hands-on thighs, taking heavy breaths. Unassuming. About thirty-something, perhaps. Black hair, hanging lank over a dark face, mud-caked boots peeling off onto the floor. The dog was much the same again, shaking herself off and dirtying Kildreth's floor with specks of brown, some in the shape of pawprints. Ah, the price of charity.

Kildreth gave them a few moments, then elected to have little further to do with them until he could get them out.

"You're welcome to the bed." He gestured to it. "I'll sleep in the chair. You're also welcome to food in the cupboards and on the worktop, within reason." He pointed to them, over in the opposite corner to his chair, near the empty hearth. "There's food in there, and you're welcome to start a fire." And he pointed to it, along with the logs and kindling next to it. I'll have to ask you to be gone by morning, though. There'll be accommodation in the village, I expect." And, job done, he shuffled back over to the chair, ready for sleep more than ever.

"Thank you, sir," said the man after a long pause. "I had to find somewhere to rest, we've just come from the woods-"

"Yes, yes," Kildreth interrupted as he winced himself back into his chair, soft cushion slowly beginning to ease his back. "I'm sure you've both had quite the journey. But I need my sleep, if you please."

The man looked at him a moment, face crunched up in confusion, and then for a moment flashed a look of what seemed like relief before he simply shrugged. "Of course, sorry. Thank you for your hospitality." Then he turned to the dog and gave her a little nudge with his foot. "Go on girl, by the fire." And she did just that, shaking herself off and nestling by the fire close as she could. He let himself smile a moment. Pick had loved to do just the same. Kildreth had never minded the cold, nor been particularly bothered by fires unless it was for cooking. But he'd lit them for Pick all the same. He'd fallen out of the habit these last few years.

The stranger picked up a handful of kindling and two small logs, tossing them among the embers, and tried to get a spark with flint he'd dug from his pocket. Eventually it took, and in a minute the shack had a warm glow to it. It made a change to sleeping in the cold dark, he supposed.

Kildreth was surprised to find himself opening his mouth again. "My Pick used to do just the same, curled up by the fire."

"Eh?" The man turned his head back, frowning.

Confused by his own outburst but determined to see it through, he shrugged. "Dog." He nodded. "My old girl used to be just the same."

"Oh, aye." The man smiled, first at him, then the dog. A smile that struck Kildreth, even in his general ill-ease with people, as a little forced. "Yeah, I think most are."

"What's her name?" Kildreth found himself asking, "And yours, of course."

"Oh." The stranger started shaking himself off, hanging his ragged coat on one of the free hooks aside the fire and wiping some of the wet from his face and beard with the back of his hands. Took an awfully long time about it, too, Kildreth noticed, before he finally decided to speak. "I'm Iven," he said, "and this is Rags."

"Rags?" Kildreth felt himself frowning for a moment, but soon supposed that a dog cares little for its name. After all, Pick hadn't been a very inventive choice. He cast his eyes back to the scruffy mutt, heavy black fur quickly drying in the warmth of the fire. "Rags... suppose she does look a little ragged, doesn't she?" He found himself smiling again, teeth and all. Must have looked quite the old fool. Soft as shit.

The stranger gave a sharp chuckle and nodded. "Aye."

The two of them stayed there for a moment, in the near-silence, with the rain pattering heavy on the roof and the wind whistling. Both of them lingered on the dog, the man taking out a small waterskin and taking a smooth sip from it. Before long and for reasons unknown, Kildreth found himself talking again.

"So, what happened to you both?"

The man coughed a little on his water and shook his head, brows closing together as if in concern. "Well... we just came through the woods back there."

"Aye, you mentioned."

"Right..." muttered the stranger, taking off his sodden overshirt now. If you could call a beige rag an overshirt. He hung it by the fire and turned to one of the cupboards. "Hmm..."

"Yes," Kildreth beckoned him on. The man had evidently been through something.

"Right...well... " He scratched the back of his head and he looked through the admittedly bare cupboard. "We came from a village not too far the other side, me and her. Ran into some trouble, and, well, had to flee. Of course." He flashed a rather unconvincing attempt at an easy-going smile. "Bastard chance to get caught in this rain."

"Aye," Kildreth echoed, "bastard chance."

"You mind if I help myself to this?" The man pulled out a glass jar. The one Kildreth used for his oats.

"Aye, of course. What kind of trouble?"

"Oh, uh. Nothing much. A misunderstanding is all." The man busied himself. Spoons, a pot, a little water from the bucket on the top, giving it a mix before he set it over the fire. As if he couldn't do two things at once. Kildreth stroked at his chin, felt that niggle in his shoulder and an unhappy feeling in his gut. "The guards seemed to think I was somebody else."

"Somebody else?" Kildreth chuckled. "A killer, aye? A thief or somethin'?" He likely shouldn't have been poking, nor prodding, nor even talking. Maybe he should have gone to sleep after all. Maybe he shouldn't have let him in. But once you're in a mess, there's no point trying to get out of it. Give it all you've got.

"Ha," the stranger let out a dry laugh, "something like that, I suppose." He gave the now slowly-bubbling pot a prod. Rags got up, shifted herself a little and sat back down in much the same position.

"What was it then?"

"Oh..." He shrugged then sucked at his teeth. "They'd thought I was someone I wasn't, and they weren't having any of it when I tried to tell 'em otherwise. Thought I'd been involved in some tavern incident the night before. Called me an aggressor. So we had to clear out fast as we could. Didn't even have time to pack my things." He gave another irritatingly awkward chuckle.

"Tonight?"

"Aye, tonight."

The two closest villages, to Kildreth's knowledge - which he thought to be pretty good, considering there were seven decades of it - were Evren, north out of the town on a dirt track through a load of wet trees, and Orever, east if you walked by the river or south-east if you reckoned on the road. But both of them were at least eight, nine miles out from here. Not something you'd undertake on a late evening, even if your safety was on the line, not if you really were innocent, Kildreth reckoned. And especially not in the gale outside. But he had another thought just then, too.

Why'd he stumble upon this shack? Why stop here, and not somewhere else in the village? The roads came into the village nowhere near here. Someplace else would have taken him in. Unless... The woods behind his shack were direct to the south. Thick, they were. Knotted and heavy with bramble and vines. Not like the trees at the roadside. You'd have to know 'em well to find your arse in there, never mind anything else. 'Weeper's Woods', they called 'em. Sounded dark and ancient and mysterious. In reality, it just never seemed to stop raining, everything always slick with wet. Made good ground for burying bodies, though. No one ever really went there.

Except, it was now obvious, this stranger.

"You come from downriver?" Kildreth asked, innocuously as possible. "Can imagine it's overflowed by now. Be the same down in Orever."

"Aye, likely has." He paused a moment to stir again. "Was bad luck to be caught out in all this."

"Mhm." Kildreth nodded along. "Bad luck." He eyed the stranger again, tried to pick him apart. Nothing special about the raggedy clothes he was wearing, nor did he seem to have anything in his pockets. Maybe he really had fled. But there was something in the way he carried himself, the way his story seemed... forgetful. Convenient. Loosely stitched.

Relying on the kindness and foolishness of an old man.

Kildreth bristled with anger at the thought of being taken for a fool. And then once again after he thought what the lying bastard might do if he found out he knew. There were measures to be taken. Not physical, of course. Kildreth knew he couldn't stop him from fleeing, or worse. But he was smarter.

"May I recommend a little crawsalt with your oats." Kildreth pointed with his quivering right hand to the cupboard. "It's just in a little clay pot at the back. Wonderful stuff. Just a little sprinkled over the top." And he winked like old men were supposed to when then said something canny.

"Can't say I've heard of it..." the stranger trailed off as he met Kildreth's eye. "But aye why not. Plain food never sits right with me." And he hauled himself up, rummaged through the cupboards and took out the little pot. He set himself down again and sprinkled a pinch of it in the pot, easy as anything. "Oo..." He stuck his nose in the pot. "Smells like-"

"Lavender?" Kildreth was surprised at how easy it was, but kept it to himself.

"Aye." The stranger beamed back a moment. "Lavender. Odd, that." And then he stuck his spoon in and started eating, each spoon wolfed down greedy as a pig, each one with a smile. Though he couldn't blame him. Even criminals get hungry. Moments later the bowl was cleared and he set it down aside him. He held his stomach. "Aye, not bad that."

"Adds a little something to it, at least." Kildreth kept his eye on him, each second waiting for him to seize, each moment dreaming of another way the stranger could kill him. Not blinking, not moving. Seconds stretched out as their eyes made contact.

"You alright, old man?" The stranger scowled at him. "What are you-" He clamped a hand to his chest and jerked, breath snatching in his throat. Another heavy jerk and he kicked over the chair, slumping to the floor, face already burning red. He jerked again, banged his head on the fireside and twisted, arms writhing uselessly at his throat, eyes rolling back into his head, purple froth dribbling from his lips.

Kildreth simply watched and smiled. The dog didn't do a thing, except watch solemnly from the fire, apparently content.

"You're not even his dog, are you?" He shook his head with a bitter grimace. "I knew it."

"Wake up," muttered Kildreth. He slapped the man's face with a sharp flick of his good hand. The man's mouth was still sticky with purple-tinged drool and as he stirred the straps across his chest, legs, wrists and shoulders moved, just a little. But they were secure. Kildreth never did things by halves, after all. He'd had to make sure the man could still breathe, had to remove the gunk from his throat. That took a good lot of the night. Then it'd been an arseache to get him down the ladder, having to rely on the craw to do its work and keep him sedated while gently lowering him to a distance he could drop without too much damage. He'd had to shove the boy off the table and bundle him unceremoniously in the corner, upsetting his normal rhythm. And then he had to haul the heavy-set bastard onto the table and strap him in. That took near an hour by itself. Elders, it might even be light outside now. Just coming up dawn. But Kildreth was been willing. He'd been waiting for this for a long time, even if he hadn't known it. A living specimen.

Someone that no one knew about. That no one would miss. Better still, a criminal. A fugitive. Someone that should already be dead. It didn't matter what he'd done. He wasn't getting out. And no one was coming for him.

"Wake up," Kildreth said, voice sharper than even he intended with another slap to match.

The man's eyes bolted open. First, his face was blank, no more than the stare of an idiot. Then it scrunched in confusion, candles around the edge of the room reflected in his ugly pinprick eyes. Then along with a futile twitch of his arms, realisation, eyes wide and breathing suddenly become quick through his gag. As if it might help.

"Good evening." Kildreth turned away to the shelf at the back to retrieve his tools. His favourite blade, of course.

The one he'd used to slit open the boy's wrists just yesterday. Clean and razor-sharp, glinting beautifully in the dim light. He took the small bowl and the spoon beside it then placed them carefully next to the man's head, who was still desperately trying to get a look at what he was doing.

"Settle down, now." He waved the blade in front of the man's eyes. The man responded with a soft, pitiful whimper. Something like a chastised dog.

Kildreth wandered the length of the table, eyeing his specimen's stripped body. Muscular, and well-built. Well looked after. A soldier, perhaps. Or a bodyguard. Or a thug. Several old scars across his chest, arms and legs suggested it could be any of them. But nonetheless, a body in its relative prime. He had to bite down on his tongue to stop himself from smiling. The glee was starting to seep in, bit by bit. He already felt more alive. If the ecstasy of yesterday was anything to go by, this would be quite the experience. He stopped at the foot of the table and caught the man's terrified eyes.

"I'm not going to tell you why I do what I do." He leaned forward, blade just brushing the man's calf as he lowered his voice. "But this is going to cause you a lot of pain. No one is coming for the likes of you, and I will draw this out as long as possible. I am well practised with the human body and I will relish every second. I will wring the energy from your body, sap every piece of relief you can give me until you are dry as a desert well."

The man whimpered and once again, for reasons unknown to Kildreth, struggled in his restraints.

"Now..." Kildreth stood straight and grinned, blade eager in his left hand. "Where to start?"

Don't Feed the Goblins

Year 669

"Aw." Elis bent down to the small, mud-green creature before him. It stared back at him with big, empty black eyes far too big for its head, which was in turn too big for its wrinkled, grubby little body. "It's kinda cute."

His companion sniffed, wiping the chicken grease from his face as he chomped on yet another leg. "I wanna boot it."

"You're not bootin' it Dev," Elis groaned. "And where do ye keep getting those legs from? That's the fifth since we left, slow down big fella."

"I'm hungry," he said between fat, wet mouthfuls, "can't help it."

"We left town an hour ago. You had three bowls of oats."

"Got a long journey ahead."

"Aye." Elis elbowed him in the shin. "So quit eating all the supplies."

The creature shared its gaze between the two of them; its long, thin nose twitching like it smelt something it didn't like. Or maybe something it did. Elis couldn't tell. He wasn't even sure what it was.

After a moment's silence, Dev reshared the only opinion he had. "I wanna boot it."

"You are *not* booting it, Dev."

"Nah, nah," Dev said between bites, "it's cute. But just morbid curiosity, you know? I just wanna see how far I could kick it."

Elis rolled his eyes and stood up, not taking his eyes off the little beast. "You sure you know what those words mean?" He chuckled at his own remark. Not like Dev was going to. "Well we're not doing anything with it, alright?"

"Yeah." Dev shrugged. "But it's just so... little. Only about the size of me boot." Elis shot him his side-eye glare, which Dev waved away. "I'm just sayin', is all."

"Ears 'bout the same size as yours an' all."

The creature continued to stare up at them, unblinking. Unmoving aside from the occasional tilt of its unfortunately large head and the licking of its scraggy lips.

Elis gave Dev another nudge. "Hey, give me ye bone."

"What?" Dev furrowed his unfortunately large brows for a moment before understanding, "Oh, right."

"Idiot." Elis snatched the bone from him, waving it in front of the thing. "You want some of this, little guy?"

The creature made a gargling sound, followed by a sniff of its cavernous nostrils. Then it licked its lips, beady eyes following the dripping, dangling bone before it.

Dev laughed, bits of chicken tumbling out of his mouth, "Heh, bet it's hungry. Stupid little bastard." He took out another leg from his seemingly bottomless satchel. The sound of teeth ripping into juicy meat was little more than a dull drone to Elis' ears now.

He sighed. He spent a lot of his time doing that, it seemed. "Yeah. I know what he feels like." He dangled the bone just a little over its mouth now, teasing it like some sort of dog. "Eh, we should be off anyway." He dropped it and the creature grabbed it mid-air, many serrated little teeth tearing into what meat still clung onto it. It took one last look at the pair, then scurried off into the undergrowth with a series of muffled grunts. "Huh. Sharp little teeth on this thing."

"Uh-huh." Dev nodded, already making his way through another leg, barely noticing what had just happened. "They're like that."

"What do you reckon it was?"

Dev took a last bite of the leg and stuffed the bone back in the bag. "Goblin," he said, as if it was obvious.

Elis scrunched his face. "That was a Goblin?"

"Hang on." Dev drew his heavy brow again. "Where'd it go?"

"Doesn't matter, we're off anyway." Elis nudged him and started making his way back to the road. "I just gave it the bone and it ran off."

Dev's piggy eyes widened. His fat jaw dropped, giving Elis a full view of half-chewed chicken. "You what?"

"What?"

"You don't feed Goblins." Dev snatched Elis by his collar and shook him like a purse. "You don't *ever* feed Goblins!"

"Get off!" Elis wriggled free. "What're you talkin' 'bout?"

"You don't-" Dev was interrupted by a shaking shrub at their feet. Another behind them did the same. Something scuttled amongst the trees. "You don't feed Goblins," he breathed, staring around with twitchy eyes.

Something in the bushes growled a high-pitched growl. Then two. Three.

Dev and Elis looked at one another. Elis swallowed, and Dev nodded upwards. Two pairs of black eyes glinted in the tree above them. Something rustled in the undergrowth. Somewhere behind Elis, a twig snapped.

They looked at one another again.

"Run."

The Dragon Knight

Year 703

"I said, it's loud in here isn't it!" I shouted at the beer-bellied man sat on the stool next to me.

"What?" Ale breath and spit slapped me in the face.

"The music, loud!"

"What?" More spit.

"The mus..." I paused. *So much for trying to start a conversation.* "Nevermind." I stood up, took the last sip of my watery ale and wound my way back through the jostling, sweating bodies to a long table, with eleven men and women sat around; a man with a silver-streaked beard at its head.

"Tomos, you've decided to join us!" The Captain beamed, clapped me on the neck and gestured for me to sit down on his left side. *Well, at least I can see the whole mess of a tavern this way.*

"Yes, Captain," I sigh.

"Well seein' as the lot of us are 'ere let's talk business." He rubbed his hands. Gruff but always cheerful and though you'd never guess it after the obvious amount of times his nose had been broken, sharp as an oiled dagger. Not book-smart, perhaps. But a man that always had a plan. And the only person ever willing to take me in. "So, as you know me and Owen picked this up a few days back and scoped it out this mornin'." He thrust a scroll onto the table. "Burned Wolves. Stupidly-named group o' bandits settled up in the forests just east of here, in some caves. Apparently been giving the guards here in Viken a trouble recently but they're

139

too few to go and root them out. Not too poor to pay us to do it for 'em, though." He scanned the table with that glint in his eye. "We ready to 'ave a crack at 'em?" The eleven mercenaries around the table loudly grunted various versions of 'yes'.

Then he turned his glinting eye on me. "Tomos? You want to come?" My mouth dropped a little, went dry but I soon clamped it shut. You can't show weakness in a group like this. They'd call me hanger for weeks. *And no, not really. I thought my first proper job might be one where I could hang at the back whilst we tracked down one, single, very undangerous man. Maybe a band of runaway sheep. Not bandits that were enough of a problem for the Empire itself to place an official bounty on.*

"Sure." I nodded. *Elders, what the fuck did I just say?* "About time I did a real job with you lot!" said my mouth without any input from me. *Oh Tomos, you idiot.*

"Settled then," Captain continued, "set off tomorrow morning then." He pulled a wide grin. "But for now lads, drink up!" And they did so without complaint. The Captain leant over to me and nodded his head. "Tomos, come 'ere for a sec lad." He put a hefty arm around my shoulder and dragged me slowly, firmly, to one side.

I spoke before he got a chance. "I know what you're going to say Captain, but I know I'm ready for this. I've been with the group for the past four years now, I know how-"

"Tomos, Tomos. My boy, I know you're capable." He kept his hand on my shoulder and looked right at me. "I've known that for a while now. Just keep yourself away from the bulk of the fighting tomorrow, if you can. I don't want you getting killed on your first outing." He grimaced a moment as he glanced at the table. "I'd rather no one did, but I don't reckon that'll be the case."

"Thank you, Captain. I won't let you down."

"I know you won't. Besides, new recruits are too 'ard to come by, don't go gettin' yerself killed on me." He let out a dry chuckle and smiled, his crow's feet creasing. He slapped me on the back again and ushered me to my seat.

The tavern door banged open. The lutes and drums stopped mid-beat, notes hanging in the air. The tavern's many heads turned. A figure stooped through the doorway, head just making it beneath the top of the frame. Black-iron plates clung to a mass of chain and leather and a great, wide sword hung by his side, one hand resting on its darkened pommel. Silence grasped the air.

"Eskel!" Captain bellowed. You made it!" *Elders, he's loud.*

"Wouldn't miss it for the world you old shit!" The figure yelled back, voice echoing in his dark, battered helmet.

Captain turned to one of the barmaids walking by. "Lass! Get my friends and I another round!"

The music struck up again as the man strode over and took off his helmet, shaking out a great mane of greying red hair. Captain gave one of his great, beaming smiles and gripped the stranger's hand with his before they pulled each other in for a great, manly hug - grunting and all.

"Now this is someone I'd like you all to meet." Captain turned to the group expectantly. "How many of you have heard of The Dragon Knight of Kervir?"

"Aye Captain," said a few. The rest simply nodded. I winced from the incoming months-worth of jokes at my expense. *Get it over with.*

"Who, Captain?" Silence over the table. I swallowed. The stranger broke into a smile from ear to mashed ear and laughed. A great, rumbling, larger-than-life laugh that everyone else soon joined in with. *Is this good? I hope this is good.* After a few seconds, still clutching his sides he sat down opposite me. He greeted the men sat beside him, smiling all the while, showing a shining silver tooth. No, teeth. The whole top row. *Wonder where he got those?*

"Trust you to be the only one not to know, eh laddie?" Captain shakes his head. "That man there is The Dragon Knight." *So you've said.* "Best sword I know and not a bad friend either. You never heard of him?"

"No."

"Huh." He stroked his chin. "G'won Eskel, tell 'im."

"You know I don't like to brag." Eskel's voice was heavy, with a breathy rasp.

"G'won."

"Rather let the lad find out." He took a sip of his drink and smiled a big, smug smile. *Find out what?*

"Still the same I see." Captain let out a hefty sigh. "Maybe the boy can guess."

"Not likely." Eskel looked right at me with his big, dull blue eyes. Tired eyes, ones that were much like the Captain's.

"Well, I'll let you two get acquainted. He turned to Eskel. "You're gonna have to make sure the lad survives tomorrow." Captain gestured to me and lowered his voice, but I just about heard. "Green." He took the tankard in front of him and made his way around to the end of the table, leaving me alone with the stranger.

He was at least fifty. Lines all over his rough face like the captain, with more than a few scars. Two big ones on his forehead, slashing down through one of his big, bushy brows. Red cheeks, and a wild grey-red beard. His slightly sinister silver teeth caught the lantern's light as he grinned.

"So Tomos, is that right?" The man swiftly necked his tankard and smacked it back on the table, easy as breathing.

"Yes sir," I mumbled out.

"Ha! No need to call me sir, I"m not a real Knight. You shoulda gathered that by now. Just Eskel."

"Not Dragon Knight?"

"Ah, just something I picked up," he sighed, "party trick that got out of hand. That's all you're getting." *Why? What's so important and why won't anyone tell me?* It's not like I wasn't used to it, but it still stung.

"So what about the teeth?"

"Sharp eyes on you eh? Least sharper than the rest of 'em." He flicked his head to the right and I followed. True enough half the company was either passed out or well on the way. "Not drinking?"

"I've had one ale, that's enough for me. At least one of us has to be alert." *And it tastes like piss.* The man drew a wry smile, took out a hip flask and inhaled the contents. *Alcoholic or just dramatic?* "Not some trick, is it? An illusion?"

"Nope," he said, wiping drink from his grey-grizzled chin.

"A family symbol?"

"No. Sure you don't want a spirit lad?" He offered the flask.

"Yes."

"It'll get some hairs on yer chest, one swig won't hurt. Alcohol helps with things you wouldn't even think of." And he arched an eyebrow.

"No, thanks." *It helps with making a fool of yourself.*

"Suit yerself." He shrugged and his eyes darted to an unattended ale. *Oh, don't.* He snatched it and down in one it went. *This is going to be a very long night.*

"Everyone, keep low to ground," Captain whispered, "they don't know we're comin', and I wanna keep it that way." Eskel tailed him, and I tailed Eskel. *My minder. Brilliant.*

Last night had droned on but we all got up early - even the ones that had been complaining about aching heads and loud noises. The morning's Whitelight was barely present, what little there was cutting between the shadows of the treetops. We crept up the steep woodland path, coming to stop just inside a clearing, letting the few stragglers catch up. Tall, thin trees all around us, with fallen leaves over the mossy, muddy ground. *Low ground, too. Not exactly a great place for an attack. A brilliant place to defend, however. Shame.*

"Everyone up 'ere?" Captain asked. He received a round of grunts in reply. "Good. Their hidey-'ole is right up there, should be easy enough to spot. Everyone remembers the plan?" Another round of grunts. "Right then. Tomos you go with Eskel, he's your best bet of stayin' alive." I go to protest, realise the futility, then hold my tongue. *He won't listen. Fuck.* I take a look at my babysitter, who'd slunk off to take a piss up against a tree, hip flask in hand, cock presumably in the other. Less than a few hundred strides from a group of murderous bandits. *If he's my best chance I best say my prayers now.* A man that didn't bring his helmet to a bandit camp raid on account of 'not sure where I left it'.

After a few moments waiting for the infamous Dragon Knight to relieve himself, we continued up the slope. I took another look around, felt everyone starting to get tense. Captain, axe in hand, fingers rippling over the haft as he led us up. Owen, fingers tapping on his thigh behind me. Vik, a few strides to my left, white-knuckle gripping her daggers and mumbling as she did. People avoiding eyes, every sound that wasn't ours initiated a grouped pause. Aside from Eskel of course, who seemed to be looking around as if on a morning stroll, finger jammed in his ear as if he might find one of the bandits there. *We're nearly there.* I kept my eyes on the treetops above me, up through the thinning trees, down where we'd come from.

A mechanical spring swiftly followed by a pained yell. Owen screamed, his shin gripped by the ugly teeth of a bear trap. A whoosh past my head. A sharp thud as an arrow hits a tree. Then a second, wetter thud. Owen slumps to the ground, eyes crossed at the shaft between them. *Shit.*

"Ambush!" Captain bellowed. A ringing of drawn steel and iron, a chorus of shouts and roars.

Bandits poured from the trees, all clad in dark leather. Ten. Twenty. *Shit, more.* Eskel shoots me a glance and a wink before gleefully drawing his sword and storming off into the coming fray. His blade cleaved through one helpless bandit's chest in as little as a breath. *So much for my protector.* The forest, silent just moments ago, descends into mayhem. *Captain. Where's the Captain?*

I saw him, some thirty strides distant, axe hacking away at some unfortunate before being tackled to the ground by some big, screaming bastard.

Weapon. The fear spikes my spine as I pat myself down, breath stuck in my throat and sweat on my face. A sick turn in my stomach as I see a bandit smash apart Vik's jaw, chunks spattering the trees. *Where's my weapon?* The grip of my axe, by my side. *There.*

The bandit saw me, a grin stretched on his face to rival Eskel's. Perhaps less mischievous and more deadly. He sprinted for me, ugly lump of metal in the air as he charged.

I raised my axe just in time to feel the weight of the his mace ricochet up my wrist. I yelled out but a fist crunched into my mouth and shut me up. A sudden white light in my head, blood on my tongue. My axe flails. *Just raise it. Better than nothing.* Another crashing blow, the axe ripped from my hands and I'm sent sprawling back, ground tumbling beneath me before I thudded into the dirt.

No sign of Captain. No sign of Eskel. *So, this is it, then.*

The bandit towered over me, wild grin painted over his blood-spattered face, mace gripped tightly in one hand. He raised it.

A sword cracked down his skull, gore flushing from his ruined face as the tip protruded from between his eyes. His mace thumped to the ground and he gurgled something incoherent before the blade was wrenched out. He slumped as his head hushed with blood. A whole new feeling swept over me, adrenaline quickly turning to disbelief, disbelief to disgust, then disgust to annoyance as I looked up.

Eskel stood there, red blade in one hand with that big, silver smile that'd make you think he'd just welcomed his firstborn.

"Need a hand lad?" And he offered one down as if some grand hero from a story book.

"No, but thanks anyway." *Great, now I owe him.* I got up by myself and shook myself off, one hand rubbing my aching jaw. I spat out a glob of blood, felt one of my teeth wobble a little far for comfort. "Shit..." I tried to say it under my breath, but I've no doubt he heard, "shit."

"You dropped this." He hands me my axe. "Be more careful."

"Uh-huh." I reluctantly take it.

I glanced at the forest. Over as quickly as it had begun, the forest suddenly quiet once again. Not even so much as a breeze.

Bodies littered the floor. All of the bandits but a lot of the company, too - Owen, Ethan, Vik. A few others I didn't know so well strewn over the clearing, their blood staining the mud, bone poking through ugly gouges in leather, chain and flesh. Myself, Captain, Eskel and two others. Kel and Seren, I think. Seren brushed herself off, started to nurse a leaking gash on her cheek, muttering something about luck. Kel nonchalantly floated around the bodies like a crow. I worked my jaw and rubbed my aching temples. *How do people do this for a living? Maybe I should go back to the organising side of things.*

"Fuck." I looked up to see Captain with hands coursing through what little reminded of his hair. "Fuck!" he yelled, kicking a bandit's corpse.

"It's not like the wolves won either," Eskel chimed in, already taking a little sip from his flask. *His version of a celebration, perhaps.*

Captain span on his heel and stormed up to him, eyes wide and mouth frothing. He was half a head shorter but shit if he wasn't twice as scary. "You fucking what, Eskel? They didn't win?" He snarled out every word like it hurt. "I don't know if you've noticed while you were busy pissing around, but my entire *fucking* company is in the fucking dirt!" Eskel stared blankly back, grin disappeared, Captain inches from his face. "Didn't feel like helping? Didn't feel like it, no? This is your *shitting* mess in the first place!" *Is it?*

"You know it's not as easy as that, not in a place like this. Look around, mate." Eskel's face stayed stone as he waved his arms. "We're in a forest. Not exactly prime territory."

Captain scrunched his face up, jaw clenching white, veins in his forehead working so hard they looked fit to burst. He took a moment to breathe. "Well, we can't stay here. We have to finish the job. We need the coin. And I'm not letting these bastards away." He spat the words out like poison. The he jerked a finger at me. "Tomos, this time stay close to Eskel or you'll be added to this lot." He gestured to the floor. "Come on, with me," he growled and strode off up into the trees.

Eskel's eyes met mine and I noticed for the first time a sharp furrow to his brow. The lines in his face forced to concern. He gave me a grave nod then followed the Captain off through the trees.

The cave was nothing special. An empty, dark hole in the side of a wooded hill. No telling how far it went down. Black as the Void down there, and quieter too.

"Right," Captain muttered, "Seren, Kel, behind me. Tomos behind them, Eskel in the back. I'd rather not have any more unwelcome surprises."

"Right you are," mumbled Eskel, voice strangely muted.

The tunnel was dank and narrow. Captain had to bow his head to his chest, and behind me Eskel had to stoop to a point it would have been comical, had I not been shitting myself. Silence, aside from the squelching of our footsteps and Eskel's armour occasionally scraping the craggy walls, always followed by a grumble. The path headed down and only down, the floor beneath my feet sloping more and more with each step, the stench of earth stronger and stronger. *Fuck.* My fingers gripped the haft of my axe. *As if I can do anything with it.* It was a comfort nonetheless.

We turned a corner and a dim glow formed on the cave walls, outlining the three shapes in front of me. A brighter glow comes from up ahead.

A gruff whisper comes from up front. "Quiet now. Light." Captain.

Another, more gravelly whisper from behind. Eskel. "What's the plan?"

"Don't know. Can't see any of 'em yet. Just light."

"Shall we take a look, Captain?" offered Kel, voice a little wobbly. "Nice and quiet-like."

"Aye. Eskel, keep him out of trouble." And even in the dark, I felt his finger jerk at me like some sort of liability. *He's not wrong.* "Seren, with us."

"Right you are," Eskel grunted, "we'll hang back a little."

The shapes dropped down, deeper into the cave. All was quiet.

A few moments later I felt a hand on my shoulder and a whisper behind me. "You're alright, lad. Low, and slow. Follow them. I'm right behind you."

"But-"

"Get movin'." A firm hand pushed me forwards.

And so with a breath of cold, damp air I sank down and crept along the passage with Eskel just behind, armour clinking slightly with every step. *Have to hand it to him, a man in half-plate and he's near quiet as a mouse.*

Up ahead, round another corner the glow grew only brighter, the three silhouettes cutting clear shapes, even stuck to the walls as they were. The passage began to open, too, wider than the entrance and opening into a large, well-lit chamber at the far end. As it did the tightness in my chest only grew, that gnawing sense of danger. Captain might have called me paranoid. He always said I worried too much. But if right then, in the dark, with less than quarter our number, with traps and bandits just waiting to spring wasn't the time to worry, when was?

The three stopped just either side of the chamber entrance, just enough room for them to huddle either side. Turning heads and aking amall, pointing gestures. I was about thirty strides away when I felt that heavy hand on my shoulder again.

"Hang back," Eskel murmured, "we need to see what they're doing."

"They need us." Captain was nodding inwards to the chamber now. "We're down enough as it is." I tried to nudge Eskel's hand off my shoulder only to be met with a light but resoundingly strong *you're-not-going-anywhere* squeeze.

"He asked me to keep you safe and I intend to. So you're staying here until I say otherwise," he half-growled, half-sighed.

I tried to put my best growl on in return but it came off more like a whine than anything vaguely intimidating. Still, I stuck with it. "I thought you'd want to get it done, get the money, and be on your way."

"This is about more than money, lad."

My face scrunched as I turned my head back to him for a moment. "What's it about then?" Meant as an angry question but it came off as a whinging complaint.

His face was set hard, now. Even more so than in the forest. With my shadow blocking most of the light it made a yellow cut over one of his eyes, suddenly tinting it with a lean edge. "Never you mind." And from seemingly nowhere, his flask appeared in his hand and he took a sip, eyes never wavering from up ahead once.

But enough was enough. I felt the anxiety in my chest grip, felt the cathartic release of the quietly angry words as I shoved my finger in his face. "What is it with-"

He clamped a hand over my mouth. "Shut it. Look." And he jerked one finger to the chamber.

They were moving in. One by one, slow and weapons drawn.

"Right," Eskel murmured, eyes flashing in the light again as he crept around me. "Follow me, and stay on the right side of the wall." He stuck to the left and made his way along.

I did as I was told.

From up ahead came a muffled yelp, a ring of steel cut short followed by two more cries of surprise, then three gentle thuds.

Eskel gave a dry chuckle. "He's still a sneaky fucker."

He quickened the pace and then we were up against the side of the chamber entrance, yellow light washing down the hallway. Eskel peeked out from his side, familiar grin returned to his face for just a moment. He nodded for me to do the same.

Captain, Kel and Seren each hunched over a body, rifling through their leathers as blood pooled underneath them. Torches adorned the circular cavern space, two similar exits into yet more tunnels over the other side.

"Bastards." Captain muttered. "Nothing useful."

"Me neither," muttered Seren.

"Nope," Kel grunted.

"Nothing to do but go on then, aye?" Eskel said, nodding towards the other tunnels.

"Aye," murmured Captain, as if the word made him nauseous. We go right. You go left."

"You never did like left forks," Eskel jibed.

"Nor you right. I recall." And for a moment, beneath the grimace he'd held most that day a smile flickered.

"Can I not come with you?" The words tumbled out of my mouth. But it was too late to do anything but double-down. "I-"

"Stick with Eskel. He'll keep you alive."

"But-"

"No, Tomos," he growled. "You're safer with him." He sighed, and nodded his head back to the tunnel. "I'll see you both on the other side." And with that the three slunk off, quickly swallowed by the shadows.

I looked at Eskel, taking another sip of his flask. "How is it he thinks my best bet at staying alive is being with you?"

"Aye," he grunted and working his shoulders. "Beats me, lad. Come on." He stood up a little and made his way to the left fork. "Places to be."

How long had it been? Five minutes? Twenty? Thirty? I couldn't say. But the path seemed to go down, the ground grew damper, the musty smell of earth stronger than ever.

Eskel was in front, this time. He stopped every now and then, to peer around blind corners or listen for unheard sounds. He'd scarcely said anything since we'd split up, just odd mutterings or grumblings. I'd said nothing either. It wasn't as we had much to talk about. All I wanted to do was leave. The way we'd come was free. I kept eyeing it, wondering if I could slink away without him noticing. But however careless he seemed, however uncaring and obtuse he came off, it wasn't quite real. And leaving him meant leaving behind the captain, leaving behind the only life I knew.

And considering my usual luck there'd likely be a bandit hiding around the first corner I came to.

He stopped us yet again and motioned to an orange glow on the approaching corner. "We've got something."

Fuck. That was my only thought. Of course it had to be us.

He eased his way to the corner, whispering in that gravelly rasp. "Right. These are likely going to be some very dangerous men. If we've found who we're looking for, you stay right here. Understand?"

"I don't-" I started.

"Understand?" He repeated, sharper this time.

"Fine."

He gave an half-exasperated, half-relieved sigh, then peered around the corner. "Fuck." He hung his head, and slunk it back into the shadows of the tunnel, eyes staring at the ground. "Fuck."

"What?"

He looked at me for a moment. Just a moment. Even in the dim, I saw his eyes flicker with uncertainty. Saw his lips purse with concern. "He's there, alright. But have a look." And with one arm he gently nudged me around the corner, just enough to see.

"Fuck." A man with his back to us, armoured with a great, heavy-looking axe hanging by his side, spattered with stains. A number of others scattered around a large room, shadows from those I couldn't see. But what snatched the breath from my chest was the shape kneeling in front of him. Captain - a shining, dark red mark down his face, hands tied behind his back.

Eskel's arm dragged me back. The urge to run gnawed at me more than ever.

But I couldn't. So, as if I thought I'd be any help, I asked the only question I could. "What do we do?"

"Fuck if I know," grunted Eskel. "I really didn't plan for this. He was always the planner. I was the doer." He scratched his beard, scrunching his face up as if there might be an answer in that fat head of his. "What do you think?"

I went to retort, then realised what he'd said. "What?" My turn to be confused.

"What do you think we should do?"

"Me?"

"You see anyone else around?"

"No, but-"

"Then give me a plan," he hissed. "You've been with him for five years. You must have picked up something."

"Uh…" I stuck my head out for a second, looking over the scene as the man paced, as the shadows danced around the glowing room. Muffled swearing, unheard insults. I slunk back. "How about you just… walk in?"

"Charge in like a wounded bear, aye?" He stifled a chuckle and grimaced instead. "That sounds just perfect, maybe I'll even kill one before I'm speared through the back of the head."

"No, no," I clarified. "*Walk* in. You said this was about something bigger, and I don't know - or care what." My voice sharper than I'd intended. "But if he's captured Captain, and not just killed him then that might just be true." Eskel went to speak but I cut him off with a hissing whisper I hadn't known I was capable of, "I don't care. But you're going to get in there, and do your fucking hardest to save that man. He'd do the same for either of us, and we've not exactly got a lot of options."

I finished,and let myself have a breath. *Where the fuck was that earlier?*

Eskel stared at me for a moment, blank. Slowly, a curl formed on his lips. Then a grin, silver teeth and all. Smug as the Emperor. "Heh. Maybe he did rub off on you." He stood up, and rolled his great, wide shoulders before drawing his sword with a quiet ring. "Well, then. We'll see how well your plan goes, aye? Do me a favour - stay out of sight and if it goes wrong, get the fuck away from here. I'd rather not fail twice in one day."

"Aye," I said.

"Great." He flashed me a grin and wink before turning off round the corner. I watched him go, trudging down the cave towards the light. *Leave? I don't fucking think so.* And I slunk off after him, keeping tight to the shadows.

"Hello boys," Eskel rumbled, arms spread wide, sword flailing around as if he hadn't ever held one in his life.

"Who's this, boss?" Someone said. I tried to peer around Eskel's frame, look into the room but he took up the entire opening.

"Him," said another, voice even more hoarse than Eskel's. Barely more than a husk in its sound. Hollow and scratchy, but loud. "Welcome, Dragon Knight." A pair of feet in front of Eskel turned around. The leader, then.

"Well I wouldn't miss this, would I?" Eskel's head nodded from side to side. "I really thought there'd be more of you, though. It's a small party."

Meaning... quite a few, I imagine.

"Bold of you to show your face," said the leader. "Stupid. Brash. But bold."

Another man voiced a complaint. "Why don't we just gut him n-"

"Quiet!" Roared the leader. "This is between me and him. You stay out of it, and do what I pay you for."

Eskel chuckled and pointed his sword down. "Aye, I know what it's like having underlings that don't do what they're told." He clicked his tongue, then sighed. "Arseache, really. Who could be bothered with that?" And I saw something behind him. His left hand, reaching into a back pocket.

The complainer started again, "Oi, I'm not-"

"Shut it," said Eskel, voice biting. "Right. Shall we..." and he shrugged as if everything to be said had been said then swung up his sword. He took a step forward.

"Ah-ah-ah..." said the leader, "we do this my way. I might not win. But you've got to lose something."

A glint of metal. A sick thud. Captain sagged to the ground between Eskel's legs, face planted in the mud.

I froze. Felt the bile in my stomach lurch. My throat seize. My hands tremor. "No..." The most pathetic sound I'd ever heard, straight from my own mouth.

Eskel didn't do a thing. Not for a few moments. Just let it hang in the air. The thing in his hand sparked. A bright orange spark with a flick of his wrist.

"You fucker."

His left hand whipped upwards and from his mouth erupted a roaring orange flame, deafening and pressing. For a moment it was just him, a rough black silhouette against the raging fire. Brief but loud enough to wake the dead and bright enough to blind a star.

Then it stopped. From its absence came shrieks and the stench of torched flesh and earth.

Eskel leapt forward, sword crashing sideways into a flame-wreathed bandit. Something crunched. An audible rip as Eskel tore his blade out and swung back. A sharp crack and a figure toppled over, leg cleaved from underneath him. A third, silver arcing through his chest and through the shoulder. Another from behind caught on the backswing of Eskel's sword, shining bright with blood and fire as it bit into his jaw and was launched back.

"You wanted a fight!" Eskel roared, jerking his arms and storming forward. "I'll give you a fight!" His voice was hoarse now but rumbled like a long-brewing storm. He swung forward.

Steel on steel, scraping and hacking as he carved his way forwards. Only his dancing silhouette and another against the crackling flames, against the thin veil of smoke pouring from the room. A sword against an axe, grinding, clanging, grunts and growls of pain and rage.

Another torrent of flame. A howl of anguish. A horrid crunch. Silence. Only crackling fire. One silhouette fell. The axe thudded to the ground.

A defeated, resigned snarl came from the one left standing. His head dropped and he pitched his sword in the earth.

"Fuck." I sprang from my hiding spot and into the room.

Ashes and smoke. Five bodies lay amongst it all, four still burning. Cloth and leather smouldered, thick smoke clogging the air. Eskel stood hunched on his sword, staring at the one before him. The leader, whoever he was. His eyes flickered to me for a moment, suddenly weary, face marred with ash a fresh gash on his cheek. No trace of the man of yesterday. Then we both turned to the only corpse left untouched by the fire, blood pooling and sheening bright underneath.

"No..." the second most pathetic sound I'd ever heard, again from me. A hole in my chest, and the swaying of the floor beneath me as my head swam with grief and smoke. "Why..." my eyes began to water, my lungs stung. "I don't..." *Why would anyone subject themselves to this life? Why did I think I could?*

A long pause.

"Neither do I," rasped Eskel. "But the past is hard to let go of. Best you learned that now, rather than in a few decades time." He gazed around for a moment, blank face and empty eyes looking over it as if it were no more than another day. "Come on." He sheathed his sword. "We need to go." He slid one great arm underneath the Captain's limp body and hauled him over his shoulder. "Back the way we came, Tomos."

To Still A Bleeding Heart

Year 274

"Shh, Isaac, it's ok. It's ok."

He strains in my arms, muscles tensing. "How- nghh," he grits his teeth, jaw clenching hard as the breaths wheeze through his nose, "how bad is it?" I take my bloody hand away from it and inspect the gash in his side. *Bad, very, very bad.* Blood seeps out and into the dark orange cloth of his tunic, dribbling over his broken chainmail.

Feigning calmness I say, "You'll be fine. We'll get you to a healer." I look around at the hundreds of others fallen over the now-quiet battlefield. Fathers, sons, daughters, maybe even mothers. Shapes move through the quickly-settling fog. Dirty scavengers already stripping bodies, soldiers searching for comrades, soon-to-be corpses crawling through the tangle. And the crows. So many crows. Rain pitter-patters around us. The mixed stench of shit, blood and mud doesn't even phase me any more.

"Adah, I can tell when you're lying." A sad smile hits my face and his eyes meet mine. "I've known you too long for you t-" he clenches his jaw again, wheezing in and out, eyes barely keeping focus on me. "Too long to lie to me." He grunts, trying to push himself up against the rock he's leaning on.

"Shut up. I can't stop myself from smiling despite the welling of tears.

His jaw drops dramatically. "You would tell a dying man to shut up? Why I never-"

"Oh you know what I mean, idiot." He smiles back at me. A moment of silence. *Filled with what I wish I'd done, what I wish I said.* I feel yet more blood trickle through my fingers.

"So," he asks, "how was your battle?"

"Good, good. I'm alive, aren't I?" *I'm only lucky archers are far away from the action, and that I was lucky it stayed that way.*

"Ha," he chuckles heavily, biting his lip. "Way to rub it in."

"I'm not the one bleeding out in a ditch." We burst out laughing for just a moment, Isaac thumping the ground to keep up with his heaving chest, spluttering into a cough. Tears run down his face as he giggles to himself. *As long as they're happy ones.* He gives one last, sharp cough and a some blood dribbles from his lips into his beard, joining the mud that already knots it. Another moment of silence comes between us before he speaks again.

"Hey, do you remember that time in the barn? We were... eleven or so. When we got chased out by that old bastard with a pitchfork?" He gives another chuckle.

"Uh-huh. How could I ever forget? My Ma gave me a right hiding for seeing a boy from another village. Said I should be more careful."

Isaac glances at a body skewered by a spear a few metres away. "Well, look where careful got you." He sniffs and gargles, coughing up yet more blood. "That was... fun, wasn't it?"

"Yeah," I say, knowing exactly what he's aiming for. "That was fun."

"We had good times, didn't we?" *Never a bad moment.*
"Always."

"A-a-and..." he took a deep breath, "and do you remember that time we made that promise?" *Please don't.*

Tears well in my eyes. "Yes," I reply slowly, the words harsh against my throat.

"What did we promise?"

"To protect each other, nno matter what."

"And?" *Please don't.*

"To do whatever the other asked as their last wish."

"Well, it looks like I get to collect on that." And he smiles that gentle smile of his.

"No, no, no Isaac. You- you'll be fine. You're always... fine." I take my hand off his wound again, covered in layer after layer of his drying blood. I wipe it on my tunic, staining the green a dirty red-brown.

"Adah," he whispers, "I think we both know this doesn't have a happy ending." He moves his head to try and make eye contact but I can't. *I can't.* "Please." I give in, his dark honey eyes solemn yet still so full of light. He grins at me through gritted teeth. *That grin. Always could get me to do anything.*

"It's just not fair," I look up to the sky just as the rain becomes a little heavier, the drops beginning a dull drumming on the ground. "It's not fair..." *This fucking war. Athons, Suthires, not one of the dead here gives a shit the reason who or why.*

"I know, I know." He takes my hand in his, gently rubbing it. "It's ok. It'll be ok, I promise."

I swallow. "What... what do you want me to do?" Without a reply, he carefully reaches into his belt and draws out a small dagger. He places it on his lap and points to his chest. *To his heart.* "Gods, Isaac... I-I-I can't do that."

He takes my hand and pulls me in a little closer. "You made a promise, Adah." He looks up at me again. I've never seen him this serious. He moves my hand to the dagger and I take it. He lets go. *I'll never have another chance to tell him if I don't now.*

With one hand I point the dagger to his chest and with the other I sweep my hair from my face. Mud and blood tangle it, clumping it together in grim knots. My cheeks are warm even in the bitter wind. "Isaac, I... um..." the words clog together in my mouth.

He takes my dagger hand, eyes gazing into mine again. "I know. Me too." He pulls me in without warning and our lips come together, a kiss of sweat and iron. He puts a hand around the back of my neck. With the other, he pulls my arm and the dagger moves forward. He grunts and twitches as our kiss deepens. I push the dagger a little farther and then it stops. His lips go limp, and a tear that is not mine runs down my cheek. I pull away just in time to see the light from his eyes wane. I put a hand over his face and close them for him.

I look around at the field of orange and green bodies. *I know not why they lay here.* House Suthire won, not that you could tell by the corpses. Including one that now lay before me. *Enemies on the battlefield, but only because others had willed it.* I sit down next to Isaac and rest his limp head on my shoulder. I will not leave his side.

May Your Blood Stain the Sand

Year 512

The lion lunged, all teeth and anger. Cyrus dove to the floor, caught a face full of sand and leapt back to his feet. The beast padded the floor and bristled its back, bared its yellow teeth in a feigned show of dominance. Its time was running out, and they both knew it. The seeping wound along its side. The slashed back leg dripping dark red on the sand, the gash across its nose where it had got a little too close for comfort. Each time Cyrus had gone for the kill, tried to end it quick but the damn thing fought back each time, twisted away. Too proud for its own good.

Poetic, some might say. Not that there were many poets among his people.

Cyrus twirled his spear and beckoned it, challenged it to come again. Hushed words and hisses. It took the bait and pounced. He sidestepped and left a thick gouge of red across its chest and spatter of warm blood on his arm. The lion hit the ground whimpering. A pang of guilt - he should've hit deeper. But his scales still rippled with excitement. He didn't enjoy much these days, but he could still appreciate a good fight.

"Got you." He drew a wry smile and flickered his tongue. The lion circled back around, limping, wheezing. The gladiator twirled his spear and readied himself. He heard the cheer of the stadium's crowd around him, of the bloodthirsty spectators but is was distant to him. Dull. They did not matter nor truly care. The lion roared, but that too was hollow. Nothing more than a death mewl. They circled each other, ten strides distant. Cyrus feinted a quick stab, to which the lion simply snarled. Each waited for the other to move first.

Bait the beast. Wait for the opportune moment.

The lion rushed, feet pounding at the ground. Eight strides. Cyrus steadied himself, grip on his spear strong. Six. He would not die today. He drove his feet into the ground, spread his weight just right. Four. His fingers rippled over the haft of his spear and he took a breath. Two. The lion's gaping jaw lunged for his throat. One. He darted sideways and and as it hurtled past he plunged his blade deep into its flank and let go. The great beast roared in pain and tumbled to the ground, painting a spray of red over the yellow sands. It mewed and growled and tried to get up but its leg was pinned and its eyes were fading. No more than a breath away now, and in terrible pain.

Cyrus drew the dagger from the back of his belt and made his way towards the sorry creature as the crowd began to cheer ever louder, and the howls and cries of *kill it* became an ugly chant.

The lion's eyes swayed. Its paws tried to reach for him but there was no will left in it now. Its eyes, empty and sad. Its body, broken and bloody. It just needed a ending. Without ceremony Cyrus found its throat and slit it. The lion gave a final growl, a final kick, then was still.

The crowd roared as if each of them had scored a great victory; as if each of them had been gifted a great honour by the Masters. They bayed for more blood, for the next fight, for a show of victory.

Cyrus looked over the lion and sighed. "You were worthy. I am sorry."

Then he wrenched the spear from the fallen beast and held it aloft. Another victory. Applause, deafening and violent. He pumped his weapon in the air again for another wave of that noise. It was all about appearances here. Something he'd learnt that the hard way. Showmanship never came naturally to him, but it was better than the alternative. He let out a roar himself and then turned his narrowed gaze to the Ssentarr's seat at edge of the arena. Closest to the fighting but sheltered from Volutem's blinding light, hidden beneath a sandstone canopy and extending out into a balcony in the circular stadium. The Ssentarr stood and stepped out into the daylight, ceremonial silver mail glinting evil bright, red scales sheening dark. A gong sounded, deep and echoing. The crowd was silent and Cyrus awaited his inevitable judgement.

The Ssentarr's pallid-scaled advisor spoke to the crowd. "Ssentarr Virrion will now decide the fate of the warrior!" Cyrus stood motionless, already knowing the verdict.

"The Fallen will fight another day!" Virrion's voice boomed around the arena, which erupted again with applause. Each time it was worse than the last. Cyrus eyed him and Virrion looked back, if only for a moment, before turning back to his seat.

"Bastard," Cyrus growled, just to himself. Another fight tomorrow, then. A scyk perhaps, or an adult rythrak or two. Perhaps if Virrion was feeling particularly malicious he'd send another poor newcomer to fight him. A good show for the crowd, if Cyrus made it last. But nothing more than a cruel exercise in extending his misery. As if his title, as if his entire life wasn't already enough. He hadn't had a fight that truly tested him in so long. Where he felt that fire of fear in his heart, that edge of a blade whistling past his face or that rush of blood through him.

Nevertheless he raised his fist to the crowd. One last roar from them and he made his way to the stadium gates. He had to rest for tomorrow.

Cyrus hummed to himself, quiet and sombre as he removed his leathers and placed them beside his bed. He couldn't really carry a tune - most Drakka couldn't, even the supposed artists. Drums, that's what they did. Drums, that's what Drakka did best. Beaten out of metal, stretched from animal hide, whatever you could smack with a fist or beat with a stick. Loud, brash and with little nuance. But had there ever been a Drakka that wasn't? He'd heard of peoples in places far from here that could sing beautifully clear, craft pipes made from wood to whistle like the wind and pluck hair-thin strings in ways that his clumsy fingers could never likely manage. He'd always wanted to see them. But he was older now, and less foolish. Not to mention never getting out.

He examined his scales carefully, checking for wounds. None new, but plenty of old scars that reminded him of past victories and failures. He was tired. His body ached all over. Couldn't stretch like it used to. No longer did he move as free as the water, as he'd trained to for so long. He was strong, and still faster than most of his fellows but long past his best. Getting old. Death could not be far off. Natural in a few years perhaps, after a life full of fighting. Or no doubt a stupid mistake sometime not soon enough. He fought nearly every day but he knew when the time came he would have little fight left. Approaching his forty-seventh year was daunting and yet... it brought a strange comfort. Virrion would have his wish. He'd have been worked to death. But he would be free.

"Great fighting out there today old man." The purred words made him snap back to reality and was suddenly aware of a figure leaning in his doorway. The only one here he had time for. Scarlet scales and a tongue sharper than her teeth.

"Hello, Leva," he sighed.

"Never woulda been able to sneak up on you a few years ago." She smiled playfully at him. "Old age is startin' to get to you."

"And overconfidence never left you," Cyrus retorted as he threw his wristguards on the floor.

"Cheer up." She punched him on the arm. "You won. What's wrong with you?"

"Need you even ask?"

"Yes, yes, oh woe is you." Anyone else but her had said that and he'd be baring his teeth. But all he could do was roll his eyes. "Heard it all before. It's not going to get any better if you just spend your days wasting away." Cyrus moved to take off his shin guards. He'd heard all this before. But still she persisted. "You know that right?"

Cyrus looked down. "I'd appreciate it if you could not make such light of my fall from grace."

"Oh come off it, you know what I mean. Besides, it's just the way of things." Her face softened and she placed a deceptively gentle hand on his shoulder. "Come take your mind off it. They're feeding us well tonight - that beast you killed today is taking pride of place on the table."

"I'm not hungry."

She gave him a light push then turned to leave. "You're coming and that's final."

Cyrus allowed himself a smile the second she left. He would've resigned himself to death much earlier if it weren't for Leva. Ever the optimist, she had helped him many times in only the year or so she'd been here. He'd been here ten and before her people had generally left him alone. And even though he'd never admit it to her, he'd grown fond of her. He'd often thought the colouration on her scales was quite lovely. Scarlet red that shifted into a fire-bright orange at the top of her head. 'Firecrest' was a fitting title. He lay down on the worn bed, still humming his tuneless tune thinking about her offer. He'd wait until he was a little late and then go. If only to aggravate her.

It was just them now, in the middle of the long table in the soft light of the torches. He was on the bench, she sat on the table, looking down and leaning on her elbow. Fellow fighters had come and gone, feasted on what they were allowed to - meats and alcohol mainly. The true diet of any warrior, caged or otherwise. Some had left by choice, some by being thrown back in their cells by the guards after a few too many drinks. Leva took one of the decanters and sloshed out some dark liquid that stank of spice and headaches into their cups, then pushed it over to him.

"So, Cyrus." She sipped her drink and winced, though she tried to play it off. "Why don't you throw fights? They'd kick you out for sure if you kept losing."

"No," he sighed. She asked him as much before. Or at least to the same effect. "Virrion would just keep me here no matter what." He sipped at his drink. Bitter and sickly all at once, and weak as water to boot.

She took a moment to think, then shrugged. "Why don't you ask for greater fights? Something that the crowd would go wild for." She leaned in, slurring her words a little. "The will of the people is a powerful sway."

"No point," he said, a little too bluntly. The drink wasn't nearly as strong as it needed to be to compensate for its taste. "Anything I do Virrion has a counter for. I spent the first few years trying it all. I throw fights he doesn't let me fight at all. He won't give me hard fights in case I die too quick, and because if I do win..." He shrugged, swilled the drink around his mouth and swallowed. "Then they might shout for me to be released. He can't have that." She poured another measure for them both and he gladly took it.

"How about refusing to fight?"

"What's this?" He snorted. "You're giving me advice now?"

"Wouldn't dream of it," she scoffed and pulled a look of surprise. "But it's been a long time since you tried. Maybe it'll be different."

She gazed into him for a long moment. Sadness, in her big yellow eyes. Pity, perhaps. By the Masters, he'd have been disgusted with himself at one point in time. Now, though? He didn't know. He'd always brushed it off as realism. Comfortably solemn with it all. Maybe... he perished the thought.

"In the arena?" He raised his brow. "I'd be crucified as a coward. You should know as much as I do, to refuse to fight is to die, and-"

"To die without fighting is to die without dignity," she finished for him, voice inflected with disgust. "Fuck dignity." She took her drink and slammed it on the table, nostrils flaring. "Have that bastard!"

A voice shouted from around the corner. "Quiet through there!"

Leva just grinned. Then she continued, quieter. "Why don't you just gut him?"

Drunk suggestions, nothing more. "He's the Ssentarr. I couldn't get close if I tried."

"Challenge him to a Rovaca, just like he did to you. He can't refuse." Cyrus' head hung down. "Not in front of everyone."

"I'm too old. He's eight years younger and he's beaten me before." He felt a ghostly pang in his side. The scar was even uglier now. The memory of his smashed gut and of the agony of being kept alive. "I'm happy ending my days here." Happy was the wrong word, but it would do. He gestured to the dusty orange walls of his metaphorical tomb. The barred doors, the rationed food, the slitted windows. "The spark's gone. He's won. There's no reason to take it farther. I had my chance, and I lost it."

"He's only won if you let him. And if you lose, then you die. Isn't that what you want?" She was close now, talking hushed with hot breath in his face. But he could see she believed every word.

"I'd die looking like a fool," he said softly, "in front of thousands."

Leva went to say something but stopped herself. Her face fell for a moment with that awful, ugly pity in her eyes again. Then she smiled and gently took him by the shoulder.

"Maybe, but at this rate you'll never know."

A loud clanging on his door jerked Cyrus awake. He squeezed his eyes shut, just for a few precious moments more. A jangle of heavy keys. A rusted lock clunked. A heavy bolt slid open.

"Get up," grunted the guard. "Something special for you today."

He opened his eyes. Light shot in through the barred window above his bed, into the dingy space he called home. Every bit of dust and grime was visible even with his weary morning eyes. He drew himself from the bed and put his leathers on. Greaves strapped tight, the worn leather creased so much it looked fit to give. Pteruges around his waist and over his thighs; leather so thin it barely protected his dignity. Vest over his head and fitting just not-so. Vambraces stained with years of blood and stitches. Pauldrons battered so much they were no longer identical. But it all served. And it was this or nothing.

He allowed himself one more sigh and went out into the hall.

No more of last night's quiet, empty space. The room stank of arrogance and sounded like a brewing battle. Fighters of all shapes and sizes drilled with weapons of all kinds, grunting and shouting with each swing as they chopped and swiped thin air. Some sparred with each other, steel and wood and iron clashing and scraping, swords and axes, spears and daggers. Insults were hurled and growls exchanged even only in passing as warm-ups for today's matches. Cyrus struggled to find a quiet corner, where he could sharpen his blades and practice in whatever calm he could find. As he pushed through the fray he wondered how many would be dead by the day's end. Then he wondered if there were still bets among them. He'd participated in them once upon a time. Done well, too. Earned extra rations, and a little respect. The fun faded after a while but luckily for many they wouldn't be alive to collect or lose either way.

He felt eyes on him as he made his way over to the weapon racks at the far end of the hall. Narrowed, suspicious, cautious. Mouths whispering, hissing idiotic lies and painful truths as he walked past. He was often a source of talk among the others - a former Ssentarr resigned to his fate among the slaves. But no one ever did anything. He'd never held too high an opinion of himself, but he was better than every single one of these and they knew it. Words bear no weight if those using them are lighter than yourself. He reached the rack and picked out a shortsword. Gave it a few swings. Fast, light. Felt right today. A shield, too. Worn and freshly splintered, a dark red smear across the front, likely from some unfortunate the day before. It would serve. He didn't know his opponent, but that didn't matter. He always won.

He walked over to the quietest corner he could find - a bench right at the back, around a small corner where just a few others stood trading nothing but practice blows and curses. He sat, took a whetstone from his pocket and began running it down the blade. Scrape and sheen, blade ringing softly with each strike. There was a serenity in preparation for battle. The peace before a storm, the gentle breeze before a tornado. A steady rhythm of singing that he hummed along to.

Something special for him today, the guard had said. He wondered again what that meant. Maybe today would be a good fight. Maybe he would feel that thrill. Death just a whisper away, just one error. But with death no longer feared, would the thrill be the same?

He thought about Leva, wondered where she was this morning. Still in her room, perhaps. Or maybe he'd missed her in the press of bodies in the hall. She'd find him sooner or later, no doubt. He spent a lot of last night about what she'd said. Mulled it over, thrown it around his mind. But it was all just talk. She knew that, didn't she? The idea had of it excited him but he knew he'd never do it. He'd tried before and found fate was tireless and unforgiving. Better to accept it than struggle against it.

A few hours had passed and Cyrus had practised, drilled, rested, and drilled more in preparation for the day. He had watched as corpses of beasts and gladiators were dragged in, smearing the floor. Wheeled in carts, if there were more than one or two at a time. Fighters stumbled in battered and bloody, missing an eye or an arm or a hand. In one case half his tail, leaving a thick trail of blood as he was hauled in by one of the guards. Still no word on who - or what - he would be facing.

"Cyrus to the gate!" cried a hoarse voice.

Cyrus gave himself a breath, then made his way over. The huge, rusted gate of iron that he'd seen every day for the past decade, the yellow-orange sand of the arena and the dark shadows of faces in the crowd. The guard gave a grim smile and pulled a lever on the wall. The gate clanked its way upwards and disappeared into the ceiling.

"Get out," spat the guard.

Cyrus made his way into the stadium, sand warm on his feet and the Volutem's pale light washing harsh over everything. The crowd cheered as he emerged from the shadows and his spine tingled. The nameless faces. So many of them. He saw Virrion reclined in the shade, attended by his many servants.

He reached the centre, unsheathed his blade to a roar from the audience and twirled, pumping his fist in the air as he bared his teeth. All about show.

The announcer bellowed to the crowd. "Drakka, I give you - The Fallen!" The crowd roared again, eager as ever. "And his opponent..." Cyrus turned to the far gate, sword and shield raised ready to fight. "The Firecrest herself!"

"No." His weapons lowered themselves, arms suddenly heavy with dread.

The far gate clunked open, and Leva stood motionless in the shadow for a moment.

"A rare treat to see a fight of this standing..." the announcer drawled on but it was just noise. Deafening and quiet all at once as Leva limped into the arena. Weaponless aside from what looked like a dagger in her left hand. Her non-dominant hand. What had they done to her? He turned his gaze on the Ssentarr to see a grin on his face, to hear a racket of laughter from him and his sycophants. This was nothing more than a game to him. A dark growl rose from the depths of Cyrus' throat. He clenched his jaw, grated his teeth and spat. Leva stopped ten strides away and looked up. She didn't need to say anything - the marks across her face said more than enough. Their eyes met.

Cyrus spoke softly, "I will not fight you."

"Just make it quick."

He looked between Virrion and her. His past and present. One he hated and one he...

"No. I refuse." He threw his sword and shield to the ground, glaring up at the balcony. "I refuse!" he roared, echoing throughout the suddenly quiet arena. He nodded at Leva, who managed a gentle - if pained - smile back.

The announcer choked a little. The guards shifted. The crowd murmured.

Eventually the Ssentarr himself stepped out into the light, grin and mail glinting. "You will fight," he rumbled. "You will fight like your life depends on it. It does." He sneered at them and sneered. Their eyes locked for a moment, and Cyrus felt the challenge. Felt his jaw clench harder and his breathing deepen, felt that long-dead spark flicker, just for a moment.

"I will not fight either!" Leva followed his lead, throwing down her dagger.

"Is that so, Firecrest?" He raised a palm. "Will you not fight?"

"Fuck you and your games."

"A pity," he said, and dropped his hand.

An arrow flew from the stands and thudded softly into her neck. Her eyes shot wide. She dropped. Cyrus caught her but she was dead before she hit the ground. Her eyes glossed over, and he closed them. He clutched her tight, his forehead pressed softly against hers.

"Masters, take her to your side, let her go with glory." He mumbled long-forgotten remnants of a prayer. "Ortis, her soul is yours."

"Send something else in to keep the spectators happy." Virrion said. "Just make sure he lives." And he chuckled.

Cyrus clung to Leva's still-warm body. He looked up to the baying crowd and brushed away the welling tears. Virrion turned away and despair quickly turned into burning fury. He laid Leva softly down on the sand. The dead spark became an inferno. Blinding, scorching and with a need to be sated.

"Virrion!" he bellowed.

The announcer started, "You will address the Ssent-"

"Quiet!" Cyrus didn't bother with him and instead glared at the big, cowardly bastard. "Virrion!" He made sure everybody heard him. A deep boom came from his chest that even he had forgotten he was capable of. "Rovaca!" A murmur swept over the Stadium. "Here, and now. You and me." Virrion stopped.

No answer came. Ever the thinker. Ever the schemer. But that was one thing Cyrus always admired about his people, no matter their faults and his many, many gripes with them - it was all about appearances. A challenge, from a slave to a Ssentarr? It could not be allowed to go unmet.

He picked up his sword and hailed the crowd, lungs burning as he roared. "Is this your leader? One that cannot even give the simplest of answers?" The crowd bristled with each question. "One who will not honour our traditions? One who tortures and kills for brutish pleasure?" He pointed the blade at Virrion. "Answer me!"

Virrion took his time with each spat word. "You can have your duel, your few minutes of dignity." He paused and turned his head. "And then I will beat the life from you myself." The Ssentarr swept on his heel and leapt over the balcony, thudding down heavy on the sand.

"My weapon!" he boomed at the attendants. One of them hefted it from beside his throne and threw it down, landing in his hand with a resounding thunk. Virrion threw it hand-to-hand, weighing it. Cyrus remembered the Ssentarr's favoured weapon well. He could almost feel the sting from it smashing into his gut as it had a decade before. An avos. A pole of pure, black iron wrapped in studded snake-leather with a thick spearpoint at one end and a heavy, spiked mace on the other. A big, brutish weapon for a big, brutish bastard. A symbol of strength and honour, carried by a weak coward.

Cyrus picked up his shield and observed his opponent. Virrion strode heavy and slow toward him, but his size hid a dangerous speed. His glinting silver mail clinked with each step, encasing him in a thin metal sheet save his head, hands, feet and tail. This fight would not be won easily. His opponent had every advantage. But he also had something to lose.

The two Drakka faced each other, studying one another. Cyrus gripped his sword, held his shield close and adopted a low stance, ready to face what was coming. He couldn't be stronger. He could match his speed. But he was smarter. Virrion stood tall, holding his weapon like a blacksmith's hammer.

The stadium was tense. Odd hoots and strangled whispers came from all around, puncturing the silence.

"Your move, hatchling," Virrion snarled. But Cyrus didn't move a muscle.

Bait the beast. Wait for the opportune moment.

Virrion growled. "So be it." He launched himself, bringing the mace end of his weapon down upon Cyrus, who raised his shield and deflected the blow downwards, metal striking sand with a hard thud. He stabbed at the brute's side but was batted away by a swing of the tail. Before Cyrus knew where he was the avos came again, whooshing past his face.

On the back foot already. But he could handle it. He'd been waiting a long time for this. He could wait a little longer.

Virrion smashed it down again and again in big, sweeping movements. Cyrus's shield took each blow with a clanging glance; just quick enough to brush them aside. Momentum kept him strong. Break the momentum, find the moment.

Another heavy strike from above aimed right for his head, but this time Cyrus went under and crunched his shoulder into Virrion's side, sent him tumbling sideways and kicking up dust as he landed. Cyrus lunged for the throat but caught only air as Virrion rolled out the way just in time. Cyrus covered his flank while Virrion leapt up and realigned himself.

He hissed and Cyrus responded in kind. Their eyes narrowed. The stadium roared. Cyrus took a breath.

Virrion twirled his avos. He came again, aiming for Cyrus' legs with the spearpoint. Cyrus darted back, dancing with each step and batting the strikes away. One strike lingered too long and he seized it, smashing his shield down on Virrion's hand and butting him in the head, sent him staggering back with bloody teeth. A whirling mace came for him but he was already strides away, free as he pleased.

"You've improved, Cyrus." The Ssentarr grinned, his bloody grin on show. "Seems your years here have done you some good. And here I thought this would be nothing but an execution."

Cyrus would not engage in timewasting. "You are not fit to bear the title of Ssentarr."

Virrion simply growled and shrugged.

He advanced again, avos becoming a whirlwind of whipping blows, mace thudding against the sand moments before the blade rung against the rim of his shield. He had the precision to make every strike a threat and the stamina to keep it up. Cyrus worked to dodge the heaviest, parry the lightest, each time no more than a breath away from something fatal. A thundering strike came from his right, the avos' spike ripping across his shoulder and putting him off-balance. He raised his shield just in time to catch the next blow on his shield, carving into the splintered wood.

It stuck.

He yanked hard and Virrion came with it. Cyrus crunched the pommel of his sword into his face before the momentum carried them both crashing to the ground, him on top and weapons flung somewhere across the sand. A fist to Virrion's nose and blood spurted over his chin. Two more crunching blows to the side of his head. The bastard would pay for everything. He raised his fist again, felt a cold shock in his side and saw Virrion's fist next to it, covered in blood and gripping a short blade. Dishonourable bastard. The bloodstained smile on his bloodstained face, that same primal thrill Cyrus used to feel etched all over him. A wave of disgust. Then the red-hot pain screamed again and fed that fire inside. His side burned, his legs went weak just a moment too long. Virrion cracked his jaw up and sent him off tumbling into the sand.

He groaned, tried to right himself. Virrion strode toward him, sword in hand and started stabbing. Cyrus rolled and rolled again, scrambled back as the blade sheened with murderous sharpness. He caught his bloodied reflection and for a moment wished he hadn't spent all morning on it. Then it came down right beside his head and he was brought back to the present. He grabbed Virrion's wrist, dug his claws in and shoved it sidelong as he scrabbled to his feet.

Back to neutral ground. As neutral as he could be without a weapon. Virrion swung the blade about, grunted, wiped his mouth and spat blood. He paced, six or seven strides distant. Just a good lunge away.

Cyrus did nothing but breathe. Breathe and rid his mind of the pain. The gouge across his shoulder, the dull ache in his jaw, the short knife still lodged into his side, stemming the worst of the blood. Likely keeping him on his feet if he was honest. He coughed and hot blood dribbled from his mouth.

He looked around bleary-eyed. The shield was off to his left, the avos off somewhere to the right. He wouldn't get to one before Virrion got to him. He reached for the blade in his side, and gripped the sticky handle.

Virrion pointed the sword at him and whispered, his voice hoarse. "I will rip the heart from your chest. I will have you struck from records. I will have your corpse defiled and marked for Crutorem, never to be freed!"

"I expect you will."

Virrion snorted, fingers rippling over the grip in anticipation.

"You never could take second place..."

Virrion snorted and snarled.

Bait the beast. Wait for the moment.

The Ssentarr roared forwards, blade hefted high, clumsy and obvious.

With a roar of his own Cyrus wrenched out the dagger, stepped back from the whistling blade, and slashed the back of Virrion's hand, made him drop it. He howled; Cyrus curled his arm around his neck and knocked his feet out from under him, taking them both down to the sand in a tangled mess.

Virrion wrestled, tried to get away but Cyrus held tighter than ever, feeling his strength spike but knowing it would soon fade. He slashed, hit flesh and heard a deafening howl in his ear. A mess of sand and blood and darkness. He wrestled for control but Virrion was still stronger and Cyrus was left struggling beneath his weight. Sand in his eyes. Hands gripped his throat. Claws in his flesh. Everything burned. The comforting grip of the knife in his hand. He jerked forward and provoked another violent grunt. For a moment between the haze he saw Virrion's face, teeth bared and eyes wild. Cyrus slithered his hand up.

His knife thudded up into Virrion's eye and it popped. Virrion's grip loosened and he howled like a wounded dog. Cyrus's knuckles pressed against the warm, oozing socket and he twisted the knife deeper. Virrion squirmed back and it was torn from his grip.

"I am the Ssentarr!" Virrion shrieked. "I will not be beaten by *you*!"

One last victory. With a wheezing breath he gripped the back of Virrion's head, yanked it down and skewered his forefingers up into the other eye. It squelched wet and hot over his hand as he gouged, hissing all the while. The Ssentarr gave yet another visceral scream as Cyrus shoved him flailing off onto the sand, choking and spluttering.

Then silence. It was over.

The fire inside went out and there was nothing but ash. He suddenly felt very weak and very cold. Felt the slow drip of the blood from his side. The lightness in his head. The rasp of his breath. Peace with death had been made long ago. He twisted his head, saw nearly nought through his fading vision save a motionless silhouette lying somewhere over the arena.

"I will see you again."

Cyrus looked up into the Volutem's blinding light once more. He let go.

Inky

Year 463

I can't remember what I was doing when I found out my family was dead. The memory's nothing but haze now, these years later. Maybe it was the way time froze. Maybe my heart was thudding so hard I couldn't hear anything else. Maybe, even in the gaping realisation of the moment, I knew I was only feeling guilt, not sorrow. I was too damn selfish. But whatever the reason, I still can't.

What I do remember is sprinting out the gates. Fleeing from where I'd longed to be for so long. There's a lot of them, now I hear. Secretive communities of learning that not everybody would approve of. Gods know my parents don't.

Or didn't, I suppose.

Places to learn things that some people wanted banned. That were banned, up until we seceded from Chea. That was before I was born of course, but it was still an uphill struggle. Places to learn magic. Not some high-flung, Gods-given power you had to be a priest or a Knight to wield. Heretical, some called it. Fiendish, and only for those willing to damn their souls. Places to learn blood magic.

"I want to go," I'd told them both, for weeks on end. "I can go, learn a few things. I can be back in a year to help with the crops. I promise, it could help us. It's for us!" That wasn't strictly true. I'm small. I always have been. Never very strong, nor very fast. Some young boys dream of being great warriors - sticks as swords and lances, swung in valiant battle in the defence of a maiden or a helpless village. Some want a simple life, working the land and following in the footsteps of their father. I wanted neither. I wanted to know things. To ask questions and to find answers. To play with the fabric of our world, to understand its nature, to know why those that fear magic fear it so.

For many, their childish dreams never come true. We grow up and life shows us a path we didn't want. We are given our lives and made to like it, or least politely pretend to. Rarely do we get a choice to change our fate, yet here I was, mind ripe with questions and a chance to do just that. Only I was stuck in a dingy village surrounded by nothing more interesting than fields with people that, to my idiotic younger self, asked questions no deeper than the next's day weather.

There was a part of me that knew I could help them. I didn't know anything about what I was getting myself into, but I was sure it'd help somehow. It was magic, after all. What harm could it do? More importantly, what good?

"Please let me go!" I'd practically begged them both, this last time. Tugged at the hem of my Mother's sleeve, pulled at my Father's arm. Gods, I must've looked pathetic. I can still hear that awful, wheedling note in my voice. "Please, I'll save my wages, find extra help on the farm before I go. Abby's old enough to help anyway now, she's fifteen. I can go and be back in a year!" I had no idea if that were true, but I was prepared to say whatever it took.

"No. I need you here." That's what Father said, in the gentlest way he could manage. Which for a man as broad and gruff as him, wasn't very. There was no arguing. Unless, of course, you were my Mother, in which case he had an irritating soft spot for you.

Unfortunately for me, she agreed. "Your Father's right, we need you here at least for the next few years. Until we can get a bit of money together."

"But I'll find someone who can replace me." I'd said, tugging a string that shouldn't have been tugged.

"Oh honey," she'd said, trying to brush a hand on my cheek which I nimbly avoided. "Nobody can replace you." At the time it made me feel sickly and embarrassed, even only in their presence. Now I'd give anything to experience it here again.

"She's right," Father had said, "you're invaluable around here." That felt like a lie, but I never truly found out. I remember the way he broke into that half-smile as he slapped me on the back. "Besides, who'd look after Inky?"

The black-as-night cat sat on the windowsill, bathing in the morning light. I'd bought the damn thing to help clear rats out of the barn and house. Saved up some wages. I couldn't do much maybe, but I'd thought a cat could. At the very least thought it might make the rats think twice. But no, instead all he did was sit in various warm spots around our little home. A windowsill, the table, an open doorway. Most often, my bed. And he certainly never went further than the front gate.

"What, that fleabag?" I'd said, not meaning it. After all, he never left the house enough to get fleas. "He'll be fine." I loved him, we all did. But he was useless. Mother often reminded him so. Father paid him little mind other than the odd scratch behind the ear. Abby only ever noticed him on rare occasions. I bought him to help but he only became a burden. So naturally, he was mine to bear. To teach me some responsibility. Something to help me leave, now keeping me here. Life has a way of being ironic.

"Please, let me go. I know you need me here but I promise I'll be more useful with what they can teach me."

"No," my Father said again, his voice suddenly sterner. "No, I don't like that stuff. I don't want you hurting yourself."

"What if you get it wrong?" My Mother sidled up to him, her hand on his shoulder. "I won't let you hurt yourself to help us." They meant well, looking back. But back then it felt like they were saying whatever they could to keep me under their roof.

I remember the way my parents looked at each other, in that same way they used to in times like this. Their signature move. One of his hedgelike eyebrows raised and eyes pointed at the floor, her nostrils flared and her own brows high pulled in tight. The look of 'we need to do something about this'.

But I knew the look too well. It only meant it was never going to happen. At least not yet. That look, in fact, was the very thing that 'needed doing'. It signalled that the conversation - if you could call it that - was over.

I remember lying awake in bed every night for weeks thinking of going anyway. Running. I knew me, and I knew I'd never do it but the thought gnawed at me like Inky did at his fur. He always kept me company, spent every single night on my bed. On those nights I would talk to him about my dreams, my wants, my wishes to have more than what this life had given me so far, blissfully unaware of what it had already had.

It's funny, really. I remember all these fantastic details of the days before, have all these memories that seem so trivial now. But I don't even remember who told me about the plague that swept through the whole of Lithale. About when it hit my little village. As sudden as a bolt of lightning, gone the same moment it had come. To this day there's been nothing official said. But I remember seeing the devastation for myself afterwards.

I'd been gone less than a year and I'd learned more than I thought possible. The primal and pure schools and their principles. The flow of blood through objects and through oneself. Even some ritual blood magic - only in theory at first, of course. They said it was too risky, which looking back I agree with, frustrating as it was back then. What was I thinking?

But Gods my time there was fun.

My new friends and I flinging blood-dripped pebbles at each other. A little grim, perhaps, but most of us were there for the same reasons; the same escapism. In that place we were all equals, all just looking for a way to help others. It was nice. It felt like I belonged. Like I'd really found my purpose.

For the first few weeks after fleeing home I felt guilty. I wanted to write letters, tell them how sorry I was. I wish I had. But I couldn't. I couldn't even bear to receive a disappointed letter from them, never mind ever seeing them face-to-face again. I'll never have that chance again. I just kept telling myself I had to do it to help them.

Another night I left I'd been lying awake, restless as usual. And so I left my room and crept down the stairs, careful to avoid each known creak-spot. Halfway down I heard sniffling, followed by gravelly muttering. Once I was down I went through the hallway and peered through the cracked-open door. I saw my parents with their backs to me, sitting at the table his head in his hand, her head on his shoulder. She was crying.

I held my breath and listened to them talk. Their land - rather, the land they were charged with maintaining, along with the rest of my village - was going to be taken away if they didn't produce more by next harvest, and they'd be pushed out. We'd had a bit of a dry spell the year before, many livestock had died in a freak storm not long after. We had little money to purchase any more, and of course we wouldn't be allowed to borrow money. But the landowner said he'd find replacements if we couldn't get it done. People from the cities, perhaps. Less than half a year. It was an impossible situation. Even I knew that.

And so I made the decision.

I packed my things - no more than a spare set of clothes and the ones I already wore, along with a few keepsakes. I left a heartfelt note on my bed and kissed Inky goodbye. I woke up Abby and gave her a hug, just in case. She was confused, I wouldn't have known her awake if she hadn't squeezed me back tight enough to crush my shoulders. She was always quiet, but maybe she knew, that night. I gave her a kiss on her forehead and said I was going back to bed. I looked in on my parents through a thin crack in their door as they slept.

I wanted so badly to say goodbye, to explain myself with words.

But I couldn't. They wouldn't understand. And so I didn't.

I left the house and I didn't look back. I slunk through the whole village, walking past every house, clinging to the shadows and hoping no one was still awake. I didn't stop until I reached the foot of the Divide all those miles later. The start of a trail I'd heard that led up the mountains and through caves, leading to a supposed haven for would-be mages. I remember the way the mist clogged my vision the same way anxiety clogged my throat every step of the way. The way the cold chilled my neck, the thin rain spat at my face, the sky loomed grey above. But I pushed through. I was in too deep to stop now. I was lucky and found some fellow trailers early on, and we made camp every night along the various stops of our journey. Dark mountain caves and deathly-steep ridges, bare plateaus and thin peaks, still tiny amongst those high enough to break the sky. Views I hadn't dared to dream of. A farmboy amongst all this vastness. The spectacle got to me more than once.

Eventually we made it. I won't speak the name of the village, but it was a haven. For me and all others than shared my desires. Farmers, the orphaned, the helpless, those that just wanted the tiniest bit of power over their own existence. Some authorities, out of fear, out ot stupidity, out of some misguided religious belief will tell you blood magic is a path to darkness. That it will consume your soul until you are but a husk, an unliving, unbreathing, unfeeling thing. That it is only used by those who desire control.

That's a lie.

It's beautiful. I'm not going to lie and tell you that it's pretty, no. It's *blood* magic, after all. It involves wounding yourself even for the smallest of applications. It can get a little gory and it can remain unnerving for a long time. But any feeling of apprehension soon turns into a thrill. That's the stomach we went there to develop. That's what I wanted. I could shift rocks without a sweat, far heavier than I ever could with my muscles. I could make my own blood a tool, or even weapon. And I felt like for the first time in my life I was good at something. Not amazing, perhaps. Certainly not a prodigy like some. But I was good.

Later into my first year I could commune with the Elders themselves - the sessions on ritual magic were always my favourite. I could speak to them, in a way. They were only ever silent in return, but you could feel them in your mind. A sort of familiar, tugging weight from the Void. We were taught of the two Ritual principles - promises and exchanges. Promises are unknown prices, to be paid when an Elder sees fit. Dangerous, but immediate. Exchanges are prices that must be paid before you receive the asked prize. Bargains. I could know the knowledge I wanted to know, see things I wanted to see. I saw reality anew, knew my place in it all, knew why magic was feared and yet was now able to dismiss it as nothing but fear of the unknown.

But as I found myself and as I found these answers, I think I lost something on the way. That's not to say I regret it - these events made me who I am today, these powers made me capable of much I couldn't have achieved otherwise. And I know now I couldn't have stopped that plague, whatever it was. But the guilt's still there, hankering away at the back of mind. I know it's stupid. I know I can't blame myself. But it's not going anywhere.

No, I lost myself in my new identity. I became enthralled with it all - the magic, the knowledge, my new life. At first I didn't send them letters because I couldn't stomach a reply. But before long that turned into not sending them letters because I was too busy in my second life to appreciate what I'd had first. And if I felt guilty then, Gods, it's nothing like I do now.

And that's when I found out. I recall little of it. Like the memory has been torn out of my brain. Like a book with a missing page. But I remember the tears streaming down my face as I ran to my room. I remember the splitting in my chest as I hastily stuffed things into my sack. I remember the furious speed my feet carried me back through the Divide. Alone, this time. And with half the sleep.

When I returned to my village it was all so peaceful. So quiet. Frozen in time at the moment I'd left, even with the fine drizzle of rain.

Only this time bodies littered the dirt. Pale and green, spotted with decomposing flesh. I had to wade through them, through the stench hitting the back of my throat. Some I knew well, most I at least recognised. We all worked for the Lord and Lady Lithale. Or rather, the families that served them. There were too many in-betweens to count, our landowner included. Mr and Mrs Bridger, the couple that married just weeks before I left, laid out together in the middle of the road being pecked by crows, flies buzzing around their glassed eyes. Old Mrs Rone out on her porch, infectious smile gone and replaced by a gaping maw, jaw hanging off at an angle as the breeze slowly rocked her chair. Everyone splayed out in grotesque mockeries of their last moments. Whatever it was, it had struck with the fury and the precision of an vengeful God.

Some foolish, stupid, childish part of me clung to the hope they were alive. I should have turned around, accepted their fate and fled back. But once again, I'd come too far to stop now. That insatiable curiosity needed an answer. The walk through town felt like the truest walk of shame there'd ever been. Long, cold and trudging through corpse-strewn mud.

I came to the door and rocked on the creaking wooden boards for a moment. Then I knocked. Stupid as it was I kept clinging, knowing how futile it was I tried to hold on.

And when I didn't hear anything I knocked again. A little harder.

The door swung open. They were home, at least. Father always locked the door if he was out. The bile crept up my throat. The bitter fear of what I knew I was going to find. And yet it didn't prepare me for it at all.

I nudged myself into the hallway. The stairs stood to my left, Abby's door to my right. I pressed it open just a little, went to whisper her name.

The shadow of a limp arm cut across the floor and I slammed the door shut. I swallowed, forced any tears back to where they came. The guilt welled in me stronger every second. But I couldn't see that.

I knew. That was enough.

I pressed on, each foot filled with lead, each step causing the old floorboards to groan in pain, deafeningly loud in the silence. Before I knew it, before the groans and creaks swallowed me whole I stood in front of the door. With a stone in my throat and watering eyes I pushed it open.

There they were. Through the haze of welled tears I saw them slumped in a dark vision of how I had last time. Father, face blank and leant back in his chair, one rotted arm slung around my Mother, flies feasting on it. Her head on his shoulder, mouth horridly agape, her bright emerald eyes glazed and now the colour of wet mould.

Cold tears ran down my face.

And then I saw a piece of parchment in front of them. A quill, resting in my mother's hand. Father couldn't write. 'Never had the time', he said. Mother wrote anything we had to.

My heart dropped so low I thought it might never come back. I crept to the table, the smell of my own decayed parents throttling. I knew in that moment that it was all my fault. I could've seen something no one else did, got them out before it all happened. Maybe saved them. Could I have done that? Or would I just be rotting elsewhere in this house?

Everyone's always told me 'no, don't be stupid' or 'there's nothing you could have done'. But that doesn't ever stop the thought from creeping back in.

I had to see that letter.

And so I took a last look at my parents, their motionless faces ever etched into my brain, and snatched the letter from the table. I shut the door behind me.

I swept the tears aside and tired to read the letter in my quivering hands, desperate to give me some relief. To tell me that they loved me no matter what, that they were sorry and couldn't wait to see me, to tell me how proud they were, I don't know - anything to make me feel less alone in the moment. I opened it.

It was blank. Only a few shapeless, black scrawls on ragged paper. They'd died before they could even start. An exhausted sigh escaped my lips as tears fell heavy on the parchment. I shoved it into my bag.

My heart sank so low I didn't think it possible. Like someone tied it to a stone and dropped it in the ocean, never to see the surface again.

I couldn't think of anything, mind as blank as their eyes. I just wanted to wake up. For it to be a late night in bed dreaming about how I could run away and learn everything about everything but knowing I wouldn't ever do it. How I wished it could be a late night with Inky, talking all this over with myself and laughing at how stupid it was, asking him questions then laughing again because I was talking to a cat.

Inky.

I hadn't seen him. Could he be alive? I sped upstairs, carried all my hopes as if I were suddenly a much stronger man. I shot up like I had nothing else to lose.

And there he was, on the bed. My heart fired through my chest and hung there for a moment as I dropped to my knees. My boy was alive! He was there, peaceful as the night I left it all behind.

Then I touched him. He was cold. Stiff.

No tears. No shaking. No pulsing blood behind my ears. No breath. No despair. No longer did I feel the overwhelming pain of it all. The guilt gnawed no longer. It swallowed me whole, like a drop of water in the Void.

Emptiness. Pure, black nothing.

In the midst of it all, that water drop became something. From the whirlwind of my mind came the screaming sound of defiance, clear as ever.

I would not be powerless. I would not let this consume me. I was too weak to help my family when they were alive. I was too selfish and too late to help them when I finally could and now they were dead. Because of me. I knew I could do nothing to help them now. That was beyond any power I could invoke.

But there was one thing I could do, one tiny sliver of power I had. One piece of control that flowed through my veins. And seeing Inky before me gave me the opportunity I needed.

I threw my bag to the floor and took the blade from my belt. I tore my sleeve and wrapped it below my elbow as a tourniquet. Tight and secure. Numb. I drew the blade across my skin, watched the red trickle across my paling arm, my teeth clenched so hard they could crack, the pain carving my arm barely noticeable through my focus. I jammed my hand over the crimson wound, squeezing all the fuel I needed from my body, let it spill forth and through my fingers. With bloodstained hands I painted the floor, swiping in the archaic patterns I needed - all jagged lines and sharp circles. Then the blood drop of Ichoth, the Elder I needed to call upon. With the last stroke I laid my hand over Inky's body, his night-black fur stamped with a wet red handprint.

And then I called him. The Lord of Blood himself. Ichoth.

"My Lord," I pleaded, "grant me the life of this animal." I remember the way my tears stung my skin, the way they seared more than the gash on my arm. "Grant me this life in exchange for a favour," I yelled between breaths that scraped against my throat. "Whatever vestige of life you can bestow, give it to him and I give myself to you." I knew the danger this promise posed and I did not care. I already had nothing. I slammed my hands against the floor and pleaded a final time. "I am your servant, Lord! Grant me this!"

I clenched my fist and sighed, aching to know his answer. I didn't know what I would do if he didn't. I didn't want to think about it.

A rustle of cloth. A warm nuzzle against my face. A soft, tired purr. I had been blessed. Grief had chewed me up and spat me out, it seemed. I looked up and a pair of brilliant blue eyes looked back at me, alive as they'd ever been. I gave Inky the biggest hug I'd ever given.

These years later I still wonder if I had other options, still wonder what I could have done differently. Could I have asked for an exchange, perhaps? Done a deed first? Did I have to read that letter? Could I have stayed in the village in the mountains, content with knowing my parents were dead and not having to see them myself? Could I have never left home at all? Could I have just stayed in my room that night, blissfully unaware of the conversation my parents had? Could I have been a different man? A better one, perhaps?

But it's all worthless. All what-ifs and maybes. As I sit writing with Inky nuzzling my shoulder, I wonder what will the price of my guilt will be.

Ichoth has called me, summoned me to his service. I will find out soon enough.

Last Breath

Year 69

"Go!" Samson pushed another of his comrades through the last set of doors as fire consumed the chapel. "Go, go!" Another beam crashed to the floor, showering splinters over the broken pews and adding more fuel to the growing inferno. Hair clung to his sweat-drenched forehead and thick smoke invaded his lungs as he desperately looked for more survivors.

"Samson! Sams-" a dirty cough reached his ears and his head swivelled to the sound. "Samson, over here!"

"Abel!" he cried, rushing over. The boy was stuck under a burning beam, one leg twisted beneath it and blood shining on his forehead. "Hang on boy," he grunted. He took the beam under one aching arm and extended his other as he drove his boots into the ground, thighs burning. "Hang on." Flames crawled up the wood, licking at Samson's face, hotter with each moment. "Come on!" He willed himself, spurred by the fire in his chest as much as the fire around him.

"It's coming loose," cried Abel, his panicked breaths sharper each second.

"Take my hand, boy!" Samson ordered, using every bit of strength he had, arm throbbing, chest heaving, heart pounding loud and dull. Abel finally took his hand and Samson yanked him free, letting the beam smash to the floor in sparking fragments. "You alright?"

"I- I don't know-" He shook his head, blood dripping over his face, hand cradling his gouged thigh.

A crash came from the great doors opposite. They were here. The Butcher and his vile followers. That soulless bastard wouldn't have a thing so long as Samson still walked these halls. Another quaking thud against the doors. Screams and yells from all around, stained glass windows shattering as burning rocks were flung through and crashed against the pews.

"You'll be alright." Samson offered his shoulder. "But you've got to get out of here, right now." Another thud. Shouts beyond the doors, feral and lurching. It would cave any second. With the boy leant on him, he carried him over to the doorway and thrust him through. "Soon as you can, see to that leg. Follow the rest out. Don't look back."

Samson drew the sword from his side, the shield from his back and turned toward the fire. Another smash from the far doors, the tip of the ram visible through the gaping hole beginning to form in the once-beautiful doors. All of his years fighting. All his years of service to the Sons. All of them led here. The smoke of his life's work surrounding him. The sorrow of the smashed stained glass. The crumbling stone of the chapel he had built. The golden sword and scales of Uras hung high above the far doors, glinting now with a terrible fire.

"Samson, what are you doing?" Abel's pleading words reached his ears even over the chaos.

"What every Son of Uras should." He planted his feet firmly on the stones he had called home for the last forty years. For the last time.

"Samson we can get out!"

The boy was wrong. The doors bought them time, but not enough. They would flee the chapel. Get to safety, find some kind of refuge. But only if he bought them more time. There was but one course of action. One he had been ready to take for a long time.

"Samson!" The boy cried again,

The old Knight bowed his head, and much as it was against his wishes, he turned to his apprentice once more. "Last breath, Abel." No panic in his voice. No fear. Only a deep solace in what he was about to do.

And the hopelessness in Abel's face faded, the glimmer of tears in his eyes stifled by a steel Samson always knew he had. He nodded. And Samson knew that he understood. Turning to face the fire once again as the back doors slammed shut behind him, the metallic clang of the bolt sliding shut on the other side gave him comfort. It would not be much time. But it would be enough for them to survive. A shattering crash from the far doors.

A breath.

The battering ram smashed through the doors; the room suddenly swarmed with heathens.

Samson gripped his blade and kept the shield tight to his weary chest. He would die today. But it would not be without a fight.

They came all at once. Leather armour and shouts. A black, frenzied mass full of dark zeal and darker robes swathing through the smoke and fire, defiling this holy ground with their stench. But like the rest of their kind they possessed no skill. And a sword is nothing without a grindstone.

A sharp thrust and one down, scarcely even dead before Samson tore out his blade and whirled it into another, splintering the haft of his axe and crunching into his shoulder. A cut-off scream as Samson kicked him back. A blade scraped against his shield; he shoved it aside and crashed his sword down, sending the weapon flying from his enemy's hand. Samson cracked his fist against his chin, snapping his head backwards. A sword through the side saw him done.

More.

Hacking blades descended upon him in vicious turns, but each was twisted away by his blade or deflected by his shield. Any foolish enough to overextend themselves was punished severely by his hand. An axe cleaving for his head, skiting over his shield as his sword plunged into the wielder's throat.

More.

But he would not cave. His sword was a whirlwind of impenetrable silver, his shield a barricade that would not break. Two more in one motion of his swishing blade, their guts spilling on the hallowed ground. Another behind them, his expression a mask of fear and rage. No older than Abel and already lost to the Elder's darkness. Samson's sword found his heart in less than a beat.

More still.

He was one man. A step back to cover his flank, a bash deflecting another wretch to the floor. An arrow pierced his thigh but he barely felt it. With a grit of his teeth and a swing of his blade another dropped to the floor, dead before he hit it. And another, Samson's blade across his eye with a shriek.

A mace braced by his shield, the force ricocheted up his arm and sent him staggering, back smacking the door. His chest heaved, spittle dribbling down his chin as he silently willed himself to carry on. Every second he kept them at bay was another second his people were free.

A blade, stabbing into the wood beside his head; its wielder too slow to recover. Samson punished him for it.

Another arrow lodged itself in his shoulder as steel hit steel. They kept coming. Another arrow in his hip threw him to his knees. On nothing more than instinct he raised his shield, a sword ringing off it and allowing him to gut yet another, guts sputtering out onto the slabs.

A knee found his face. Blood stained his teeth. Iron on his tongue. His blade, knocked from his aching hand. A fist thumped into his temple as he tried to stand; a blade in his foot dashed it completely. With another great effort he flew his own fist forward, only to have it twisted and crunched down. Something cracked. The last thing he saw was the muddy heel of a boot.

Samson stirred, his head throbbing. Was he alive? He limply shrugged his shoulders. His right arm couldn't move. Blood still lingered on his tongue, tangled his beard. He spat. No more than a dribble. A dull pain coursed through his side. Blinking only brought him pain; one of his eyes would not open at all. If he was alive, it was only barely. Barely, and cruelly.

A hoarse voice called something out. Then another.

"Draval!" That name caught his attention. So, he was here. The Butcher of Manarn. A monster, even by their heathen standards.

Arms hoisted Samson up and he was jerked viscously along the floor. Black shapes moved across the room, sifting through the rubble of his home.

"Where is he?" Harsh, heavy footsteps echoed through the chapel. "Where's that Son?" Samson had heard half his face had been charred off. He'd never believed someone could survive such an injury - but perhaps it was true. He'd seen stranger things, and blood magic was known for its perversions.

He was shoved to the floor.

"Ah, there he is." His voice was as unnatural a thing as Samson had ever heard. Raspy and bestial, like a wolf given speech. Though Samson could barely see through his haze, he saw the cracked smile on Draval's half-blackened face. The Bloodpriest continued with a breathy chuckle. "How the mighty have fallen." He took Samson by the chin, cold metal gauntlet pressed against his skin. "How do you feel, Son of Uras? How does it feel to see yet another of your precious chapels burn?"

But Samson said nothing. His body was alive, but only as Uras' Vessel. If he was still alive, he still had work to do. The Gods don't work in half-measures.

"Oh," Draval chuckled, pushing away Samson's face, "I understand. He has taken his last breath." He turned to his followers. "He will not speak another word. What is it they say? 'You cannot kill what is already dead, and what is dead may never speak.' Is that it, Sir Knight?"

Samson kept his head bowed. He would not be baited. The monster could talk all he liked. Silence is a virtue. Silence kept one's mind at peace, slowly turning, waiting for the right moment to strike. Silence was the greatest weapon he possessed now. His unbroken hand crept down to his hip.

"Well then, Knight..." Draval stooped down to Samson's level, breath hot and ugly on his face, each word a spiteful taunt. "If you will not talk, then I will make you scream." The beast had taken the bait.

A breath.

With a grit of his teeth Samson ripped the arrow from his hip and thrust it through Draval's jaw, hot blood gushing over his hand. For a moment, the monster looked only surprised, charred mouth gaping open. In the same second a sword was thrust through Samson's back, breath punched from his lungs. But even as his life faded, even as pain wrought through his chest he held his fist firm and forced the arrow ever upwards, squelching, knuckles locked in place, arm searing with the last of his strength. Even as his vision became blotchy he would not look away, holding on until what little light in his enemy's eyes faded.

And as they did, Samson allowed himself a smile. A last, weak gasp crept through his lungs and he slumped to the floor, duty fulfilled.

Valley of the Demon

Year 687

"It's scorchin' out here, ain't it?" Scis retreated into the shade of the Ssentarr's imposing hut and picked at the scales on the back of his head. The Volutem was just starting to disappear beyond the crack in the sky, giving way to evening. "Ssav, what do you reckon about this new contract then? Think the boss'll get it?"

"Course he will. Ain't another option for this town." The older of the two Drakka stood still, soaking up the warmth and chewing hungrily at his jerky. "Be nice to get working on an easy job." His tongue forked out. "And don't call me Ssav again."

"Easy?" Scis licked his teeth and swallowed. "You reckon?"

"Just guarding a caravan, ain't we? A single-track road from here to Magnacuss." He took another savage bite, throwing the meat around in his mouth.

"You do know which road that is, don't you?"

Ssavak stopped mid-chew and spat the soft red pulp at Scis' feet. "Don't tell me you believe in that scyk-shit. No damn Demon out there, it's just a myth to scare travellers."

"Then how'd you explain us gettin' this job?"

"Well they need new caravan guards, don't they? Don't be stupid." Ssavak rolled his shoulders and closed his eyes, dark scales sheening in the light. A low growl seeped from his cracked black lips as the ridges on his spine twitched. Scis was no coward but like any good Drakka he knew fear, and fear meant respect.

Still, questions gnawed.

"Why?"

"Why what?" Ssavak snarled.

"Why do they need new guards?"

"Because the other ones-"

"Got killed by the Demon!" Scis blurted.

"No," he said, "no they didn't. Quiet. Boss'll be coming out any moment now, and I want some quiet before the smoothskin bastard does."

The thought still ate at him. "They did I bet."

Ssavak leapt at him, one hand a sudden vice-grip around his scrawny neck. "Are you Drakka or some good-for-shit whelp?"

"Drakka," Scis spluttered, uselessly trying to prise the claws from his neck.

"Right then." Ssavak pressed his forehead against his, burning orange eyes flaring. "Act like it."

"All I'm saying is-" he didn't know what he was trying to say. His eyes strained and bulged.

"That thing's as much a myth as Krakens." Ssavak forked his tongue and leant in for a menacing whisper. "Does it scare you?" From the back of his belt he drew a large, serrated blade and brought it to Scis' eye. "You think we work with cowards? You want to be scared, boy?" The knife curved its way down his quivering cheek.

"Ssavak!" A bright voice called out from behind them. Florus strode out the Ssentarr's office and didn't waste a second. "Playtime's over, get back to the others."

Ssavak dropped Scis spluttering to the ground and spat out another ball of pulp. Then he growled at Florus for his trouble and stalked off.

Scis gulped in a grateful heave of air and ran his finger around his neck. "Crazy bastard."

Florus had always found it distasteful to spit, never mind waste food. Maybe it was a human thing.

"Known him eight years and he still hasn't learned any manners," Florus said. He offered Scis a hand. "You alright?"

The young Drakka took a puzzled look at it before pulling himself up. "Yeah. Thanks, boss."

"No worries. You'll get used to him." Florus knew that was a lie, but it didn't hurt to offer the newcomer some hope. You didn't get used to Ssavak, you just learned to let him do his thing. It was the only way he knew how to work. But he had his uses. "You go find the others and tell 'em I'll be there soon."

"Yes, boss," he wheezed, hands still rubbing his throat. "Will do." He ran off through the dusty little outpost toward the local watering hole.

"Of course." For all their talk about honour, glory and competition there was another element to Drakka they never seemed self-aware of. Something that held true for them all. They were fantastically predictable. He supposed that was why a human was their boss. He started his slow walk over to tell them the good news.

"We got the contract."

With those words Florus re-ignited the fire inside his men and a raucous cheer erupted around the table. He only wished they kept this mood up all the time. After a dry spell like the last few months though? He couldn't blame them. It wasn't his fault. Just not much work around for a group of nearly thirty mercenaries. Drakka settlements were never short of mercenaries or sellswords or guards. Every settlement he'd ever been to had a good, healthy population of lizards with loose morals for sale. And that was without having to split the reward up. Drakka didn't like to share. Even thinking about the last time he'd asked for something from one of them made him on edge. Valus had snarled like a wounded dog until Florus had swore on his life he was making a joke.

"So what is it, boss?" one of them shouted from the end of the table. "What are we doing tomorrow?"

Florus took a small sip of the burning, dirt-brown spirit he'd been given, an all too familiar taste of things chucked in a barrel and left to fester. Drakka liked to drink. Shame their tastes were horrific. He swilled the small glass again - at least he had something to drink at all. Same couldn't be said way out in the sands. He necked the last bit and slammed the cup on the table. The plan was always a big moment.

"So boys." He stood leant forward with a dry smile. "Who feels like being the heroes for a change?"

The table erupted once again in vicious cheers, fists slamming against the table so hard dust leapt from it, the few other patrons in the place looking over with distaste. Or perhaps envy. Another thing a lot of Drakka were good at.

"Well, feast your eyes on this." He drew a scroll from his back pocket and threw it on the table. The others scurried to open it as he continued, "That right there is a map from here in Raiva, all the way to Magnacuss. Some small mining town out in the middle of the hottest desert these lands know. Our job is to transport and guard a caravan of vital supplies for the inhabitants of the town. Barreled water, food, tools, nothing special. Four to six of us at a time will have to pull it, the Ssentarr's advised me against using mounts out in the desert. Easy targets and extra mouths to feed." He pointed to the bending red line drawn between two crosses. "This is our path. We leave before first light, to avoid the worst of the Volutem-"

"Come on, boss. We're not all gonna burn up like you," Ssavak spiked. Always had something to say. Florus always let him. Let him have his moment, then reestablish control. Play his little back-and-forth.

"Well Ssavak, we're not all heat freaks like you eh?" He turned his gaze back toward the map as the Drakka finished up another shot. "So, once we've left we should have a three day or so journey ahead of us. Day one will be spent here." He jabbed a finger at some dunes. "Dangers are all things you're all familiar with. Desert scyks, sand goblins and the like. Should be able to find some cover to sleep. Any questions so far?" His eyes scanned the table; a sea of scaly faces stared back. If a Drakka wasn't angry, horny or hungry you had no real way of telling what they were feeling. "No? Good. Day two will be spent getting over the last of the dunes. Around midday we should hit the valley. For those that don't know it's a small, narrow canyon. But it's safer to travel through there than out in the dunes to the east, or mountains to the west." He passed his finger over the paper. "Day three should be a half day if we make good time. And they've promised us a place to stay for the night as a bonus. Anything changes or we meet a problem we sort it at the time. Any questions?"

The table was once again silent. That normally meant he'd done a good job. But Florus knew uneasy eyes when he saw them. He raised an eyebrow at Scis.

"Uhm… " the boy stuttered, "is it really safe in the Valley?"

"According to the Ssentarr, mostly."

"What about the Demon?" The table was set alight with whispers.

"Quiet, quiet boys. What 'Demon'?" The Ssentarr hadn't breathed a word about a Demon. Florus knew he'd been touchy about the whole thing.

"The Demon of the Valley, boss. Locals say he holds the Volutem's fire in his hands, and he…" the boy stopped to collect himself as the words spilled from his mouth. "That he moves so fast you can't see him at all. That he leaves no one alive. That- that he has horns the size of-"

"Yes, yes." Florus raised a hand to silence the boy and the whispers. "Yes, I get it. So you all… believe in this Demon?" The whole table nodded, save Ssavak who sat in unmoved silence. "Fuck sake…" Florus muttered. But he always knew what to say. "Do you want the money?" The whole table nodded. "Then it's decided. We go, we do our job, we get paid. We're mercenaries. You all knew that when you signed up. Don't tell me the mighty Drakka are afraid of some soft-skinned runt hiding in a cave?" The shameful murmurs told him they agreed but no one said a thing. Drakka were superstitious, but not cowards. But something about this one was different.

Before he could say another word a raspy shout came from the back of the table. "He's right!" Ssavak stood. "There is no 'Demon'!" His talons dug their way into the table. "But if he is real, and if this smoothskin has the guts to fight him." His bright eyes narrowed in Florus' direction. "Then we should be ashamed that we cannot. Come with us or I'll kill you myself."

If Florus ever wondered why he kept Ssavak around, this was it. A loose leash does wonders. The table began to nod and the nervous whispers became eager conversation. He breathed a sigh of relief.

"Well then," Florus announced, "I'll see you all in the morning. Be ready."

The morning went off without a hitch; the crew had met before light and been underway for hours by the time the Volutem appeared. As always the desert was harsh; the wind so dry it made Florus' throat long for last night's drink. But he'd have to settle for drips of water.

The Drakka didn't seem to mind. Most of them didn't even seem to notice. Some soaked up as much heat as they could before trying to cool off a little in whatever shade they found along the roadside. Rocks or the occasional desert tree. The caravan itself if you got in the right spot and walked alongside it. But Ssavak was different. He loved it. Adored it. In all his time spent here not one of them compared to him. Seemed almost like he got off on it. He'd spend hours muttering to himself and if you ever got close, he'd growl at you until you backed off. Made sure to see every rise and set, too. Florus had never asked him why. Ssavak wasn't the kind that gave a straight answer.

There was a lot he knew he didn't know about his Second: his age, his birthplace, his history. Sometimes even why he was his Second in the first place. Gods knew what had possessed him to do that in the first place, but it had come in handy at times. Last night was a perfect example.

Still, Florus had to admit Drakka had a right to be superstitious. Some of the things that lived out here? Defied any preconceived notion of sparse life in the desert. There were more things willing to kill you out here than even the dense jungles at the edge of the land. Apart from goblins, of course. More of a nuisance than anything else.

"So Ssavak." Florus caught up with him at the front of the Caravan. With a look around to check they were out of earshot of the rest he asked. "What do you reckon about this job?"

"Should be nice an' easy. Just guard duty."

"Be nice to do some real good for a change, too."

"Sure," Ssavak hissed, "if you like that sort of thing."

Florus smirked. He knew Ssavak hated it, and that made him smirk wider. "I do. It's nice to do some good that isn't just killing a rampaging beast or putting down some nutjob warlord."

"What do you want, boss?" Straight to the point like always. At least he was consistent.

"What do you think of this 'Demon', then? Really?"

"Truthfully, boss?"

"Always."

"Heh, sure," he scoffed. "Not real, like I said."

"You think? The rest don't agree."

"Then they're cowards." There it was. That glint in his eye. Absolute, burning hatred as the word fled his mouth.

"Cowards for believing in stories?"

"No." The Drakka snarled, teeth glinting in the pale light, "cowards for being scared of something that hides. If something hides, it is a coward. And if one is scared of cowards, then that makes them worse than dirt." He spat. "These lands are sacred, Florus. I will not have cowards here."

Was that zealotry? Passion? Refreshing, at least. The thought crossed his mind to drop the subject, but Florus had to push again. Had to eek out as much information as he could. It was a chance he wouldn't get again.

"So what's this Demon supposed to look like? What does he - *it* - do, exactly?"

Ssavak sighed. "You're really that interested, huh?"

"I've got no stake in if it's real or not. I'm just saying if it, I'd like to know what to expect."

"Hm. Fair enough." Ssavak shrugged. "People say he came here near a century ago. Not sure when exactly he arrived, or where exactly he came from. One day he wasn't here and the next travellers were disappearing in the pass. Any that survived were delirious by the time they were found, rambling about some towering, robed figure that could hold fire in the palm of his hand. Horns the size of spears, and too fast to see. Most never got that lucky."

"Disappearing?"

"All the time. After a few months the settlers got the message and moved their routes. Since then, very few people go through the pass. And since then, the attacks have stopped. My bet is that whatever was there moved on - maybe it was some kinda desert beast I ain't seen before, who knows? Or it died. It's been a long time, and most drakka, beasts or humans don't last that long."

"And I haven't seen a Drakka past sixty. Doesn't mean they don't exist. Besides, what's to say it just stopped attacking because people left it alone?"

"Everything in this land attacks what it wants, when it wants. Nothing weak survives here. That's because Drakka live their lives, smoothskin. We don't prance around trying to look after ourselves all the time, trying to protect ourselves from death. Look around you." He swung his arm around to the group. "You see a single one of these wearing as much armour as you?" Now that he mentioned it, Florus was the only one wearing leathers that covered his entire body. Most wore a simple skirt, some semblance of a chest piece at most. Not a single pair of boots on their clawed feet. He'd always assumed it was a preference the Drakka had for the heat but apparently he was wrong. "We do or we die. We aren't..." he hissed with a flick of his forked tongue. "Cowards, like most of you."

"And how many humans do you know, Ssavak?"

The Drakka's burning eyes trailed him up and down. "Enough." He stalked off round to the back of the caravan.

Never mind. One foot in front of the other. It helped when he didn't think about the dry ache in his heel every time it twinged. They had to complete this contract, and

Florus had a knot in his gut that told him tired feet or a bastard Second might be the least of his worries.

The next day had started much the same as the last; up early and off before the light. Florus had swapped to the back of the group. A change of pace was nice. As it was for things to go smoothly for once. Normally someone had been injured by this point, or there'd been a scrap. Gods, they'd fight over anything. Food. Drink. Accidents. Stories. Petty insults, intended or not. The time one of them had killed someone over a piece of smoked meat that wasn't even his to kill over. And then everybody had moved on as if it'd been a playfight in the sand. That didn't seem normal, but then again, maybe whenever he finally met another human he'd have a sudden urge to fight them to the death. Who knew? He kept his judgement to himself.

"Boss!" Florus was pulled from his thoughts as a voice called from the front of the group. He didn't need an explanation. "We're here."

A deep cut in the flesh of the desert. Two enormous, rust-red rock formations rising from the sand, the western side forming up steady and jagged into the sheer mountains above. A single path ran between them - no bigger than the width of two of the caravans at the widest point he could see. Dark and shadowy, the daylight ending about halfway down and trying its hardest to brush the ground. A little daunting and the perfect territory for a predator but after the burning heat and endless dunes? Shade would be nice.

"Right," Florus raised his voice at the shuffling group. "Double file, all of you. I'll take point. Ssavak at the back. Weapons out. There might not be a Demon." He grimaced and drew the spear from his back. "But there's plenty else. Be on your guard, and remember if you die the rest of us get more."

A few nervous titters came from the Drakka as they lined up, but most didn't make a sound. It was never nice when they went all quiet. The knot in his gut twitched again as they made their way toward the entrance. The two walls loomed over so high their edges disappeared into the pale blue sky. He gave a nod to those behind him, and they nodded back.

"Let's move."

Not so long later and they were deep in the pass, going steady through the midday shadows. There'd been a few scuttles, a few odd noises but nothing much. Probably just goblins for the most part. They loved places like this.

The path was worn. Old. But unused for years, if what Ssavak said was true. Rusted weapons and broken armour lay in its crevices. Bits of cloth, spear tips, arrowheads. Waterskins and scraps of leather. Littered with it all. Something had definitely hunted here. Whether it was still here, or whether it was really was a Demon? He tried not to think too hard about it. The safety of his men came first, and he'd fight anything for them.

The wind cut through the silence like a hot knife, whistling past the red stone like it wanted to be anywhere but here. Understandable. Florus didn't feel much like being here himself. But the choice had never been his. In these lands, you took what you got given. Damn. Ssavak was right about something.

A corner. Florus held a fist up to stop the company. He gripped his spear and readied himself. "Scis, stick close." The young Drakka raised his blade and followed. Moving low and slow, Florus crept round the corner. Nothing. "It's all clear, come through."

"Boss," whispered Scis, "what's that?"

Florus followed his pointing, shaking finger to a spot on the wall next to his head. Scorched and black as coal. He rubbed a finger against the rough surface, smudging it over his finger. Charred. A torch, perhaps? No... Fire. Could it be? He turned back to Scis and his eyes were frozen open, lips quivering.

"Scis, keep calm." Florus put a hand on the youngster's arm, but his eyes didn't budge from the wall. Even as the words left Florus' mouth his heart began to beat a little faster. The hair on his arms twitched. Scis stumbled back through the group, into the caravan. The others started muttering, all fearful whispers. "Scis. Everyone, quiet down. We keep moving." The wind seemed to turn. The knot in his gut sank further. A dead, immovable weight dragging him down. He couldn't believe he'd thought this would be an easy job.

"F-fire..." the boy stammered.

"Fuck..." Florus sighed and looked down the path, past the corner. More heavy, black marks pocking the stone far as he could see. The men behind him grew restless, all grumbles and snarls as they waited.

"Forward!" Florus tightened his grip on his spear and started walking.

"But-" an objection came from behind him.

"These supplies are vital," Florus growled, "they need them to survive. We've also been contracted to do a job. Which means we're going to do it."

Not a single word.

He wanted to be a good leader. And unfortunately, that sometimes meant he had to do things he didn't like. He shoved any fear deep down. "Right?"

"Yes, boss," a few of them muttered.

"Good. Now let's get out before-"

An almighty explosion; Florus was flung back and smacked against the wall like a flopping doll. A few, short, screams. Roaring white-orange flames. Scorching heat.

"Ugh..." Florus grabbed the back of his throbbing head. Ringing in his ears, dust clouding his eyes, cheek pressed against the coarse sand. Flaming debris littered his vision. At least seven bodies lay around the inferno that was once the caravan, flesh seared from their bones. Something stank of meat and coal.

He pulled his head from the ground just long enough to make out a white cloak. Just a blur but he was certain that's what it was. Maybe it was in his head. Were there two of them? Could have been five for all he cared. Ten. They'd just destroyed his next payment. Killed his men. Destroyed vital supplies. He planted a fist in the ground and drove himself to some semblance to standing.

It was standing there, surveying its destruction. It didn't even notice him.

"You will pay for this, Demon."

It turned, seemed to stare at him for a long, perfectly still moment. Scis and Ssavak were right, those horns were huge. Each at least size of a shortsword, clear even through the hazy orange dust. Its face was grey and dull. It didn't make a sound.

A roar. One of the Drakka leapt at the Demon from behind, hammer raised in a brutal swing readied for the face. The Demon ducked, batted him to the dirt before unleashing a torch of white flame. After a moment of screaming it was over.

The Demon's visage turned back to him. Every muscle burned as he tried to move forward, legs threatening to cave with every step. The ash in his lungs scraped his throat and the ringing in his ears was vicious. But he raised his spear nonetheless. Today was not a good day to die, but at least he would die fighting.

He charged. Something sharp hit his neck. One last grit of his teeth as the ground swayed beneath him. The dark closed in. He didn't even feel his body hit the floor.

Florus groaned as he stirred, head still aflush with throbbing and eyes clamped shut. Was he in a bed? Something covered him, at least. A rough, scratchy cloth but he was still grateful. His eyes fluttered open and it took a few moments to adjust to the candlelight. Some kind of small cave - the room couldn't have been more than a couple of strides wide. The same red stone of the valley. He couldn't be far, then.

Someone attacked the caravan; that he could remember. A blast of some kind. Food and water shouldn't have exploded like that. Nothing should. He'd never seen anything like it. Nor felt anything like the dull ringing that still pierced his ears. Something had knocked him out cold. The ghost of the prick in his neck still stung. Had he been captured? There weren't any shackles on his wrists, and the doorway only had a thin curtain over it. No. What would a Demon want with him? Maybe someone had survived, pulled him to safety?

All the thoughts were too much; his head slumped into his hands as he pushed himself to sit up against the wall. His mind ran like a dog chasing its tail.

"Gods..." he massaged his eyes, forced himself awake. Blinked once, then twice, then thrice. A heavy sigh escaped his dry lips. It was as if all the energy had been sapped from his body; his muscles like paper, even his bones seemed... floppy. Water... was there water? He fumbled for his belt, but it was gone. Only in his undershirt and trousers. Reaching blindly down by the side of the bed his hand stumbled upon a cup. "Oh thank..." he gulped it down in a messy rush, the cool liquid dribbling over his chin and spattering the floor. Nothing had ever sated him so much.

Gazing around the room again he noticed now the candles were not yellow in flame but white. White. A hazed memory flickered in his mind - the Demon had used white flames, hadn't he? Only fragments came to him but he knew what he'd seen was real. Shivers crawled up his neck and down into his heart. He hadn't been rescued at all.

He bolted up and gave the room another once over. Nothing he could us. Not even his leathers were there. He was disadvantaged in just about every way except one. The Demon didn't know he was awake. Or at least, he hoped. He had to. Maybe it wasn't even here. That really would be a Godsend.

With held breath and a steady hand, Florus pulled the curtain a little; just enough to peek out. Absolute darkness greeted his eyes. That probably meant it wasn't out there; but it also meant he had to take another risk.

"Godsdammit..." he growled to himself and snatched one of the largest candles from the rock shelves. Shining it through the gap in the curtain, yet more red stone revealed itself - a corridor of sorts, stretching both ways, both shrouded in blackness. Right or left? Left or right? He shrugged, determined to not let the situation mess with his brain. Enough of that already. "Right it is," he suggested to himself. Brushing the curtain aside he stepped into the darkness; brilliant white flame illuminating the craggy corridor.

As he tip-toed his way through the winding, tight space, his feet seemed to fall a little harder on the ground each time. Each step a little longer than it was before. Was he going down? That didn't seem right. There weren't even supposed to be caves here, let alone any that ran this deep. Yet he couldn't deny his senses. Maybe he wasn't where he thought he was. How deep was he already?

"What the fuck have you got yourself into this time?" His bitter self-questioning echoed around the cave a little too loud for his intent. "Every time something happens. Every damn time with those bastard lizards. If they hadn't stopped..." He knew he didn't mean it, most of them were good company on a good day; but they were hard to deal with. And good days didn't come very often. Always fighting, always wanting more, always competing with each other. No matter how much he said, pleaded to leave him out of it. Maybe it was a human thing. He owed some of them that much; a few of the elders of that group had partially raised him, even if they were all gone now. He owed it to them to at least see if any had made it out. Report their deaths. Take revenge on that bastard Demon. If he could.

At last an exit up ahead, covered by another rough curtain. A faint white glow seeped into the hallway as the muffled sound of bubbling reached his ears. Slow, steady. A spiced scent reached his nostrils and he inhaled. His stomach growled, twisting as it demanded satisfaction. When was the last time he'd eaten? That he even had to ask wasn't the best of signs.

"Is that..." he sniffed the air and took a cautious step closer. Hot spices, fragrant herbs. Wispy steam. The smell of warm meat pulled on his nose, bringing him closer and closer to the entrance. The hunger gnawed at his gut. There had to be someone here. Maybe he had been rescued after all. Demons couldn't cook like that.

Edging closer yet to the door, the smell grew more potent and bubbling louder. A Drakka-made stew if he'd ever smelt one. They weren't much for anything that hadn't once been alive - but they did it well. Should he go in? Was it worth it? Even if it wasn't a Demon, they might not be friendly.

"Come in, dear." A voice from inside. Like none he'd ever heard before. Soft, wise, with an unusual lilt of kindness. All the same, Florus's heart skipped a beat. "It's alright, you're safe here. Not going to hurt you boy." He figured that would be the best insurance he could get.

"How do I know that's true?"

"Just get in here before I drag you in myself." Suddenly the lilt was gone. That was more like it. Still, the offer took him by surprise. "I think you'll enjoy this." No more hesitating; Florus brushed the curtain aside and eased in.

A hooded figure sat hunched over a large pot, a crackling white fire underneath. Steam rose to the high cave ceiling, obscuring it from view. The cave larger than he expected, with two other visible entrances, both roughly curtained. Next to the figure, perched atop a rock lay the Demon's head.

Florus scowled, then frowned, then gave it a proper look. A helmet, dull and heavy-looking. Long, thin, curved horns sat atop it, curved and sharpened to points. Unmistakeable, even if last time he'd barely been able to see them. The helmet itself was nothing but a blank steel face - devoid of any expression except for two eye slits. He supposed a helmet was better than a head.

The figure stirred the mouth-watering stew with a large spoon. Almost comically large, in their small hands, in fact.

The hands were like his. Certainly more aged, but more like his than any he'd ever seen. Not covered with scales, but skin. Not clawed, but with nails. Soft-looking and rough

225

all at once. His heart skipped and at the same moment the figure turned to him and pulled down their hood.

"Hello, dear." She smiled with unsharpened teeth. She produced a wooden bowl from a makeshift shelf behind her. "Would you like some stew?"

Paralysed with questions, Florus simply nodded. It was like looking in a mirror. If the mirror made him a woman. And older. But that skin was like his. That hair, even her eyes were a shock of blue that Florus hadn't ever seen in a Drakka. Only in his own reflection. "I-"

The woman raised a hand. "Let me stop you right there dear. Yes, I captured you. No, I'm not going to kill you. No, I'm not going to eat you either - though things do get desperate out here." She grinned. "Yes, I saved you. Yes, the stew is safe to eat. And no, I'm not a real Demon."

"I can see that," said Florus. "You're a human?"

She chuckled deeply as she loaded the bowl. "Yes, boy. Perhaps I put too much toxin on that dart."

"Dart?" He remembered before as the words left his mouth, a hand rubbing over his neck. "Oh, right. No, no. I've just... uh..." words failed him as he continued to stare at the woman.

"Yes?"

"Oh, right." He shook his head, sat down and tried to compose himself. "Sorry, Still confused. You're a human."

The woman snorted. "Well observed."

"I've never met another."

A moment of silence befell the two as the woman realised he wasn't joking; then her face turned from smiling to a befuddled frown. "How does that happen?"

"I-" he stopped himself, unsure of whether to continue. Should he divulge all his secrets? All that he had kept from nearly everyone he knew. Near thirty years without seeing another Human - he could die before seeing another. "I've lived in Drakka lands all my life. My parents were... exiled. That's what I was told. But they died when I was young. I don't remember their faces, nor know their names." It felt strange to say out loud. A weight had been cleansed from his chest, yes the sting of his words caught him by surprise. "I was raised by a mercenary group that found me. Now I lead them. I suppose our work never takes us into Human lands, or even near anywhere they might be if they're to be found here."

"Heh, our people are a long, long way from here boy. Besides, who'd want to visit?" She shrugged and started spooning out the stew. "Unless you like everything hot, dry and angry."

Florus snorted. "The lizards or the desert?"

"Why not both?" She handed him the bowl with a grim smile on her lined face. "There you are. Expect you'll need it after the past few days."

"Past few days?"

"I've been tracking you since you left. You made good time, honestly. Glad you came this way, too. Always makes things easier than ambushing from the desert. No cover."

"I knew it," he murmured, "knew something was off. I knew something was watching us."

"Oh please." She lay back against the wall and put her feet up on a small stool. "Could've had the lot of you if I'd tried." She was probably right. They hadn't stood a chance.

He began shovelling stew into his mouth and asked. "Tracking us? Why?" Now that he came to think of it, she'd just attacked a caravan full of supplies. Was this stew those supplies? The thought made him sick. Shame it was so damn good. "Is this..."

"You're not very bright, are you?"

"Uh..." He froze again.

She grinned a moment before continuing. "The caravan of so-called supplies you were hauling exploded. What does that tell you?" She arched a silver eyebrow in suggestion.

"That you... destroyed it?"

She leant forward, eyes lit golden by the fire. "No. That the cart was full of black powder."

"What?"

"Black powder."

"What's that?" Florus shrugged and kept eating the salty, heavily spiced meat and whatever else was in it into his face, savouring every mouthful like he'd never eaten anything so good. Eating only jerky and dry biscuits most days will do that to you.

"Oh. Well, simply put - makes things go boom. That cart was loaded with the stuff."

"It was supplies," Florus said between chews, "the Ssentarr told me himself. For... where was it? Magnacuss, small mining town out in the middle of nowhere. Food, bandages, water. Good, safe coin."

"No." The woman gave him a hard stare whilst taking stabs at the beef in her own bowl. "It was black powder. And it's going to be used to destroy."

"But we checked, the boys told me it was-" Florus stopped himself. No, he hadn't checked. Ssavak had checked the caravan the morning they left. Come to think of it, Ssavak was the one who'd recommended him the job. "That scaly prick..." he thrust the spoon into the bowl and took it into his mouth. "Bastard." It'd explain why he was so adamant to get it.

"I know that look. One of them got the better of you, didn't they?"

"Mhmm," he growled, "Ssavak. My second."

"Always is," said the woman, setting her bowl down, "always is." There was something weary in her words.

"Meaning?"

"I mean it's always those close to you that fuck you over. She shrugged and stabbed the spoon at him. "Now strangers - that's where the truth lies. A kind friend is expected, but it only hurts more when they stab you in the back. A stranger can't ever betray you. And if you find one that's kind - that's a rare find indeed."

Florus supposed that was true. But then he didn't often find himself with friends either.

She leaned forward, the white flames shimmering off the buckle of her sand-stained cloak. "Does this Ssavak have black scales?"

Florus nodded.

"That one got away. Slipped away in the confusion. Too quick to catch. And he wasn't the only one."

"That sounds like him. He's a good fighter. Headstrong and bloodthirsty, but he'll run the second he knows he can't win."

"I expect he bagged some of the powder in case things went south. Make sure he could make a profit." She grimaced. "I've managed to stop most the caravans, but every now and again things slip past. Many more and I'll have a proper fight on my hands. They'll burn this place to the ground, and me along with it soon enough."

"Them?"

"The Magnacuss and Raiva Ssentarrs." She gazed around at the walls. "This place is special. Not just to me, but to all of us. They just can't see it. Or they can and simply ignore it, in which case it's worse than I thought."

Florus couldn't see much remarkable about this place. Looked the same as the desert outside. Dry and lifeless. "And what is this place, exactly? A bunch of caves?"

She stood, and with a flick of her head beckoned him. "Follow me. I'm gonna show you something."

"My name is Florus."

She cocked her head. "That's a Drakka name."

"I know." He didn't need reminding of that. If he'd ever had a human name he'd never known it.

"Well then Florus, I have something to show you." She beckoned again, but Florus did not move.

"What's yours?"

The woman sighed and gave him a slow look up and down. "Atara. Now come on."

Atara led him down yet more tunnels, a steady white flame in her hand guiding the way. She'd not said a word, despite his admittedly incessant questioning. Whether she didn't want to or simply didn't care he couldn't tell. Drakka wore their emotions on their sleeve - even if there were only three of them. She was much harder to work out. Were all humans like this? Was he? Maybe that was why the Drakka found him so confusing. And the fire... The beauty of it was mesmerizing, to say the least. All at once warm and cold. Bright as the Volutem itself and somehow drawing in the darkness around it.

"Where are we going?"

Atara only chuckled. "Patience."

"You're leading me further and further down into caves that shouldn't even exist." He slapped a clammy hand to his forehead. "They don't even appear on maps."

"This place is older than any map you've seen. Trust me."

For all his questions, she never gave a straight answer. It was infuriating. Understandable, though. Alone in a strange land, the only one of your kind? Enough to put anyone on their guard. Even after all this time, even after calling these lands home for so long he couldn't remember anything else - it had never truly felt like it.

"How far down are we now?"

Nothing.

How long had she been here? How old was she? He wanted to say seventy, sixty or so but that was difficult to judge. Ssavak said the Demon had arrived about a century ago but that couldn't be true. Did humans even live that long?

Atara stopped. "We're here. You ready?" The edges of her lips curled upwards, like a goblin about to pounce.

"Ready for what?"

"Good enough." She pushed him into the cavern.

"Oh my..." It was enormous. The ceiling so high as if it didn't exist, lost in darkness despite the flame, walls so far apart it could be a gladiatorial arena. Endless, boundless space and rock. And in the centre of it all a swirling scarlet pool at least twenty strides wide, washing the orange stone in a blood-red glow. Florus had never seen anything so beautiful. Nor so ominous. "I... this is..."

"Mhmm." Atara slapped his back. "Take your time. I was the same."

"What is this place?" He stepped further into the room, his eyes stuck to the vortex before him.

"If it's got a name I don't know it. I was never an academic." She shrugged. "But it leads to a place very much unlike this. And a peaceful, if territorial, people."

"People?"

"Not Human, not Drakka. Yjorn. Far better and more hospitable than both. And I think they'd appreciate being left alone by the damn lizards."

"I bet..." Florus gazed back into the pool for a moment, letting his eyes drift into the pulling abyss. It tugged around his neck. Gentle, strong arms guided him toward it. He turned away and took a big step backwards. "So... They want to destroy it? Wage war?"

"I don't know. Could be a hundred things. But I can't let them get to it." She bit her lip and seemed to struggle for the words. "This world is worthy of preservation, even with all its flaws. And quite frankly, with all the things I've seen for all we know this pool over there could be holding it all together. I'd really rather not take the chance."

But that didn't add up. He wandered back to her side, still taking in the cavern. "If it's so important, why's it not already guarded? You said it yourself and Gods know I've seen enough to know the world looks after itself."

"Oh that I can answer." She smirked and the flame in her hand zipped to the other side of the cavern, illuminating the far darkness.

A skeleton so big its teeth could've sliced you in two with size to spare. Long, thin fangs attached to a gigantic, snakish skull. A gargantuan spine and ribs trailing deep into the dark. Where it ended Florus couldn't see, but he was glad it was dead.

"A Basilisk. It was lond-dead when I got here."

"Shit," Florus mumbled, "that's one big fucking snake."

"Heh, yeah."

Silence fell upon them as Florus processed everything that had happened in the last while. Was he really here, staring into some magical pool guarded by a long-dead Basilisk? After meeting another human? One that could wield magical fire? He pinched his arm and felt the twinge. This was all really happening. With every moment another question felt the need to burst forth from his lips. Who was she? Why was she here? How long had she been here? What kind of power did she have? But there was one that overruled all the rest. One that he had to know more than any other.

"So, all this... why show it to me? Don't- don't get me wrong, Atara this is all amazing..." he paused, unsure of his words now they were spilling out. "But why me?"

She shrugged. "'M not entirely sure. Guess it's nice to talk to someone. When you've been away from people this long you tend to forget how nice conversation can be. Though I must admit, I was never sociable with my peers."

"Peers?"

Atara waved her hands. "No personal history. Just suffice to say the order I was a part of and I disagreed on some crucial matters. I was exiled, just like your parents. And I think fate may have brought us together for a reason."

"Stranger things have happened," Florus said, still gazing at the Basilisk. "That sounds rough. And you've been hiding alone all this time?"

"Not hiding," she said, "protecting."

"Ssavak said if something hid, it was a coward."

"Not all hiding is cowardly. It's about being content in your own company. Being alone isn't so bad. Being lonely is what gets you." Atara stroked her chin as if musing out loud for the first time in forever. "I felt more lonely in the order than I've ever felt here."

"Huh." The words sucker-punched him in the gut. "Guess so."

A few days later, the two sat conversing over another pot of bubbling stew. His head felt clearer now and the ache of his muscles had mostly worn off, replaced by a sense of ease and calm he'd scarcely ever felt. Being inside for a few days had also done wonders for the peeling burn on the back of his neck and the sweat on his clothes.

"So, this fire... I've never seen anything like it. It- it looks like-"

She cut him off. "From the White itself?"

"Huh?"

"Oh." She rolled her eyes. "Of course. The Volutem - what humans call the White. The ball of fire beyond the crack in the sky."

"Right." Florus nodded, admittedly confused but going along with it anyway

"Whitefire was part of what made those of us in the order special. A boon we all shared, 'from the Gods themselves, apparently."

Florus paused. "That makes sense, I suppose. I didn't know Gods could do that." This was all a little over his head.

Atara smiled as she stirred the pot. "Well, it's from the Gods, but that doesn't mean you have to be one of us to use it. That's something they like to keep under wraps."

"You sound bitter," Florus jibed.

"Heh, could say that." Her voice became more solemn, eyes staring blankly into the fire. "It's not all it's cracked up to be. It has its costs. As does everything."

Florus sensed pain in her words, wherever it came from. He moved the conversation along. "Sorry I've got to be going tomorrow, just need to get back to the group."

"It's a shame you can't stay a little longer," Atara said, grinning, "would've been useful to have a helper 'round here."

"Yeah... But the ones that got away will be wondering where I got to. Don't want them thinking Ssavak is their new leader." The thought made him sick - that slimy bastard didn't deserve the right. "Besides, I've got a life outside. Responsibilities."

"Whatever you say." She handed him a bowl of fragrant stew, the heavily spiced meat wafting to the back of nostrils like a warm hug. "But I do have a question for you, now."

"Go on," he prompted, chuckling at the irony, "suppose it's only fair." He took the spoon to his mouth.

"Less of a question, more of a proposition. A promise."

The spoon halted at his lips; he put it back down as he noticed Atara staring straight at him. A little ominous, but that was her all over far as he knew. "Um... sure. Go on."

"I need you to promise me you'll remember this place."

"How could I forget?" He resumed eating, unphased by the surprisingly transparent question.

"Heh, of course - and something else, too."

"Of course," he mumbled through mouthfuls.

"I need you to abandon the contract you signed with the Ssentarr. How you do it is up to you - ditch the place, tell him yourself, whatever you like. But I need it gone. The more that give up, the less appealing it is for others. Eventually no one will want to take the cursed thing."

"Sure." Florus nodded. "I can do that. They'll understand. We can find other work. We've been meaning to move on for a while."

Atara drew her brows in. "Just like that?"

"Yeah, sure. Least I can do after the past few days." He smiled. "This place is worth protecting."

"You really think they'll listen?"

"They'll listen to me." He leant forward a little, thinking of something else that had been playing on his mind the past few days. "Why don't you just go and kill the Ssentarr? If he's the one that wants it gone-"

"Oh I've thought about it, but I wouldn't be able to get close. You know as well as I do he has guards around him at every minute of the day. That was right. Florus had never met a Ssentarr that wasn't paranoid about their own safety. Came with the Drakka mentality. "It's a risk I can't afford to take. If I lose... " her eyes wandered the cavern. "And to be honest, I prefer the mysterious threat of the Demon rather than walking into town and burning it down to the ground."

Florus understood the sentiment.

Silence befell the two of them as they ate. Florus could only think about going back, and how much might have already changed. Maybe they'd already abandoned the job. No no, they liked coin too much. And the chance, the temptation of getting revenge on the 'Demon' would be too great. Maybe Ssavak really was their leader already. He'd put him in his place if he had to. But it wasn't them that he thought might have changed. Something niggled at the back of his mind, something that had always been there but had only just awoken. A gut feeling he knew was right but one he'd tried so desperately to ignore for so many years. He shrugged to himself and kept eating. It could be dealt with tomorrow.

"You expect us to believe that?" Ssavak forked his tongue and drew his eyes to slits. "You expect us to believe the Demon isn't only real, but that he - sorry, *she* - made you food? You want us to abandon the best-paying job we've had in months for some smoothskin? You must think we're stupid."

"Ssavak, I know you are." Florus laughed and took another step toward him. "But what I'm saying is true. I'd take you back there, but she's told me not to."

"How convenient for you," Ssavak growled. "And how cowardly."

"You saw what happened as much as I did." Florus pleaded to the group of angry-faced lizards. "Why would I bother making this up?"

The Drakka shared suspicious looks and hissed mutterings. A red-skinned one from the back of them spoke up from the back. Vass. "He's got a point, boss - we all saw the fire and scorch marks. We all though he was dead."

Florus bit his tongue. "Boss?" He asked. "That was quick."

Ssavak bared his yellowed teeth and scoffed. "Someone had to step in, we thought you were dead."

"But here I am, alive and unscathed. I fought a Demon and lived." He took another step closer to the unflinching Ssavak. "What did you do?"

"I was helping the others get to-"

"You ran." Florus grinned at the pressure he saw in Ssavak's eyes.

"At least I didn't abandon my men."

"I didn't," Florus said flatly, "I tried to fight for them." Something clicked. Ssavak was a lost cause. He spoke to the rest instead. "I fought for you. All of you. But I didn't see a single one of you come back. Fear shook your mighty Drakka strength." The shame was palpable; their eyes darting downward, their confident smiles gone. Not one of them said a word. "Keep the contract if you must."

He turned back to the desert and faded into the sands, his path clearer than ever.

"Atara!" Florus' voice echoed through the passageway. The weight of his chest had been lifted, his shackles broken. And there was only one person to tell. "Atara!" He burst through the curtain, into the room he'd first met her.

The room was empty. No pot. No fire. Nothing. His face crumpled.

Florus cupped his hands around his mouth. "Atara! You here?"

Not a sound. Maybe she was out. Not that she seemed to get out much. Florus peered around the room and his eyes fell on the cloak, folded neatly on the stool. He'd never seen her without it. It had been cleaned, too. White as a perfect cloud - her mask nested on top, its once dull surface so shiny you could shave in it. A pile of tomes lay next to them - leatherbound, crusty and dusty as everything else here.

"Wow..." He ran his fingers across one of the curved horns; the metal somehow cold as ice and smooth as silk. It had been a long time since he'd seen anything of this quality. Maybe she'd made it herself - he cursed himself for not asking. "Wow..."

And his eyes fell further, to a slip of parchment next to the stool. 'For Florus' was written neatly over the front.

Florus,

My apologies I could not do this in person. I was never good at farewells. Nor, I imagine, are you. If you have returned as I expected, you are reading this note. And if you are reading this note - well, you are taking your first steps into a larger world. If not, then fool me. But I'd rather not know if I was wrong.

I, like you, am a loner. A drifter. I have been for a long time, and so have you, even if you have only now realised it. I cannot stay here if you return. My solace is my own company, as is yours. There are other things in this world that need protecting. And so my former duty falls to you. I know you will take it well.

My robes, my helm and my books are all yours. In them you will find all you need to succeed. Even the power of Whitefire. Just be sure to take it easy. It'd be a shame if we were to never cross paths again. Good luck.

Atara

His hands fell and he felt a pang of sadness, yet the warmth in his chest remained. And he smiled.

"Hurry it up back there," Ssavak hollered, "we haven't got all day, Ssentarr wants the shipment in by dawn!" Since Florus had abandoned them a few weeks back he'd seized full control of the group. They played by his rules now - and he wasn't nearly as lenient as the smoothskin. Tight reigns, short patience. "Be careful with it, hit too many bumps and it's liable to blow."

This was the first run he'd done back on the contract - it had taken a lot of fake smiles and pitiful pleading to get the Ssentarr to trust him again. To trust anyone with this crucial delivery. Florus had taken the blame, of course. That's what you get when you fuck off into the desert like some high-and-mighty martyr. Bastard would likely be dead by now anyway - this place'd swallow him like the irritating little gnat he was. Though Ssavak liked to think he might even still be alive - he was persistent, if nothing else. The thought of Florus slowly drying up like a piece of rotting meat tickled his scales.

"Any signs of trouble?" Ssavak asked Scis, who trailed behind.

"No. Nothing." Ssavak whipped his head around. Scis hastily corrected himself. "No. Nothing, Boss."

"Better."

They continued through the valley, winding in between its dusty walls.

The silence was eerie; barely a whisper of wind, the sand still as stone. The ridges on the back of his head prickled with each muffled sound, every noise that wasn't one of his own. But it was just a routine job. What Florus said about the Demon couldn't be true. Even if it were, the way he described it didn't sound any more fearsome than Florus himself. Wasn't even a Demon, according to him. It was a human. A dirty, soft, ancient smoothskin. Not worth the effort it'd take to spill its guts over the ground.

A trickle of rocks fell from the ridge above them and thudded softly on the sand. Ssavak raised his hand to stop. Nothing. Not another sound. His ridges tingled. Someone was here. His fingers crept to his daggers.

Boom. A blinding explosion sent him sprawling into the far wall. His vision shook, ears shrieked. Flames howled like dying krysens. But he would not be taken down so easily; he sprung back to his feet, roaring through the thick orange dust. But between that and the white blaze, even his sharp eyes couldn't see a thing.

"Where are you?" He spat and hunched down, ready to pounce. "Show yourself!" A flaming white ball tore past his head seared his shoulder. He clenched his jaw and narrowed his eyes. He'd taken worse. But the stench of his burnt flesh still made his heart race.

Something cracked into his jaw. Another slammed into his chest so hard he jerked to his knees. Something sharp drove itself into his foot, nailed him into the ground. A yowl escaped his mouth as he swung wildly into the smoke, pain bursting from his foot.

"Where are you!" His voice cracked.

Nothing. Not another sound besides crackling embers and the thunderous thumping of blood through his head.

But then the dust began to settle. A silhouette cut against a whirling orange cloud. Horns like a dragon, pale cloak billowing. A white blaze in each hand. It stood with its back to him, surveying its wrath. Ssavak's blood ran ice cold and his throat dry.

It was real.

The Drakka stepped back with his able foot and felt the rocks stab against his back. It turned, and for one, painful, endless moment they locked eyes.

The Demon took a step toward him.

Fallen Stars

Year 652

A bright light streaming through the night sky, shining like a blessing from the Gods themselves. A deafening thud echoing through the forests, dulled only by the whistling midnight wind. I couldn't believe my luck.

I knew what it was. Quick as I could I got my things ready - lamp, bag, coat, boots. Left without telling my parents a thing. Already asleep and they'd only lock me in. The woods weren't safe in the day, nevermind at night. But I had to get to it. It'd be gone by morning. Sooner if I don't hurry up. I picked up my pace, boots sinking into the freshly-fallen snow with soft, satisfying crunches as the wind nipped at my frozen cheeks. It would make us a fortune. Gods knew we needed it. Not just my family, the whole village. And what a story.

I crept out the window, ran across the frostbitten garden, hopped over the gate, up and over the weak excuse for a palisade and off toward the Icewood. Wasn't long before I'd reached the wood itself and began passing between the huge, frozen pines, wading through knee-deep snow in search of... the biggest find of the century. It landed somewhere north, but as my eyes wandered the dark forest it all looked the same. White and dead where I could see, looming and black where I couldn't. My lamp only reached a few strides into the misty night either each way, every breath of wind threatening to extinguish it. The trees eclipsed any starlight. But I knew the forest well. Far better than my Mother would

243

like. Just keep pushing north I supposed. If it shone as bright as it had earlier I couldn't miss it. Like a torch being waved right in your face, except a thousand miles away and somehow just as blinding. How no one else seemed to have seen it was a miracle.

The bitter breeze chapped at my lips, my ears and nose so cold I could no longer feel them. I sniffled my way through it, pushed one gloved hand deeper into my pocket and yanked the scratchy coat tighter over my shivering body as the other held the lamp close to my chest. Some much-need warmth that kept my fingers from falling off. I kept my breaths deep and full, eyes darting around the dark for any flicker of light. Got to get there first.

Heard rumours of this sort of thing time and again, but I never thought I'd see it. Travellers, adventurers, bards - you know the type. Came wandering through the town, into my parent's tavern. Serve them a few drinks, start talking to them and once they've stopped bragging they have all sorts of amazing things to share. Mythical beasts and strange creatures, lost tombs, artefacts from before even the Empire, ancient magic long forgotten, songs and tales of battle too extraordinary to be true. And in fact, I suspect some of them probably weren't. Most of them, even. But this one had come up time and again. Mother always told me to stop dreaming of these things, said it's all too fanciful and to focus on pouring drinks. But Father was always right there with me, quizzing anyone that comes through. He'd want me to do this, even if he'd never say it in front of her.

Starcrystal. Soulstone, I've heard some call it. Rarer than diamond, more precious than any gold. More beautiful than any made-up maiden. Harder than any sword and just as deadly in the right hands. Tales of greed, some wanderers told. It corrupted the hearts of men in its glory, drove them mad with obsession. Tales of love, too. An Emperor besotted, gifting a piece to his true love as a mark of his undying affection. Tales of warning, that starcrystal should not be abused by those with ill intent lest it take its own revenge. Some said it sprouted from the very ground when powerful magic had been used. Others told me it fell from the sky when the Gods found one worthy. Stories upon tales upon stories.

I stopped in my tracks.

Something shimmered in the mist. A gruff, sing-song humming met my ears. Someone was there. The thing shimmered again, cutting a blinding swathe through the fog. A silhouette swept past it, eclipsed it for just a moment. I dropped behind the nearest tree and set the lamp in the snow behind me. I held my breath. That had to be it.

My hands trembled as I peeked around the tree, heartbeat loud in my ears. A man with a scraggly brown beard nearly as long as his torso, swathed in several different-coloured robes and a long, thin pipe in one hand. In front of him was a slow-crackling fire with a rabbit spitted over it. Warm, gamy, delicious - but I had to focus. He was sat still, puffing smoke rings into the mist and the crystal was in his hand, glowing just like I thought. Lesser than when it fell but nonetheless mesmerising. Beautiful. I had to get it.

I spotted a shrub, a little closer. His eyes are still locked to the crystal, turning it in his hands. I stepped from the tree and shuffled my way over, clearing a path through the freezing snow. Gods, it was freezing. My nose twitched, an invisible itch in my nostril crawling upwards. My eyes closed in anticipation and I clamped my hands over my face. After a few moments, nothing. I try to get another good look.

I sneeze.

"Who's there?" The man shouts out, soft as a shout can be. Warm. Welcoming, even. Yet I said nothing. "I mean you no harm, friend, but I have the means to defend myself. Though I must say that if you intend to rob me..." He gave a brisk chuckle. "I have little worth the trouble."

Sould I run? That's what came to me first. But what if Mother and Father found out and I didn't even have anything to show for it?

"Whoever you are, you might try extinguishing your lamp before attempting to sneak around."

The lamp was still by the tree, withering and melting itself into a hole. Mother would have killed me if I lost it. I sprang over, snatched it from the snow and shook it off. A little damp, but fine.

"Ah, my stalker reveals herself," the man said with a wink, still puffing at his pipe.

"I wasn't- I don't... uh, Sir." I shuffled back into the forest. "Sorry, sir, I'll go."

"No, no it's quite alright." He raised a hand. I stop. His wizened eyes gave me gentle stare before he continued."Come, sit. Tis a cold evening for one as young as you."

He raised a bristly eyebrow and gestured to the crackling fire, which itself beckoned me in. I glanced back into the forest, cold and dark. Couldn't see the treeline any more.

I turned back to the warmth of the fire. As I approached a tingle flushed through my skin... warm, dry. The smell of juices dripping into the fire, meaty and fresh. The man turned the crystal over in his aged hands, the small, rough chunk looking like a freshly-hewn block of coal. Only much, much brighter.

He offered it to me. "Come, I mean you no harm. I suspected someone else might seek this. Ever such a rare find, isn't it? We're lucky to have the privilege." Motioning for me to sit down and take it, I did just that.

"Good Gods." Dense. Warm. That familiar, filling, happy warmth you get from holding a mug of something warm on a cold night. Something in it swirled, a fine rainbow mist moving and swaying like it breathed. Its rough-seeming surfaces were smooth to the touch. Gentle, even. I uttered the only thing I could. "Wow."

The man took a deep puff of his pipe. "Truly wonderful thing, starcrystal. Forged by the Gods themselves, some say." He muttered about something else but I was pulled only to the stone.

"I heard it grew from the ground or... someone once said it fell from the sky."

"Ha!" He giggled heartily for a moment and I laughed uncertainly with him. "You're half right. But whoever told you it grows from the ground was either stupid or lying through their teeth. Though not many know the mystery behind such objects, in all fairness."

"And... you would?"

"I would. Studied it all my life, among other things."

An adventuring stranger that knew all there was to know about starcrystal? Questions intruded my mind, threatened to burst from my mouth but I kept them to one at a time. "So how do we get it? How does it work? What does it do?"

"As I said," he puffs, "you were half right. It falls from the ceiling of this world." With a single finger he points skyward. "It is what makes the stars. What you're holding right there is a fragment of the world itself."

I looked down at the chunk again with renewed awe, turning it over with glee. "And it just falls? Just like that?"

"Essentially," he mumbled, gazing longingly at the midnight sky. "It's too far away for us to really find out."

"Oh..."

"But..." He leans in. "There are other mysteries that we mortals can unravel." He beckoned with his head and so I shuffled over and handed the crystal back to him. A thick tuft of floral smoke wafts over me as he starts to explain. "Starcrystal is one of the only substances known to possess the ability to hold souls."

"Souls? I thought-"

"Souls are very much real my dear. Every mortal has one. Something we all share, no matter what corner of this world we hail from." His words are soothing, like warm, slow-running water. His mind must be wonderful. "Through magic-"

"Blood magic? Right?"

He nodded. "Yes, blood magic." He grinned in a way that made him younger beyond his very obvious years. "Thought you had something about you. Anyway..." He points back to the crystal. "It can hold souls, store a person's essence.

Among people like me it's highly prized for such an ability. Some believe it holds the key to immortality. Some say that it can even increase a wielder's magical prowess if certain rituals are performed."

"And does it?" My thirst still wasn't sated.

"It does, to an extent. Though it's not just that. Not only is it a substance of great power, nor is it that it's one of our world's most enchanting natural objects." He passed the crystal back into my hand. "Something that very few people know is that it's not simply a rock or a stone. It's alive. Not quite sentient, not capable of thought like you or me." He looked right into my eyes. "But quite capable of choosing when, and where it falls. Many, many pieces have fallen since the birth of this world, and many, many more will fall before it ceases to be. Mark my words, child - when it falls, it's always for a reason."

My eyes fell back to the wondrous object in my hand, still pulsing with tender warmth. Could it be true? Did he have reason to lie? I didn't even know his name. "Who are-?"

The stool was empty. I bolted up, eyes wide and looking around. The fire still crackled. Floral smoke lingered in the cold air. Not a single footprint in the snow.

I clutched the crystal in my hand. Mother and Father would never believe this. Now I only had to find my way back. I picked up my lamp and set off for home.

Crimson Tears

Year -173

"W-what's happening Mummy?"

I don't know how to reply. I told her it would be alright just a few hours ago. A lie. It's all been a lie. Her whole life. All six years of it.

Years since one of them last came and one is here again. Last time I survived at the cost of my parents. Not this time. This time I can't even move. Some say that's how it is. That when the dread sets in, when that yearning gnaw to see them takes hold you're already lost. All I can do is collapse as the world around me does the same.

"Mummy?" I know she's wailing but I hear it as less than a distant whisper. Her little hands tug at my arm as I stare through the shattered roof up into the cloudless sky, the midday light shining through the crack in the sky, moments from being eclipsed by the one that comes. The Elder. Which one, I wonder?

She tugs again. "Mummy!" I don't look down. Not for a second. Just pull her close, run my fingers through her hair and tuck her into my arms as we huddle, crouched and quiet among the raging noise outside. The rubble of our home lies around us like a cage, my husband somewhere within. I thought about recovering the body, briefly. A burial, even amongst this madness. But there's little point and even less time. Not unless I dig a hole big enough for two more.

"I don't understand..." My shirt begins to dampen with her tears. Warm against my skin, but not comforting. I want to explain it to her. All of it. But I can't. Even what little I do know I still can't explain. I don't know how I know what I know, or even why. It's just... always been there, resting in my mind. Reciting their names won't help. Telling her of the stories. Lying to her about how we might be able to find some shelter instead of telling her just how utterly doomed we are. How completely futile all the running is. All the screaming. The fighting. Doesn't matter what we do. She blubbers more, face scrunching against my chest as if it might help.

Finally peeling my eyes from the sky I look through my front doorframe, over the crushed mass of wood and stone. The house opposite engulfed in raging fire, black smoke pouring up, white ash floating down. The soot scratches the back of my throat and I splutter, phlegm ejecting onto the splintered floor. They're not even here and already the world admits defeat. But what else is there to do? *And the world descends as it has a thousand times before, just as it will a thousand times more.* That's what we were always told. This is life.

"I love you." I kiss her on the forehead. That, I can do. For the the nothing that it is worth.

She snuggles closer to me, clutching at my clothes. Little fingers grasp whatever they can hold on to. Through confused tears she mumbles, "I love you too." *Elders know I love you. I wonder if that's why they do this. Perhaps they hate us. Or perhaps they feel nothing at all.*

The sky begins to turn. The lifeless blue overtaken by a sick, looming sepia. Deep, rolling thunder tearing through it, poisoning the heavens. *One of them comes.* I don't know which. Doesn't matter. When your fate is to die everything else tends to seem... small. Insignificant. As we are to them. The sepia begins to turn again, a dark scarlet seeping into the sky as if the world itself bleeds.

My parents thought they saved me by hiding me the first time. Underground, with the rest of our village. All they did was prolong the inevitable. Now I have to watch my daughter die. Unable to get to shelter. Unwilling to even try. Just sit, and hope our deaths come swiftly.

Last time, there were creatures. Perversions of nature. Rabid, snarling dogs, teeth dripping with black bile. Horned, winged devils with steel claws. Horrific beasts, unnatural to this realm. I haven't seen any yet. *I hope I die before then*.

A colossal roar cracks the sky. *No, no, no...* My daughter buries her face in my chest farther, wailing muffled as I hold her against me.

"Shhh..." I turn my gaze back to the sky. *One of them is here.* My mind begins to tremble, my hands shaking and heart suddenly cold. What if I'm not ready? I slam my head into the wall behind me, the brittle wood snapping. The distraction is good. Again. A sharp crack as the wood splinters more. Again! My head bashing, something warm trickling down the back of my neck. *What if I'm not ready? What do I do then? I don't know...*

Then I feel a wriggle in my arms. She's still here. There is no hope, but she is still here. I cannot give in yet. I kiss her once more on the head and look upwards again.

The sky burns. It cracks with a mind-shattering boom, parting the crimson sky as if it were parchment. A great, looming eye peers through the rift. *I know. I know my purpose!* The eye shows me. The ruby iris gleams among the horror like a divine beacon. *I am... calm.* Another boom, the sky snapping like bones. *A smaller part of a larger whole.* The bloodshot white, the pulsing red veins. Is it flesh? Or is it just boundless being, as infinite as their cosmos?

I understand now. It's so clear.

My daughter screams. My eyes are pulled back from the sky for the briefest of moments. Her head rips itself from my chest, and her eyes look up into mine.

No, not hers.

Soulless and black. Devoid of any life. Her hands release from my waist and she lurches back. Then she wails. A terrible, splitting, familiar sound. Tears stream down her face just like before.

No, not like before.

Red. Bright blood streams from her eyes like a gushing wound as she shrieks, pudgy little hands clawing at her face.

I can do nothing but watch, panic caught and frozen in my throat. A warm tear falls down my face. I rub my eyes then take a dreadful look at my hands. Stained fresh crimson, ugly and bright. Then tears fall hard, warm blood dripping fast over my flushed cheeks and into my grinning mouth.

He beckons. It is time. We scream as one, eyes fixed on the burning sky. Just in time to see his great jaw envelop the heavens, teeth shining with welcoming warmth. Just in time to witness his true majesty. The gift of blood itself. His ruby eye turns its gaze to us. *He sees me! He sees me! Oh, joy!*

Ichoth.

Milton Keynes UK
Ingram Content Group UK Ltd.
UKHW030004260824
447288UK00004B/138

9 798224 650798